THE KING'S SUMMIT

OREJ ZANS SERIES
BOOK 1

SUKALIA BROWN

BLUE POINT PRESS

Blue Point Press
Atlanta, GA, USA

Cover art by Muhammad Waqas

ISBN: HB: 979-8-9877148-1-2; PB: 979-8-9877148-0-5

ACKNOWLEDGMENTS

First, thank you for supporting me. It means more to me than you know. To my husband, I could not have done this without you. Seriously, this thing would still be sitting on my computer, half written and full of typos. Our boys have the best dad in the world, and I am the luckiest woman to have you.

The biggest thank you to the online writing community for sharing your knowledge and encouraging newbies like me to see this journey through to the end. Thank you, Black Girls Who Write. And last but *definitely* not least, thank you, Sussie. You were the final push I needed to get this done. I'm forever grateful for your support and advice.

DEDICATION

For my mom

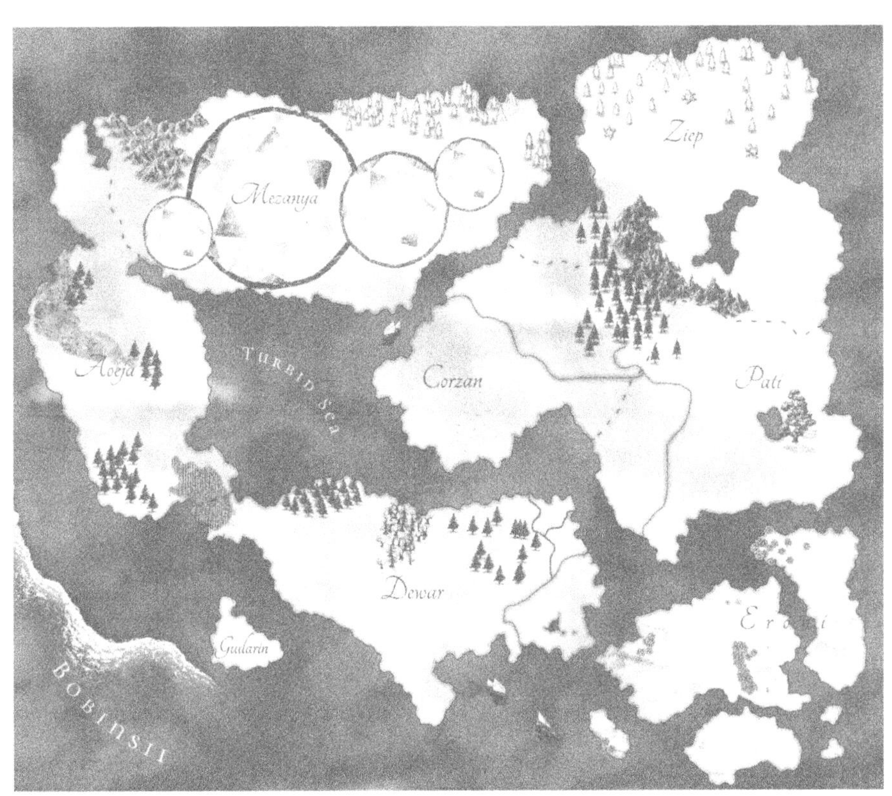

Ziep
Mezanya
Aoeja
Turbid Sea
Corzan
Pati
Dewar
Gularin
Bobinsii

PART I

WORLDS APART

1

She'd been warned. Fate had been sending Jaya signs all day that something terrible was coming, and she'd ignored every one of them— starting with the water. She was seven minutes late for sunrise training and was ordered to bring their drinking supply for the day. Two buckets, five gallons, one brutal uphill run with it all hanging from her shoulders. And she had to do it all over when some idiot took a shield to the temple while sparring and bled all in the buckets.

Then she'd accidentally called Yido by his name and not his title of Brandt. From anyone else, it was a mistake, but from Jaya, it was blatant. Disrespect of his rank and the man who gave it to him. He couldn't let that go unchecked. So she'd spent the rest of the morning with the bow-hunting party instead of having breakfast with the other soldiers from sunrise training. Jaya hated hunting, and she was terrible with the bow and arrow. Something that was made painfully obvious when she nearly blinded one of the other hunters.

Her day had been shit from the start. So really, what came next should have been no surprise.

"Brush fire in the fields," Durand said.

Jaya turned away from her view of the empty desert in time to see the smoke rise over the squash fields. "The water tanks are full. Terwin made sure of it. Alright, it's my turn."

Jaya shooed Durand out of the shady spot beneath the tower where he had been leaning, dragging sweat from his forehead into his low-cut hair. He pushed off the stone wall, shuffling forward so she could squeeze by. The walkways up on the border wall were wide enough for two people to move about comfortably, as long as one of them wasn't Durand.

"Hey," Jaya nudged Durand's shoulder, "Only one slacker at a time. You know the rules."

He didn't move. While Jaya slowly baked in the afternoon heat, Durand stood staring in the direction of the fields.

"What are you looking at?" Jaya shaded her eyes with her hands to get a better look, but it wasn't necessary. The black smoke formed a wall tall enough to block out the sun. It stretched for acres and abruptly cut off at both ends of the squash fields. Like a writhing monument, it could be seen from anywhere in Inestar.

"What the—" Jaya pulled out her walkie. "Terwin, you need to get those flames under control. Now's not the time to be stingy with the water."

She waited two seconds. "Terwin, respond. Now."

Static crackled over the channel. After another two seconds of silence, Jaya pocketed her walkie. "I'm going down there."

"What?" Durand swung around, eyes wide.

"Don't cover for me. If someone asks you where I went, tell them the truth."

"Jaya, you know —"

The tower door closed behind her, cutting off his warning. Jaya stepped onto the lift and pulled as fast as the old rope would allow. She reached the ground in record time and nearly shot out in the open without thinking. Stepping back into the lift, she closed her eyes and took two long breaths, hoping no one wandering by spotted her.

Disguise.

Right, right. Jaya made one last sweep for prying eyes, then quickly untied the purple sash from her waist and wrapped it around her head, nose, and mouth. Not great, but at least the passing eye couldn't tell her from any other female soldier.

She ducked her head out of the lift, squinting up at the soldiers on the wall. All eyes were on the fire except for one hulking silhouette. Durand's ability to telegraph his disapproval, even from twenty feet up, never ceased to amaze her. Jaya twirled her finger at him. He heaved a sigh but turned to face the other side of the wall.

She strolled out of the lift, staring at her shoes as they sunk into the sand, then tracked across hard stone. Her thighs twitched, wanting to sprint, and her throat felt like she had swallowed a flaming sword. She kept her pace until she reached the cover of the first-level houses. There she broke into a run, cutting through the maze of houses that surrounded Mount Inestar. The small, single-room clay structures passed by in a beige blur, growing bigger and homier the farther she got from the wall.

Horns blared, cutting through the quietness of the empty neighborhood and Jaya's ragged breathing, causing her to lose her footing. She stumbled into an alcove, nearly ramming her head on someone's front door. Her phone sounded in her pocket. She didn't need to check it to know what it said.

ALL EYES: Jaya Nideha, soldier. For the crime of abandoning post. If apprehended, bring to the chambers for beheading.

No point in turning back now. She tucked her feet in, brushed the sand from the scrapes running up her arm, and pushed up the wall. Just then, heavy footsteps came thundering through the walkway. Multiple, and they were in a hurry. Her window had gotten smaller just that quickly.

Jaya waited for the soldiers to pass her hiding space, then ducked out of the alcove. Ditching the cover of the houses, she ran up to the base of the mountain and took the trail that led straight to the fields. The sky was black and overcast. Flames climbed higher up the smoke wall the closer she got to the fields. It was like something out of a tall tale. The fire roared against the invisible barrier that kept it contained in one spot.

Standing at the corner of the fire, staring at the flames adoringly, was

Terwin. Jaya reached over her shoulder and pulled her sword free. She crept soundlessly until the tip of her blade grazed his neck. "Where are they?"

"I've never seen fire behave like this. The flames... they're like people, sentinels, waiting for a command to move."

"Where are your charges, Terwin?"

The press of warm steel at the base of his skull finally snapped Terwin out of his wonderment. "They disappeared. Seconds before the fire started." He risked turning his head to see his attacker. "Should have known it was you. Only you would be worried about the slaves during a breach."

"Breach?"

Terwin bent down, sifting through the sand. He found a small rock and chucked it at the fire.

"Hmm," he said, squinting at the wall as the rock disappeared into the flames. "Yeah. Bas sent out an alert for all soldiers to secure the wall a minute ago. Aren't you supposed to be up there?"

Terwin turned to her, and the flames rose at his back. Jaya sheathed her sword, holding his calculating stare. "I guess you'll be keeping your mouth shut about the slaves then, huh?" He didn't wait for her to answer. "Better hurry. Half the village is probably at the wall by now."

It was way more than half the village. Every Inestar soldier had answered the alert and was now divided into small huddles surrounding the main entrance. Up on the wall, archers had loaded their arrows and were scanning the ground for the threat.

Horace- the village medicine man- and his wife were gathered in front of the lift with the other nobles. They were careful to separate themselves from everyone else. Unlike the soldiers, the nobles had no uniform to distinguish them from the slaves. If this turned out to be a demonstration, they wanted it to be known that they weren't one of the disposable ones.

Everyone packed in close against the wall and looked around for an intruder or some sign of what this was about. Why were the soldiers still here? A group should have been sent out to do a ground search by now.

Jaya scanned the crowd for her mother. She spotted Terwin standing next to the nobles. He had already scoped out a good view in case she got caught sneaking back into the lift. He squinted across the distance at her, slowly raising one finger to his lips. Jaya turned her back to him just as the crowd fell silent.

The breach and all other concerns were forgotten as Bas emerged from a walkway with a man, a stranger. He wore rust-colored trousers and a long sleeve black shirt. Both melded to his powerful physique in a way clothes that were designed with a specific person in mind usually did. Inestar was small, and the people were not above gossiping, so word of a wealthy traveler coming to visit Bas would have made rounds by now, especially if they mentioned his glowing yellow eyes. His face was even more pronounced thanks to thick, midnight eyebrows and an angular beard that tapered down to his sternum. He wasn't one someone easily forgot.

So this was the intruder?

Bas looked none too happy to be escorting the stranger who had gotten through his security and presumably set fire to their crops to meet his people. So why was he? In all the years Jaya had known her grandfather, she had never seen him back down from a threat. He'd rather be strapped to horses and torn limb from limb. So what was it about this man that had her grandfather quietly seething in reluctant compliance?

Jaya's mind went back to Terwin's words about the fire, the odd behavior of the flames, and the people disappearing. Had he done that? He couldn't have. It wasn't possible.

"Rahmus!" Bas's strong voice combed through the crowd, plucking one of his biggest and most vicious soldiers out from where he stood in the mass of bodies. Rahmus pushed his way forward, reaching for his sword with a smirk on his square face.

And then he was gone.

Terrified cries came from all sides as everyone stared at the empty spot where Rahmus had been just a second ago. The yellow light emanating from the stranger's fingertips dimmed as he turned to Jaya's grandfather. "I'm not playing games with you. If you want to lose more of your men, that's fine, but I will find who I'm looking for."

Tense silence passed as every soldier, including Jaya, wondered if Bas would give the order to attack. Could he make one hundred and thirty people disappear at one time?

"Everybody fall in line. Soldiers to the right, except those on the wall," Bas glared at the stranger, "I'm not leaving my borders unprotected for you. If you want to check them, you'll have to go up there yourself."

Jaya moved in a haze. People bumped into her in their rush to do as Bas ordered. She was screaming on the inside, and nothing she did could pull her back to her current reality. *They disappeared. Seconds before the fire started.* All the field workers, including her mother, were gone, just like Rahmus.

"I don't enjoy being here, so we'll make this quick." He strolled to the first person in the soldier group. To Yido's credit, he didn't flinch when the stranger and his glowing hands came within arm's reach of him. He stood rigid, muscles visibly clenched, as he was examined from brow to chin like a dusty trinket. With one last tilt of his head to get a side view of Yido, the stranger moved on to the next soldier without a word.

He repeated his inspection, soldier after soldier, always tilting his head to the right, never taking more than two seconds before moving on. Jaya stood dead center in the second row. Only twenty people between her and a death sentence once she was unmasked. She shouldn't have come back. There was no way she could've gotten back up that wall. Her time would have been better spent looking for her mother and getting her out of Inestar.

"All of you, move to the back." The stranger said when he reached the end of the first row. A wise choice. He wouldn't have gotten far before a soldier up front slipped a knife into his back. Bas stormed forward with murder in his eyes. His leathery fists were clenched tight at his sides.

"You don't give orders here, glowworm," he seethed. The vein bulging between Bas' eyebrows was never a good sign. The few times Jaya had seen it, it was luckily directed at someone else, and their death had not been clean.

It happened just as fast this time as the last, but instead of disappearing into thin air, Bas found himself surrounded by metal and glass. He was visible from all four sides. On display for everyone to see in a glass chamber. A second of stupefied horror that anyone would dare to imprison *Bas* passed over the crowd. Her grandfather pummeled at the glass with his bare knuckles, yelling obscenities and threats they could barely hear.

Water poured in from the top of the chamber. Like a well that had been turned upside down, the torrent filled half the chamber before Bas even realized what was happening. In his drenched tunic and pants, he continued to wail against the glass with the force of a raging storm. He was so far gone in his fury that even the possibility of drowning in the middle of the desert was not enough to pull him out of the bloodlust. Only revenge would calm him, and since Bas was trapped, it was up to them.

"Kill the wizard!"

The call came from Jaya's left and reached everyone simultaneously. Archers let loose, firing arrows overhead as the soldiers charged over the hot sand. The stranger watched their approach with a blank expression. Meanwhile, Jaya's mind was in a cold panic as she ran toward her death alongside fifty other soldiers.

He's too calm. Can't they see that?

Yido let out a mighty yell and chucked his sword through the air like a spear. It sailed straight for the wizard's heart. A beam of light shot from the sand, swallowing the sword and the stranger as he stepped through the other side before it collapsed.

Bas' chamber shattered into fine grains of sand moments later. He fell to the ground, hacking and spitting out water. The soldiers surrounded him, blocking the other's view of him, but Jaya had seen that tremble in his hands.

"Take him to my house!" Horace yelled, already heading for the village.

She thanked the skies for Inestar's hive mentality. The soldiers and a few nobles followed behind Horace in the human shield. While the rest of the crowd panicked over the stranger coming back with an army of wizards, Jaya snuck into the lift and up the wall.

~

"How is she?"

Jaya eased the door to her mom's room closed. "Alright. Confused."

She wandered past their small and empty dining table. She should have tried to make something. There was still time. Her mom was still up in her room, patiently folding and smoothing the fabric of her robes by hand. Those creases would be crisp and permanent by morning. "She doesn't know how they got to the chambers. Her story matches everyone else's. They were locked in the cells, then they just opened."

Durand raised his hands in surrender. "I'm not here to interrogate."

"Then why are you here?" She sighed, pressing her fingers into her tired eyes.

That brief pause and Durand, still in uniform, told her all she needed to know. She went to grab her bandolier and daggers from the chest that doubled as a guest table. "Patrols have been doubled. Bas's order. And everybody's pulling an all-nighter."

"Like that's gonna do any good if he comes back." Jaya sheathed the daggers across her chest, tucking another by her ankle for good measure.

"When." Durand held the front door open for her to pass. "You heard him. He's looking for someone. We got in the way today, but he'll be back. He's not gonna stop until he finds whoever it is."

2

SIX YEARS LATER

Grunt Day in Inestar was the worst. A bunch of starved, sad, and desperate people willing to do anything to not be starved and desperate anymore. Even travel to a desolate canyon to fight a trained soldier.

"Her." A boy pointed at Jaya with a shaky and bony finger.

Great. She fought the urge to roll her eyes. The quiet snickering from the guys next to her didn't help. Jaya was called out often during these things. Being one of a handful of female soldiers, they assumed she'd be easy to beat. She tried to stay in the back, but the other soldiers would shift, making sure the grunts saw her every time.

She allowed herself one exasperated huff, then stepped into the sweltering heat of the hexagon. The six-sided depression in the canyon was probably a lake at one point, but the water had long since dried up.

The boy's eyes widened in either shock or fear as she approached. He took in her lean muscles, the red bandages wrapped around her fists, stained black with blood- hers and others. He scanned her from head to toe, noting every bruise, scar, and scratch. His hollow cheeks flushed with hope until his gaze returned to the bloody wraps.

Jaya pulled her red scarf down from around her mouth and nose and stopped at the center of the hexagon while her challenger remained near the border. Her eyes zeroed on Brandt Yido, comfortable on his shaded perch beneath the canyon arch at the head of the hexagon. She wouldn't look at the boy. She didn't want to see that look. The one all but the overly confident grunts had whenever they saw an Inestar soldier up close. Like she was a rabid animal who had crept into his home while he slept.

She could hear his frantic breathing from where she stood. Everyone could. He startled at the sound of Brandt Yido's voice. "Come forward. State your name and birthright."

The boy stood flummoxing as if he had been asked to conjure water instead of give his name and place of birth.

"Do you have a problem hearing, boy?" Brandt Yido said loudly.

Another round of low laughter rumbled behind her. Jaya shamefully wished he would say yes. It'd spare her from ruining yet another life and marking more flesh.

"No. My name is Dwayne. I'm from Monesta."

She turned, surprised to find the boy's eyes, not on her, but the soldiers behind her. He had straightened to his full height. His shoulders were thrown back with pride, face set in determination. He wouldn't go down easy.

"Choose your weapon," Yido said, paying more attention to the doodle he was drawing in the sand than them.

"Hand to hand," Dwayne replied with little certainty. Another thing Jaya had come to expect when she was called out. They always wanted bare fists. Probably because her hands were on the small side. She took a deep breath as Dwayne finally made his way to the center of the hexagon to face her and settled into the numbness of battle.

"Begin."

She struck first, a quick jab to his throat that would have knocked the wind out of him had he not stumbled back, caught off guard by her quickness. She kept coming, throwing jabs and elbows at his eyes, temple, and nose. Many he was able to block, but even that cost him. His arm blocked his view, and he couldn't see where the next blow was coming from. They kept coming, each more precise and brutal than the last. He wouldn't beat her this way. He needed a plan. *Fight back.* Maybe they'd be willing to train him if he could last long enough.

Dwayne threw his body wildly in her direction, trying to get her to the ground and get the upper hand. Jaya sidestepped his attack, but his weight propelled him right onto her knee. His head smashed into it with so much force that his body buckled like someone had ripped out his power cord. Dwayne hit the sand with a muffled thump.

STARS PULSED IN BLACKNESS, and he struggled to regain his balance and sight. They were cheering now. All around him, he could hear the shouts of the soldiers blending into one throbbing wave of sound. No longer disciplined guards performing a duty. They were spectators now, enjoying the match.

Rage and humiliation coursed through Dwayne. He charged at the female, determined to prove that she, that they, were not better than him. He swung for her head with all his strength, careful not to let his weight be used against him again. Again and again, he struck.

Be the aggressor. Strike first. Do not relent.

He had to beat her at her own game. Force her into defense. He kept up his assault, waiting for his opening. Finally, it came when she glanced back for a half second to gauge how close she was to the barrier of the hexagon.

He pounced.

Reaching out, he tried to wrap his arm around her and take her down. She caught his wrist and twisted with more force than she should possess. The kick that followed to his ribs sent him hurtling to the hot desert floor for the second time. Face down, he took staggered breaths of sand and blood. That's when he felt it. A blinding pain hammered into his side.

She had stabbed him!

Weapons were supposed to be off-limits. They told him he could choose hand-to-hand. Disgusting liars. He should have known this wouldn't be a fair fight.

"Enough. Mark him, so we can move on," Brandt Yido drawled from above.

"Wait, no! I can still fight. She cheated!"

The fight had carried them across the hexagon to where the commander sat, and Dwayne now lay face down at his feet.

He sat up as quickly as his wound would allow and looked around for his opponent. She stood back four feet, hands at her side but coiled tight, staring through him with unfeeling eyes. She had stuck a knife in a man while he was down, and she didn't look the least bit ashamed about it. "Show me your weapon! Where is it?"

Bewilderment broke her stony mask. For a moment, she looked just as surprised as he was that she was armed.

"*Where is it*?!" His eyes darted wildly, searching for it. Sand and the bright glare from the overhead sun stung. She must have hidden it somewhere. "You said this would be a fair fight!"

"Wow, Jaya. You beat him stupid. That's a first," one soldier hollered out.

Low, sinister laughter echoed around him, closing in along with the circle of soldiers. Dwayne's heart thundered in his chest. Fear like he had never known before rattled inside him as realization set in. He wouldn't let them mark him. He'd die here, in this scarred hull of a place, before he let them enslave him.

Dwayne got to his feet slowly. His ribs throbbed from the movement. One or a few of them were probably broken. And maybe piercing some vital organ, if that slow wheezing was coming from him. So he didn't have long. He wouldn't die a slave.

Seeing that they were in for a fight only amused the soldiers more. They tightened their circle around him in eerie unison. Now would be his only chance.

Be the aggressor. Strike first. Do not relent.

He locked eyes with the biggest of them, a beast of a man with a gruesome scar in the center of his face like someone had made it halfway through cutting his nose off. He kept his eyes trained on the big man until the last second, then he pivoted and struck the soldier to his right. He kicked backward blindly, hitting another.

Then they were on him. The weight of the entire Inestar army bearing down on him. Crushing him. He could make out a lone figure through the mass of arms and bodies. The female soldier stood at the farthest corner of the hexagon, looking on with those dead eyes. He focused on her until everything, light and sound, blurred around him and faded to black.

JAYA PLUNGED her hands into the freezing water before she could second-guess it.

"Red grain."

Invisible spikes splintered and raced up her arms, causing her muscles to jerk violently.

"sweet linmins, shh—short.. cake."

Breathe. Breathe.

"plum... da-daloons."

The lump in her chest tightened with each shaky inhale. She closed her eyes and focused.

"Kyne nectar, froloin, melon jye."

The relief of numbness came in on a wave. Jaya let go of the breath she'd been holding as she began washing. She took inventory as she went.

No broken bones this time. Sprained wrist. Shoulder's moving a little funny. Chest, alright. That shot to the kidney is going to bruise pretty good, though. Right knee's still a bitch. Should have seen that kick to the shins coming. The heat must have melted her senses by then. Hopefully, it won't be too much trouble. All ten toes intact.

The weight of the day settled in, and her eyes drifted closed. She was met by dark eyes glaring back at her.

You did this to me.

Jaya reared back, snatching her hands from the clay basin. For the second time in less than ten minutes, she fought to get her breathing under control. Four light taps sounded at her door.

"Go away," she yelled, hoping she didn't sound as fragile as she felt.

"Jaya, it's me." Her mom's soft voice carried through the door.

"Come in."

"You know better than to bathe with the door unlocked."

"I wasn't thinking," Jaya responded absently, her eyes on the two trays her mom juggled as she turned to close and lock the door. The smell of smoked stargan and greens drifted from beneath the lid. She hadn't eaten since earlier that morning when they were called to assemble for pre-Grunt Day training. Even the droplets of steam looked appetizing to her at the moment. They probably tasted like watered-down green juice.

"I got Sellyan to get me some greens from the garden. She also made some warm peaches for you."

Jaya's knees wobbled. Sellyan had no way of knowing how much she loved peaches, but her mom sure did. She no doubt had to finesse and bargain to get this meal for her. "Ma, you shouldn't be—"

"You can eat after you finish." She placed the trays on the small stand near Jaya's bed and returned with two brown bottles in a small bowl. Jaya's eyes tracked her mom as she sat the bottles down on the counter and nudged her aside to fill the bowl with water, looking for signs of a limp or a wince of pain. Thankfully, there were none today. Her mother moved around confidently in the small room, her purple robes clean and elegantly fitted to her tall frame, eyes sharp with wisdom and strength.

She pulled over the old worn trunk, Jaya's father's trunk, from the foot of the bed to the bathing area. Jaya soon felt the scarf being untied from her head and her curls falling in uneven lumps around her shoulders. "Sit down."

"Ma, I can wash my own hair."

"Oh really? When's the last time you did it?"

"I... I think you should use this time to rest. The last thing you need is to be—"

"The last thing I need is my child telling me what to do." Neither spoke nor moved in the next few breaths. Jaya knew that tone. And while she didn't appreciate the comparison, she understood her mom didn't need the constant reminder that her life was not her own.

The cold water from the bowl spilled from above, and Jaya instinctively tilted her head back as a shiver ratcheted down her spine. Her mom's fingers dove in, working shampoo into her scalp and unleashing sand and grit from the past few weeks. Her voice was softer now. "You are my child, Jaya. No matter how old you get or what happens. Taking care of you will always be my priority."

Jaya didn't respond. Instead, she sat down on a stool and wrapped her arms around her knees as her mom detangled her coils.

"You keep letting it get all tangled like this, and you're going to have to cut it all off."

"Well, I didn't get your small, perfect for low-cuts head, so that won't be happening."

Zora Nideha did not allow her silver curls to grow longer than a few inches. Anything more was an unnecessary burden, in her opinion. Jaya often wished she had inherited her mother's delicate beauty. Instead, she got a mixed match of small breasts and big thighs and her father's sharp nose. The only traits she had managed to snag from her mom were her almond skin and stubborn nature.

"I heard someone from Dewar is coming here."

"Where'd you hear that?"

"The guys on mountain duty. They said Brandt Yido wouldn't shut up about it."

"Well, that part, I believe."

"You know how he loves to gossip. Couldn't hold water if he were the ocean."

Jaya chuckled.

"Their king wants to establish a relationship with Inestar. After all that mess, he probably just wants to monitor what's going on here."

"And keep it far away from him and his people," Jaya finished.

"Right. The Dewarian is coming to take someone to stay on their planet for two months as a guest of their king. Brandt Yido seems to think it's going to be him."

"Well, it makes sense. He is Bas's heir."

"I still can't believe your grandfather chose him."

Over you. Jaya didn't need to hear the words to know her mother had placed a lot of hope in the belief that she would be chosen to take her grandfather's place after he died. It wasn't just a long shot, but a near impossibility. He saw too much of her father in her, physically and mentally. Bas might have torn Inestar back down to sand before he gave his title over to her.

Her mom wrapped her curls in a robe, and Jaya took that as her cue to cut her bath short. The smell of food was only making her hunger pang worse by the minute. Zora cleaned up the bathing area while Jaya got dressed. She sat at the foot of the bed and watched her mom put the products back on her stand, organize them by size and rows of four, and wipe the floor dry of the water they had spilled without making a sound.

Despite the cold of the desert night, a fine sheen of sweat had collected on her mother's skin. The glisten made the mark just above her left brow stand out. The stylized 'I' might have looked like a scar from some minor accident were it not for the red glow of the Syntia-laced ink.

"Stop staring and eat." The tone was back. Jaya grabbed the plate from behind her and began eating. She finished the greens and fish without having tasted anything. Thankfully, her mom had stopped cleaning and had come to sit on the bed next to her by then.

"I heard about what happened today."

"Yido might as well start a gossip letter- *What's Hot in Inestar.*"

Zora snorted. "Don't think he hasn't thought about it."

"Bas would skin him alive in front of the whole village."

They both fell silent, each lost in their own dismal thoughts.

"You don't have to stay with me tonight. I'll be okay," Jaya said.

"Eat your dessert."

3

Jaya stood at her post in the east tower, distracted by the children playing below. They ran around, stopping to dip their basins in the river and screaming their heads off when they doused each other with the cool water. A boy and girl, twins guessing from their matching orange robes, had worked out quite the system. One would run interference, chasing the kids away from the river as the other refilled their basin.

A slightly older child sat on a stone nearby with his knees tucked into his chest, keeping watch over the young ones. He looked like he'd rather be anywhere else. Maybe playing with kids his own age. Soon he'd be too old to play. Duty would come calling, and he'd have to figure out what he had to offer Inestar. No one lived here without offering something of themselves.

Unfortunately for Jaya, all she had were the honed skills of a killer. Her grandfather began training her at the age of four, back when he could stand to look at her. She was never taught to cook, make medicine, or construct homes. Those skills would not help her in her role as Bas. Now that she was at the bottom of the list of people in line to lead, she was here guarding the Bastian River against poachers and beating and enslaving outsiders who wanted to prove themselves useful to Inestar.

Out of the corner of her eye, Jaya spotted Durand approaching from the west. It wasn't time for them to switch yet. She enjoyed this part of her guard duty. The east tower was quiet and rarely saw any action or intruders. She could sit here all day and watch the kids play in the tower's shade. It was much better than Grunt Day in the hexagon. She listened to Durand's heavy feet clomping up the stairs and turned just as he filled the doorway, huge and slightly winded.

"You alright there, big man?"

"Would it kill them to put a lift over here? What are we, sand dwellers?"

"What are—you know what, never mind. I don't want to know." Durand had a fascination with the lesser-known and often bizarre. Unfortunately for him, his size and brutal resting face landed him in the Inestar army instead of his beloved tomes.

"What's up?"

"You've been summoned."

Jaya climbed down the ladder of the tower and headed toward the homes. The sandstone streets of Inestar were quiet in the late afternoon. Everyone was wrapping up their daily duties, too busy and afraid to waste a moment on idle conversation. Someone's failure to finish their assignments always got back around to Bas. That person would soon find themselves without a home and facing a long trek through the harsh desert to the next settlement that would take them. Inestar was not for the stagnant.

When the original settlers, exiled to the wilderness by the Carye, came upon Mount Inestar, the land was nothing but sand shadowed by hungry vultures. Rather than continue to wander from wasteland to wasteland and eventually starve to death, the settlers carved small dwellings into the mountain. They ate what they could grow or catch in the Bastian. Centuries later, Inestar was a village of one hundred-thirty, including the children, soldiers, slaves, nobles, and Bas.

Jaya climbed a stairway between a gathering of stone homes leading up to the east entrance of the mountain. Although they had built many homes outside the mountain over time, Bas preferred the dwellings of his ancestors. He had commissioned thirty slaves to work from dawn to dusk, carving out and sculpting the many shelters of the settlers into one enormous palace for him beneath Mount Inestar.

The smooth beige stone formed stilted doorways that led from one immaculate and austere room to the next. Jaya found her grandfather in the main space with the large windows overlooking the Bastian.

Today, he had ditched his usual battle tunic and armor for white linen robes that billowed in the breeze as it swept in the windows. It must be nice to have time for quiet reflection. All he was missing were some open-toed sandals and a cool drink. He didn't turn away from his view of the river, but he spoke as soon as she reached the center of the room. "I am expecting a visitor in the coming days."

He didn't ask a question, so Jaya knew to remain silent until he did.

"He's coming from the kingdom of Dewar on the neighboring planet, Okew. You may remember their ruler came here years ago."

Jaya definitely remembered.

"I had a very unpleasant talk with him while he was here. He accused one of my soldiers of attacking two of his citizens and holding one hostage here." He paused there, likely for dramatic effect because he still had not asked Jaya a question. "It seems he has recovered some of his senses. He's invited a guest to represent Inestar at his annual kingdom summit."

This wasn't news to Jaya, but there had to be more. He couldn't have called her here just to tell her he was having a visitor. Maybe she was going along with Brandt Yido as his guard, or she needed to take over his duties while he was away at this summit.

He turned away from the windows then and finally looked at Jaya. His eyes were depthless, murky pits, and his gray beard turned down with his mouth into a permanent scowl.

"You are going to go to this summit and kill the king of Dewar."

It didn't take long for word to get around that Jaya had been chosen to be Inestar's representative. Yido was furious and took it out on anyone who had the misfortune of being assigned to his command, slaves and soldiers alike.

Jaya had just finished her tower watch shift and was now packing her father's trunk with the robes and gowns that were lying on her bed when she came in. She wasn't sure if she was supposed to pack light, if the plane- no, spaceship?- would hold so much weight.

She was going to be on a spaceship.

Her chest felt like it had a deflating balloon inside it, pushing hot air up into her throat faster than she could let it out. She stopped halfway through folding a yellow dress to get ahold of her shaking hands. The rest of her continued to shake. She could get through this. She had suffered much worse during training. Just need to be quick. Get there, get the king alone, make the kill. Quick and clean. And then what? Ask for a ride home? She'd have to lie low until her grandfather sent someone for her. If he sent someone for her. This was feeling more and more like a suicide mission, but she had to do it for her.

The her in question walked into Jaya's bedroom as if summoned by her troubled thoughts. She wore her purple robe draped closely around her shoulders today as if it would hide the fresh hand marks around her throat. Seeing the bruise took Jaya back to her grandfather's main room just after he had commanded her to do the impossible.

"Aquillo has a weakness for pretty women. He was willing to risk the lives of his people by insulting me over his runaway mistress. You need to use that. Get close. Do what you must. And then kill him."

Jaya had stopped hearing. Everything was buzzing around her. Rage and disgust battled within her over what her grandfather was implying and outright telling her to do.

"I knew you were my only choice, but I also know your faults. You are strong but emotionally weak and easily swayed, just like your father was." She forced her eyes away from his to the large windows, wishing he were still standing by them. It'd be easier then to push him out of one.

"So to make sure you don't lose sight of what's important here, what's

expected of you, I'll make you a deal. You complete this task, bring me Aquillo's glowing eye, and I will free your mother."

Jaya met his stare, scrutinizing every inch of his face for any sign of deception. He let her. "By free...you mean?"

"She will be an Inestar citizen with no duties. A woman of leisure. Free to do whatever she wants, as long as it's within my law."

Truly free. Only the children of Inestar were allowed to simply be *and enjoy life, but even they were forced to into the hexagon at age seventeen. Her mother would be the first actual citizen of Inestar, not a subject.*

"Do we have a deal?"

Her mom move stiffly around the bathing area, collecting toiletries Jaya would need for her trip. It was pointless to ask her to let her do that. The bruises were no coincidence. Yido had been asking around about her mother's assignment for the day.

They both worked quietly until Jaya had her father's trunk and one extra filled to the brim with the things she'd need. She then fell back onto her bed. Her mother gingerly laid down by her side. Though neither would admit it to the other, they both felt the smothering weight of finality. But saying goodbye felt like a jinx, so they settled for being close to one another. Zora was the first to break the silence. "I don't want you to call."

Jaya had given her mom a radio phone she'd stolen off a soldier who had met his end in the hexagon before his body was carried to the pyre. Her mom had been too afraid to use it. They saw each other in the evening, so Jaya assumed she had tucked it away and forgotten about it. She probably wouldn't be able to call, anyway. Not where she was going.

"Your father called me every day when he was away. I still remember the excitement I felt knowing I'd hear his voice. It didn't matter what we talked about. Those calls were what I looked forward to each day. I set my time by them. Everything was before or after our call."

People rarely spoke of her father. It was like they feared speaking his name would curse them with his fate. Yet he had been mentioned twice today. Maybe it was a sign.

"He never forgot. Never. He always called." She nodded. "That was your father, always thinking of others. Maybe if he wasn't so focused on me-."

"Ma, don't–"

"I'm not blaming myself, but I need to say this. These years have given me time to think and maybe be a little less starry-eyed. Your father was a selfless man. He lived and died thinking of others. I can't tell you how much I don't want that for you." Her breath hitched, and Jaya knew that talk of her father had done what Yido's bruises and long heat-drenched days carving out the mountain had not. "I don't want memories, Jaya. I want you to be okay. So do whatever you have to do. Focus on you, on surviving. Nothing else matters. Not me, not your grandfather, not this place."

Jaya reached over blindly and took her mother's hand. She hoped the gesture would be enough and her mom would not force her to give a promise aloud that she knew she couldn't keep.

4

Quielle walked through the sliding doors of The Orb Center transit and install department to find his younger brother playing a mini game of pool on his desk with a pen and three orbs. "Does anybody work around here?"

"Not as much as you. We have lives." Tonure paused the game to stretch his long arms back over his cushioned roller chair. "How long are you here for? You got time to go home? You can tell me how it is you haven't been bumped down to toilet duty."

"What do you mean?"

"You know Re already talked my ear off about how 'some people' can do whatever they want with Orb Center property. *Getting stranded once obviously wasn't enough for him*," Tonure mimicked Rea's voice to the tee.

"She acts like she has to take a break from talking shit to come get me. I double up on my orbs before every trip now, after that shit she pulled- leaving me to freeze to death on that planet." Quielle flopped down on one of the empty chairs in front of a floating screen. He'd passed the two guys his brother shared a workspace with on the way in. "She needs to focus on her other Deep Exploration travelers who won't go more than two planets away."

Tone chuckled. His eyes were on the orb he was pushing around on the table, but Quielle could tell they were laughing at him.

"What's so funny?"

"You two. She does all this complaining about you, but she'll be in here riding my back about making those extra orbs for you and restocking the pods along your route as soon as she hears you're back."

"That's because she's crazy. I told you you need to watch out for her."

Tone laughed again. "Re's harmless. Besides, you can't be out here playing lone wolf, then get mad when people leave you alone. You want someone to come through when you need them, take our advice and join a team. Or leave that space cowboy stuff alone altogether. Find you a nice girl and settle down. Start popping out some strong-face kids for Uncle Tone to spoil."

"Rea still got your head gone over that little kiss from eight months ago, I see."

"It was six, and we're not talking about me."

"Yeah, okay, family man. I'll pass on the team, but I'll take any extra orbs you got."

"I tried," He said as the door behind them slid open.

Rea strolled in without sparing Quielle so much as a side glance.

"The Travel Committee got approval for an orb pod install. I need you to meet up with Sinest. He's putting together a team. You all can head out before the day's end." She dropped a gear bag on his desk.

"Good morning, Re," Tone said, ignoring the bag. "I'm sorry. Rea. Ms. Westin."

She gave him her signature green-eyed scowl, which would usually have people knocking each other down to get out of her way. Tonure, however, reclined in his chair and let his eyes drift down, slowly taking her in- the t-shirt and jeans that clung to her full figure, her hand propped on her hip- before meeting her stare. "You look beautiful, as always."

For once, Rea didn't have something snarky to say. Quielle took that bad omen as his cue to leave.

"Hey, I need your report before you go," She mumbled, stopping Quielle's retreat.

"Check your communicator. I'm sure it's working this time."

She chuckled at that. No doubt remembering Quielle's multiple distress alerts and requests for orbs that went unanswered- by her. Demon.

Since then, he had dialed back on the uncharted missions. He still traveled farther than any of the others, but now he usually returned to sectors he had been before. Thanks to Quielle, they now had nine pods in VXR 50, The Gold Plane, and Ursa Quin. Let some other fool put his life on the line so they can explore the ends of the universe. He'd done his part.

The orb transit workers installed orb pods on uninhabited planets, sometimes on occupied planets, if they could get approval from the ruling species. The more orb pods there were, the farther Dewarians could explore without worrying about running out of fuel. It was a major waste of time, seeing as only thirteen people in all of Dewar had gone through Deep Exploration training.

"Where's the install?" Tone asked.

"Hanlar LVI."

"Who all going?"

"He's still putting his team together, but it'll probably be you, Sinest, Juri, and Loak."

"Nah." He snorted and stood to hand the gear bag back to her. Tonure had always been the taller one, even though Quielle was a good six feet and three years older. Their father used to joke that height outran sense in their family.

"Excuse me?" Rea glared up at him.

"You heard me, gorgeous. I'm not about to spend three weeks on a craft with a bunch of funky ass dudes."

"You don't have a choice. Sinest has had his life threatened by half the women in the installation unit. The other half doesn't want to be in the same room as him. You guys better come up with a shower schedule." She pushed the bag into his chest.

"Quielle can be our ride. The IU ladies love him." Tone grinned slyly.

Quielle glared at his brother. He promised that if he had to deal with spits-when-she-talks Tula or listen to Hizella's 'men like you just need a good, strong woman and a home' speech again, he was going to put hands on him.

"No. Quielle has an assignment, so before you go, I need you to prep a DE kit and at least six orbs."

That got Quielle's attention. "Where's the target?"

"No clue. You'll have to ask the king when you meet with him."

"Aquillo? Why am I meeting with him?"

"He wants you to pick up a guest of his."

It took two rewinds for her words to make sense, and when they did, he looked around to see if there was another Quielle in the room. "What? So I'm dude's driver now?"

"Looks like." Rea cackled in his face, then strutted out.

You wouldn't recognize the king. The tattered gray pants with dirt on the knees and grimy, sweat-soaked shirt were more suitable for a beggar, but it was Aquillo. There was no mistaking that royal air that said, *I am Kani's chosen. My gift is your salvation or destruction if I so choose.* Plus, this was his private garden. Even kneeling in dirt, he gave off the vibe that he was so much better than everyone. He took his time inspecting every plant under their individual, neat hemispheres before acknowledging Quielle.

"King." Quielle tilted his head downward for the briefest second in Dewar history.

"So, this is what it takes to get you to come to the palace?"

"I was under the impression that I was ordered here."

One side of Aquillo's mouth tilted upward as he tapped the top of one of the domes, and it dissipated, revealing a flower. "I have an assignment that requires your special skills."

He grabbed a pair of shears from a tray and cut the flower's stem. Cradling its red polka-dotted leaves, he gently opened the petals to peer inside. Quielle rolled his eyes. He had better things to do than to stand here watching the king fondle his flowers.

"It's Syntia," Aquillo approached, stopping less than two feet from Quielle. Up close, you could clearly distinguish the irises of his bat eyes. "A unique plant that acts like invisible ink until it comes in contact with blood. Not surprisingly, it only grows in Inestar. I grabbed a sample the day you met the soldier."

He wouldn't call having a knife chucked at your face a meeting, but Aquillo's recollection of that day had always been soft, just like his response to one of his citizens being kidnapped by an interplanetary assassin.

Not for the first time, Quielle wondered what Mia saw in this guy, why she had put her trust in him. Was it his power? She wouldn't have liked the constant attention that came with being with royalty. Security? Mia had her fair share of enemies, people locked away in Gudarin thanks to her work as a seeker. She'd also had weekly training sessions with her uncle Bijöse, who she affectionately called Uncle Bee, although he was about as affectionate as a kick to the nuts. So pity? That had to be it. She probably saw Aquillo as some kind of tortured soul.

True, it couldn't be easy having a whole family and no responsibilities one minute, then losing everyone you love the next. But, thanks to him, many Dewarians had that in common.

Aquillo was exceptionally powerful, even by Okew royal standards. When his parents were killed during the last kingdom's summit, and word reached him, that power that all of Okew refer to as 'The Gift' erupted into a blinding fury that disintegrated everyone and everything within a three-mile radius of him. Quielle often wondered if the people of this kingdom ever questioned whether the energy that powers their homes and utilities was from The Orb Center or the trace amounts lingering in the soil from the blast.

"Am I going to Inestar?"

"Yes, you are."

"You said this required skill. Inestar is on the next planet. You could send a team from the install unit." Or go get your *guest* yourself. Quielle didn't say the last part out loud. Even in his bum clothes, Aquillo was still one of The Gifted, and he wouldn't hesitate to turn someone's organs to lava at the first sign of aggression.

"It has to be you. Your years in Deep Exploration have given you skills none of my other travelers have shown themselves to possess. You've gone into some of the most hostile and unknown territories and come back alive and, for the most part, mentally sound. You're strong but crafty and have a near-constant distrust of everyone."

"I'm flattered, King. Really. But–"

"The summit begins in two weeks. That's enough time for you to retrieve the Inestar chief's granddaughter and bring her to the palace. Consider this part of your duty as prince."

Pop told him he would regret taking this fake prince job, but Aquillo had agreed to personally sign off on his solo missions, and the royal stipend was ten times his Deep Exploration pay. It seemed like an easy call at the time: make a few public appearances and pretend to give a shit like all the other royals did. Now he wished he had told Aquillo to find someone else to be his puppet.

Quielle turned without another word and retraced his steps to the garden's double doors, teeth grinding hard enough to saw through steel.

"And, Prince," Aquillo called, "I expect you to be present for the summit as well."

QUIELLE DOCKED his craft in the maintenance wing and flagged down a worker, who rushed over with excitement dancing in his eyes. He must have been bored out of his mind. Travelers didn't need to come to The Orb Center unless their craft required maintenance, or they were called by the Travel Committee. Both were rare occurrences, so the maintenance workers often had long days with nothing to do.

"Hey. I'm heading out for a trip. I just need my thrusters checked."

The worker walked around the ship, noting his observations on the screen projecting from his forearm. There were no doors on the crafts.

They were completely sealed off to protect travelers during trips. They entered and exited their ships through the port stations on the dock or with orbs.

He pulled a scanner from the chest pocket of his navy coveralls, and Quielle sighed. He knew what was coming next. "You have some frosting on your left side, and one of your radars is down. I can get you a new DE-J7 model, but there'll be a eight day hold for final inspection."

Quielle didn't have that kind of time. Seemed like every time he came back from a mission, the engineers had programmed a new model into the COGs (craft and orb generative systems). The oversized vending machines were spitting them out faster than they could be validated. Aquillo visited the orb center every few months to check on his creations and re-power the COGs.

"Yeah, it was glitching, but it's been cleared," he lied. "It should reboot once I refuel."

"Alright then," the worker said with much less excitement than before. "Well, thrusters look good. We'll get it defrosted and do another quick inspection. It'll be ready for you in an hour."

"Thanks, man."

Quielle left, taking the elevator down seventy-three floors to the bridge. He crossed over, tapping the scanner and waiting for the door to the manufacturing side to open. The desk for visitor sign-in was empty, and so was the visitor center. As he walked into the first-floor training compound, the temperature dropped noticeably. They kept it freezing in there to simulate space for the trainees, so everyone else had to suffer along with them. He passed by the training pool where a traveler was easing into the water in full space gear.

The orb transit and install departments were down the hall. Transit was Mia's department back when she and his mom worked at the OC. Tomia Delu had been the whole package back then: beautiful, driven, and loyal to those close to her. A ten-year-old Quielle, gap-toothed and scrawny in clothes that were bought for him to grow into instead of out of, had taken one look at her golden brown skin and full-face smile and fell in love. She didn't pay him much attention. Even after twelve years and significant muscle gain, she still saw him as her friend's son.

They stayed close through the years. Mia took him out for drinks to celebrate his acceptance into Deep Exploration, and he was there when she opened the doors of her seeker business. If it weren't for him getting stranded on that mission, he would have been with her when the soldier broke into her place, and he probably wouldn't be headed to Inestar now.

Quielle passed the change-out room where Tonure and the rest of Sinest's team were inside, cracking jokes and laughing loudly. There was no time to catch his brother up on Aquillo's assignment for him before he left. Having two sons working in space exploration had always been a major source of pride and worry for their father, so Quielle tried to keep Tone in the loop about every mission, sending the coordinates for where he was going and a guess of when he would be back. Tone did the same. But Quielle needed an extra couple of days to stake out the area around Inestar and plan his approach, so he had to leave immediately. There was only time for one stop.

The weapons lock-up was underground, beneath the Orb Center. Hundreds of employees and visitors passed over it every day, unaware that some of Dewar's most deadly weapons were beneath their feet. Being prince gave Quielle access to this- the secret and the place.

He dug in his pants pocket and pulled out one of the orbs Tone packed in his travel kit. The ball of swirling light was no bigger than an eye. Cool and unnaturally weighted like the enhanced alloys that coated the outside of his ship. It was a product of innovation and magic, like most things at the OC. He curled his fingers around it and squeezed, fracturing the sphere and sending light spinning out of his clenched fist. It was a weird sensation. The sound was like glass shattering in his hand, but the orb was nowhere near sharp enough to scratch the skin. Quielle stretched his arm out and opened his hand. Light shot up to the ceiling before showering down to form a passage next to the change-out room door.

He stepped through the portal into an endless stretch of knives, blasters, explosives, and tools for even the most creative method of torture. There was no way he was going into Inestar with just a kit and six orbs.

5

The day of the Dewarian's arrival came faster than Jaya expected. There was no fanfare or grand send-off for her. She was summoned by Bas, who told her to get her things and leave through the main gate.

Durand at least helped her carry her two trunks out, but her mother was in the gardens giving agricultural lessons to the children. She wouldn't abandon her position to come say goodbye, and Jaya didn't think she could handle it anyway, so it was probably for the best.

He stood forty paces away from the wall. Far in the distance behind him was what had to be his spaceship. It was either white or a very shiny silver. In some areas where the sun was hitting just right, it would disappear altogether. Any other day, she would have thought it was a mirage.

He didn't look like he had just walked half a mile through the midday desert heat, not in his all-black and long sleeve shirt. His fitted pants had large pockets on the sides that bulged with whatever was stuffed in them. If the rugged attire didn't give it away, the muscular build and two curved knives- harnessed in full view for their benefit, no doubt- would have. Chaperoning was not one of his normal duties.

Jaya forced herself to stop sizing him up like they were in the hexagon. She tried to overlook the fact that he was visibly armed while her daggers had to be hidden to not give the wrong impression. If his king wanted her dead, he would have come here to do it himself. It wasn't the most calming thought, and it did little to put her at ease over the tension she felt radiating off of his servant like a red haze.

Out of the corner of her eye, Durand shifted her father's trunk from one meaty arm to the other. Might as well get on with this long walk before his chivalry runs out. She took a step forward but was stopped by a deep command. "That's far enough."

His voice was hard, and his stare, trained on Durand, was cold enough to send Inestar into its first winter. The Dewarian lifted his chin and said, "You can go now."

Clearly caught off guard by the hostility, Durand gave her a 'are you sure about this' brow lift. *No. Why would I be sure about going to space with an angry stranger?* Jaya cleared her throat and nodded, giving him her most convincing smile.

He slid her trunk off his shoulder and sat it on the ground. As he turned, he grabbed Jaya's hand and briefly squeezed before walking back to the wall. It was the most physical contact she'd had with him in the fifteen years they'd known each other. The Dewarian kept his icy stare on Durand's back until the gates closed behind him. Poor guy. He was really looking forward to seeing the spaceship.

The Dewarian's hands balled into fists at his side, then he raised one and held it mid-air. Was she supposed to do that too? Maybe this was their way of greeting. She wasn't given specifics on their customs. The invitation was cordial and to the point. His fingers spread, and light shot out of his palm in tiny white sparks.

Another wizard.

Without explanation, her angry, magical chaperone picked up Jaya's trunks and walked toward the illuminated doorway. Pausing halfway in, he turned, giving her an expectant and impatient look.

The half-mile walk to the ship wasn't looking so bad after all. Heat exhaustion be damned. Who knew what would happen once she stepped through that doorway? Maybe it only worked for wizards, and she'd be blown back, making a Jaya-sized hole in the guard wall. Or maybe she'd be sent hurtling through time and wake up a billion years from now somewhere where humans didn't exist, and giant bird lizards would put her in a cage and feed her mud rocks.

You're being ridiculous. It's just a door.

Jaya stilled herself- mentally chanting her last thought- and stepped towards the white arch. It wasn't like she had a choice. She tilted her head, trying to sneak a peek around the side. The arch was thin as a sheet of glass. How was she supposed to fit in there with her hips? Gods help her if she got stuck.

Just go in one, two... Her body clenched before she could cringe-leap through the doorway. She tried again, but her feet were stuck in the sand.

"Close your eyes." His voice took her by surprise. It wasn't that she'd forgotten he was there, but the compassion in his voice wasn't a moment ago. Jaya looked up, squinting against the bright sparks that surrounded him. His full lips were still set in a stern line, but his eyes- hooded and richly brown, she noticed from this close up- held a hint of amusement. "The glare can be a lot 'til you get used to it. "

Okay. She could do this. It was just a damn door... that could lead anywhere. Before she could talk herself out of it, Jaya clenched her eyes shut and took one giant leap forward. She probably looked like a camel jumping a creek, but when she opened her eyes, the ship's sleek navy and chrome interior greeted her.

The Dewarian, not bothering to hide his amusement now, slid past her and strolled down the circular walkway in front of them. Jaya followed behind but couldn't help looking back to see if the glowing arch was still there. It had been replaced by a chrome wall.

Navy floors ran throughout the ship. They stepped into an open area with circular walkways that branched off in four directions, including the one they had just come from. To their left was a small flight of stairs leading up to a platform that had to be used for controlling the ship based on all the handles, blue screens, and panels. A curved, blank wall was the only other thing on the platform. No windows.

The Dewarian took the second pathway, leading them to a dead end. He placed his hand on the chrome wall, which faded, giving them entry into a bedroom. "You can leave whenever, but I'll need to program your hand into the scanner for you to get back in."

Jaya nodded absently, taking in the plain white room and its three pieces of furniture: a round table with a cube for a chair and a bed at the top of a short flight of stairs.

She wasn't sure what she expected, but she reminded herself that this wasn't a luxury getaway. If anything, she needed as little distraction as possible if she was going to complete her end of the deal and get back to Inestar alive.

6

Jaya was going to die of boredom before she even reached Dewar. She would become a cautionary tale Inestar parents told their children to get them to work harder. Or maybe the kids would use her story to get out of boring morning lectures.

Storytelling was Inestar's way of preserving history, and those stories were almost always turned into lessons to ward off death.

She could hear hers now. The Dewarian would be turned into some gruesome, slimy half-man who abducted her because he was lonely. Durand would be the brave friend who fought the monster off as long as he could until he was knocked unconscious by a stray tentacle. Like all the monster's victims before, boredom would consume her within the first week.

It had been two days. On the first day, her wonderful chaperone sat her trunk down and left her to explore her space. Since then, he had only shown up to program her hand into the door scanner and given the sage advice to "not die in here". "No one but you can get in now unless the scanner is reset at the OC."

Jaya had no idea what the OC was or why he thought she'd be faced with a life or death situation in this room. She had unpacked her trunks and put her clothes in the dresser, the room's fourth piece of furniture, she discovered. That took all of twenty minutes.

Sleep had always been hit or miss for her. With the unknown surroundings and an even lesser-known near future, she was averaging a few hours in naps. So the past two days had been filled with planning, stressing, and sitting on the hard cube chair, trying not to scream at the white walls.

On day three, Jaya started to smell herself. She went to scope out her hygiene options in the bathing area, which connected to her room, expecting it to be just as plain and empty as her room. So the metal shower was a complete shock.

It was like the outdoor one they had near the training complex in Inestar. Except instead of an old bucket being tilted forward with a rope by a second person- someone you had to be okay with seeing you partially naked- and cold water being dumped on your head, there were shiny handles and a big, round outlet overhead. Showers in space? Jaya was by no means Fipy's best student, but she had learned enough in her science lectures to know that something wasn't right about this situation.

She turned the handles, watching in confusion as water rained down on the glossy white floor. When the water warmed against her fingers, Jaya began to question if they had ever left Inestar. If this was all concocted by her grandfather to make her think she was losing her mind.

She stripped out of her gray pants and shirt and stepped under the stream. It was, in a word, euphoria. Calm and bliss like Jaya had never experienced before. Amazing the difference warm water and privacy made. She took her time washing, even cleaning, and detangling her hair. The water wasn't running out of warmth, and this was better than staring at the clinical walls of her room. But eventually, she would have to get out and return to the real world. The one where she was traveling through space to take yet another life.

Padding out of the bathing area, deflated despite her shower, Jaya rifled through the second drawer to find something comfortable to put on. Whoever picked out her clothes knew she was going off planet. Their idea of

Dewar fashion was thundercloud-shaped hats and bedazzled masks with holes for the ears but not the eyes. The gaudy dresses all had long trains, and Jaya would fall flat on her face when someone inevitably stepped on one.

She closed the drawer and opened the one below it. More of the same with some extra, and thankfully solid-colored, fabric. It was long and lush. With some folding and draping, it would make a nice dress, but she'd have to get creative with where she hid her weapons. She grabbed a simple ankle-length dress that was probably meant to go underneath a much more fancy dress and slipped it over her head. There was only one towel in the bathing area, so her curls would have to dry freely.

The remains of fruit and bread she had packed and eaten were on the floor next to the table. It looked like someone had come into Horace's surgery room and dumped a load of trash on the floor. Jaya imagined that any day now, flies would materialize from thin air to buzz around the filth. Since a trash can wasn't included in her stay, Jaya picked up as much as she could carry and went to find one.

It wasn't hard to find her way back to the main area. The first corridor she took led her to a dead end. The second led to a small nook that had the makings of a kitchen. *Things just keep getting stranger.* She dumped the trash in a bin next to the walnut cabinets and noticed a small glowing sphere next to an empty mug. She reached for it.

"I wouldn't do that if I were you."

Years of combat training had given her control over her reactions, so she didn't shriek as her racing heart told her to. Instead, she turned to face the Dewarian. Even though he was sitting on the counter that reached Jaya's waist, his feet touched the floor. His eyes were on his long, nimble fingers as he peeled what looked like an orange. Oranges didn't grow in Inestar, but Bas occasionally got one from an outsider or noble in a bribery basket.

He finished working the fruit free, then unfurled his large frame from the countertop with the languid control of an apex predator. No sign of the curved knives from before, but Jaya wouldn't bet her life on him being unarmed. She shifted to the left, closer to the sheathed knives on a magnetic strip.

His unhurried footsteps were a distraction on their own, but Jaya also had to deal with how those light jeans hugged his thighs, and the olive green sweater magnified his hard muscle and umber skin. So at odds with the harbinger of death who had dismissed Durand with a look that said he would rather slit his throat. This version of her chaperone was refined- comfortable. Definitely not a slimy tentacle man.

She blinked hard, trying to gather her thoughts and catch up with what was happening. He was saying something, offering her some of the orange. Jaya took the offered slices and absently popped one in her mouth.

It was amazing. Of course, it was amazing.

She sighed up at the ceiling in frustration as the burst of sweet citrus gyrated across her tastebuds.

It was the firsts, she decided. Jaya had had too many firsts in the last few days, and it was causing her emotions and hormones to go into overload. That's why she was losing her mind over fruit and eye-banging the space wizard. She just needed to take it easy on the experiences for a while, and she'd be fine.

"How was it?" He asked.

"It was good. They don't grow in Inestar, so it's hard for me to get them sometimes," she lied.

Squinting, he sized her up from her bare feet to her head. He chuckled. "You're going to have to lie better than that, Jaya, or your grandad's going to be one granddaughter short."

A harsh silence crept into the space between them. He knew. No, he couldn't know. Jaya held his stare while she tried to devise a convincing denial. The orange peels hitting the trash bag below were like thunder cracking through the room. "What... what are you talking about?"

He tsked. "Definitely needs work. Lucky for you, you have me."

"Who are you? And how do you know my name?"

He leaned against the small island and crossed his arms over his broad chest. The picture of composure. "Jaya Nideha. Granddaughter of the Inestar chief- Bas. Twenty-seven years old. 5-foot-8. Father, deceased.

Mother, unknown. Don't look so surprised. No one comes on my ship without me knowing everything there is to know about them."

Jaya's hand slid closer to the knives.

"Wow. Violence before breakfast, huh?"

She snatched a blade out.

"Okay. Would it help if I told you a little about me?" He waited for her to answer, but she wasn't falling for this pleasant act. "My name is Quielle. I'm a Deep Exploration traveler- not a soldier, not an assassin. I'm not a threat to you. In fact, in two months, I plan to return you home myself, safe and well."

"And I'm supposed to trust you?"

Two rows of perfect white teeth flashed in a smile. "No. Trust is hard-earned, and we don't have that kind of time. But you need my help, so I'm sure you can deal with a little mistrust."

Fine or not, Jaya was about two seconds from slicing his face off. He must have heard her thoughts, or it must have been written on her face because he straightened to his full height, all signs of teasing gone. "I want to make a deal with you."

"Pass. All out of deals."

"You mean like the one you made with your grandfather?"

Jaya mentally cursed at the slip-up. Bait, that's all this was. If he knew why she was going to Dewar, he would have sold her out already. Surely the king had more to offer him than Jaya did. This was a test. If she confirmed, he'd probably turn this ship around and dump her back in Inestar. Or there'd be guards waiting as soon as they landed in Dewar. In any case, silence was her best bet right now.

"You don't have to tell me I'm right. I don't even need to know the specifics. But whatever your plan is, you better do a damn good job of keeping Aquillo in the dark. If he so much as suspects something, you wouldn't get five feet away before he turned you into a human bonfire."

Who the hell is this guy?

"So, maybe you want to think about hearing what I have to offer. I'll make us some food, and then we can talk."

7

Quielle spooned half the food from the skillet onto her plate next to the orange he'd taken the time to slice into half circles and arrange along one side. She watched him prepare everything from her perch, with the knife still clutched in her hand and pointed at him.

He picked both plates up, making sure to stay out of striking distance as he passed her.

A small, empty nook was around the corner from the kitchen. Shifting one plate to the crook of his arm, Quielle placed his hand on the metal wall, activating one of the ship's many hand scanners. How he knew where to put his hand on the blank wall was the mystery. Just one of the many mysteries that were starting to stack up around this stranger.

She should have made better use of her time these past few days instead of hiding in the small space he'd designated for her. He could have an entire area devoted to spying on her. She should have gotten up early to look around. If she'd run into him, she could've said she was an early riser and needed something to do. The lack of windows, however, made it impossible to know when early was.

While Jaya was kicking herself for being an easy victim, the blue carpet blurred, shifting to dark wood floors. A black table, set with silverware and surrounded by very comfortable-looking chairs, sprouted from the floor. The chrome walls brightened to a stark white as greenery materialized along shelves. In a few blinks, the chrome cave had transformed into a charming breakfast nook.

Jaya hesitated in the doorway. Only an idiot would think about food at a time like this. And he probably poisoned it. But the last few days of nothing but rationed bites of fruit and stale bread had weakened her resolve. She could take this meal that she had watched being prepared. She'd need the mental clarity to figure out how to deal with him.

Jaya tested the wood floors. When she was sure it wasn't a very good illusion, she walked over to the table and sat down. The chair was even softer than it looked, a king's throne compared to the cube in her room. She rocked side to side, checking its weight and if it was secured to the floor. *I'm taking you back to my room tonight.*

"How does this work, the ship?" she asked. "There's running water on here and a working stove."

He took his time chewing and swallowing his food before answering.

"The rulers of Okew were given the gift of creation by the god Kani. That," he pointed to the glowing orb on the counter, "is a little piece of that gift. And this ship is like that orb, scaled up by a thousand. All the amenities around here run on a steady stream of magic."

"Do you provide the magic?"

He chuckled, although Jaya hadn't made a joke. "No. That would be Aquillo."

Jaya glanced behind her at the small orb and tried not to let it show on her face how much the thing creeped her out. So much power in such a small, breakable shell. All it would take is her accidentally stepping on one. "Have you ever lost one?"

"No. I keep careful track of them since I need them to get in and out of here. They also power my ship. "

Jaya picked up her fork and began eating. It felt awkward with her left hand, but her right hand was busy holding the knife to his kneecap beneath the table.

"It's easier if you don't think of it as a spaceship. More like a magical, floating house."

Not much better. Her grandfather expected her to kill someone who could burn acres of crops without lifting a finger and create space houses? Either he thought very highly of her killing skills, or he hated her more than she thought. "There aren't any doors or windows."

"Planning your escape?" He gave her a knowing smile. "We're traveling very fast, and the ship is surrounded by a shield to protect us from radiation poison, so good luck."

How convenient and disorienting.

"How do you know how much time has passed? If it's been five minutes or five hours?"

"It's a little past sunrise, Inestar time, and we've been traveling for five days."

That made sense. She usually woke up before sunrise for training, then ate breakfast at—did he say five days?

"Did you say five days?"

"Yeah. We should land in Dewar tomorrow afternoon."

The fluffy eggs turned to sludge in her mouth.

Less than a day before she came face to face with the king. She swallowed, as the familiar unease churned in her stomach. A nauseating mix of panic, guilt, and fear. It was the feeling she had when she heard Dwayne's ribs crack. When she stared into his hard eyes, and they condemned her for every life she'd taken. Aquillo would be another life, another strike against her soul. "I've eaten. Now tell me what you want."

Quielle glanced at her half-full plate, then shrugged. "A friend of mine disappeared six years ago. I've been trying to piece together what happened to her, and I believe Aquillo knows. I need you to find out. In exchange, I'll help you stay alive while you do whatever you were sent here to do."

Not what she was expecting. A power grab or rebellion, maybe. That was the vibe she'd been getting from him. A disillusioned soldier who had had enough of answering to a power-drunk king. Not a man looking for answers about a loved one and willing to betray his kingdom to get them.

This was another thing she could add to Aquillo's list of abilities, making people disappear. She'd have to work very hard to not become one of those people. That's if Quielle was telling the truth. She couldn't think of any reason he'd have to lie about this, but that didn't mean there wasn't one.

It wasn't like he was asking her to do anything worse than what she was doing. And he hadn't pressed her for any sensitive information. Right now, the only thing he stood to gain from this deal was answers and maybe closure.

Beating half-starved scavengers in the hexagon was a far cry from being an emissary and royal assassin. A Dewarian ally could be the missing link to Jaya's survival. She was out of her depths, after all. There was no point in denying that. This was his planet. He knew it and the king better than she did, and he promised to return her to Inestar. Not that his promises meant anything, but his need for answers about his friend could be incentive enough for him to keep his word.

But Jaya had spotted the scrapes and worn handles on his curved knives. She'd also dealt with enough warriors and spies from the other villages, disguised as desperate fathers or defectors, to know when to be on her guard. Quielle, with his wolfish smile, too slick to ever be mistaken for innocent, probably couldn't pull off charming his way into Aquillo's confidence, so he needed her. More reason for her to think twice about trusting him.

"I'm sorry about your friend," she said, getting up from the table and visibly lowering her knife, "but my grandfather sent me here to strengthen our ties with your king. I won't jeopardize that by questioning his rule. Thank you for breakfast."

With that, Jaya returned to her room, resolved to not come out again until they reached Dewar.

THEY DESCENDED into Okew the next day, just as Quielle had said. Jaya was cataloging and sharpening her weapons- all three of them- when she felt the downward shift.

She had chosen her weapons wisely: two daggers and a garrote disguised as a ring. The square diamond that served as a pulley for the wire was fake but good enough not to draw too much attention. If these three failed... then she'd have to improvise.

Jaya paused mid-sharpen, waiting for her hands to stop trembling. She closed her eyes, focusing on the silence of the room and the distant sound of the ship nearing land.

The summit would not start for another three weeks. The other rulers would likely arrive a few days before the welcome banquet. By the fourth week, Dewar and Aquillo's palace would be brimming with foreign royals, advisors, guards, and servants. She would strike then. With the host dead, the rest of the summit would be canceled. She'd only need to play it cool and avoid suspicion long enough to leave with the other guests.

It wasn't a full proof plan, but she'd feel more confident with her odds after getting to know the royals and their inner circles. She may need to hide in one of their kingdoms until she could find a way back to Inestar.

A knock on the white wall drew her out of her musings. Jaya tossed the knives in her trunk and closed the lid before standing to touch the area of the wall where a door should be. It vanished to reveal Quielle. He was in black again. This time his outfit was more formal but just as well fitted to his body.

He took her in, eyes traipsing down over her teal bodice that flowed into an airy rust-colored dress. It had taken hours to remove the jewels that curved along the top and swirled along the side of her breasts, coming to a point where her nipples would be. Hopefully, she'd done a good enough job, and what had been there wasn't obvious. Jaya forced herself not to shift under his intense stare.

"I landed us on the southern grounds. We'll go in through the garden."

THEY STEPPED through the portal into the waning sunlight of the palace garden. The overhead clouds, a mix of oranges and deep purples, were muted, allowing the bronze accents to push through and bathe the garden in its ambient glow.

Jaya kept her head forward, chin high. If she was going to be a convincing emissary, she needed to commit to the role. That meant no gawking at the strange and beautiful trees or wondering down the many paved walkways and hidden groves. She spared no glance at the small animals who played in the water as they strolled over the wooden bridge.

Quielle was quiet at her side. He didn't say anything, even when they came to a fork in the path. One arched pathway lined with vines and a spattering of blue-gray flowers was to the left. The other was a stone staircase that led into a shaded cove.

Jaya slowed her footsteps, letting him take the lead. He steered them towards the stairs.

As they trekked into the darkening path, the foliage closed in, becoming more and more dense. Jaya fidgeted with the ring on her left hand. The square diamond bit as her grip tightened, and she prepared for... what? She wasn't sure, but the tight space and uneven ground would not be on her side if something happened.

Pitch black engulfed them, and she blinked hard, hoping her vision would soon adjust. The calling birds and gurgle of the stream they had passed over were like swords clashing.

She listened for approaching footsteps and any change in Quielle's. They remained steady, and soon her eyes had adjusted enough to make out the silhouette of his back. His shoulders were slumped, and his hands were in his pockets. Not the stance of someone preparing for an ambush, but best not to let her guard down.

Light broke through as they stepped into a small clearing covered with fallen purple leaves. Across from them were two soldiers flanking a brick archway sealed by an old but sturdy iron door. Quielle had drifted behind her again and was now spacing out at the top of the stairs. What was with him? Jaya stepped forward to give the guards her name.

"I'm Jaya Nideha of Inestar. I have an invitation from King Aquillo."

At that, both guards bowed at the waist, taking Jaya by surprise. The iron door opened with no warning or provocation, revealing the palace, a white stucco fortress that rivaled Mount Inestar in size. They were facing the back of the palace, judging by the many balconies that lined the second level.

Quielle appeared at her side. Despite the layer of crunchy leaves beneath their feet, Jaya hadn't heard him approach. She was going to have to watch out for him. He moved like a big cat, and he was just as hypnotic. She shifted, putting two feet of space between them. He gave her one of his too-knowing smiles and waved a hand for her to go first.

Like hell.

Jaya tilted her chin up and planted her feet. Bas's words from a lifetime ago rang in her head.

"Never turn your back on an enemy, Jaya. You need to see, hear, and smell every cue they give you to predict their next move."

"How do I know if someone's anemone?"

He frowned at her poor articulation. "You don't. Not until they show themselves. So what does that mean?"

Jaya squinted, trying to force the answer from where it was hiding in her brain. She hated when granddad asked her questions. They were always super hard, and she never got it, even when he gave her the answer.

"Never turn your back on anyone," he answered.

Jaya looked over her shoulder at the two soldiers sparring, then at the other ladling water from a bucket into his mouth and over his face. She turned to face them, putting her back to her grandfather and the soldiers huddled around the hexagon. She turned again, then again, flaring her nostrils wide. See? Super hard.

Jaya huffed, crossing her small arms over her sweaty shirt. Her grandfather's stone face cracked momentarily as he watched her struggle. "You'll get it." He said.

Quielle must have realized that Jaya was dead serious and that they would be out here all night if it was up to her. He ended the standoff and started up the path to the palace. Jaya followed behind, only a little smug. If only all her battles were that easy. He shortened his strides, letting her catch up to his side.

Her dress trailed over the ivory walkway, no doubt filthy with dirt and grass from their walk through the garden. Luckily, the rust color hid most of the damage. Imagine what the king would think if she showed up sweaty from a hike *and* in a dirty gown.

"Six days alone on a ship together, and you don't trust me not to kill you in front of the palace?"

Nope. She just thought about killing him in the stairway. He had to have been thinking the same thing. "I thought you didn't need my trust."

"I don't. But I'll take it if it'll help us get through this meeting faster."

"Why don't you go back to your ship? I can find my way from here."

"Can't do that."

Jaya was about to ask why when she spotted a woman opening the tall glass doors at the end of the walkway.

Her approach was swift yet poised. Someone who was not used to wasting time or having her time wasted. She wore a simple white dress. The hem crested below her long and graceful neck. Her round mouth was framed by cheeks that looked like they were in the early stages of sagging. That, along with the unnaturally black hair, had Jaya putting the woman in her late fifties.

There was a weariness to her. Not in her straight back or her proud, stiff shoulders. Those things were easy to put on and take off when needed. Accessories for the day's outfit. No, Jaya had learned from her hours of people-watching in the tower that true emotion lies in the eyes. This woman's eyes were tired and -oddly enough- longing.

Quielle's sharp exhale drew Jaya's attention. She looked over to find him staring bluntly at the woman. His hands were back in his pockets.

"Welcome." She gave Jaya a tight smile. "We weren't sure when you'd be arriving. The king is finishing up another meeting, but he's in the palace. I can show you around while we wait."

She was having trouble keeping her eyes on Jaya. As she finished her greeting, they once again drifted to Quielle.

"How long will he be?" he asked.

"Not long. He's meeting us on the roof terrace." She paused, either waiting for his approval on the delay or waiting to see if he would speak again. He didn't.

"I'm ready when you are, umm...." Jaya forced cheerfulness into her voice.

"Lenille."

Her eyes finally settled on Jaya. She looked from the low bun Jaya had wrangled her hair into down to her dress and gave another tight smile. "We're honored by your choice to wear the Dewar colors. The other guests refuse to. Not even for the summit. May I ask how you knew our kingdom colors are teal and rust?"

"Uh." She couldn't tell her it was just dumb luck, not when it could be her in with Aquillo, but saying she knew about this small custom already felt like an even worse response somehow. It was the way Lenille was looking at her.

"I told her. Now can we go?" Quielle said, stepping around her and Lenille and walking towards the palace without waiting for her answer.

8

Lenille herded them from one room to the next on the lower level of the palace. One grand marvel of architecture after another. Arabesque archways, works of art built into the walls, indoor fountains, and chandeliers with solid gold fixtures that gleamed in the late afternoon light. And Jaya paid it no attention. She was busy running that scene from outside over in her head. What was it about the kingdom colors that made her suspicious, and why had Quielle lied for her?

Jaya was so lost in her thoughts that she almost missed the man coming in the side doors of the great hall. The door clicked shut, but he didn't immediately approach.

He stood back, observing them, observing her. His hazel eyes were on her, hard and squinted in a way that reminded her of the male soldiers back home who thought she had to prove herself worthy of their attention and camaraderie. They were always outraged when they realized she wanted neither.

He couldn't have been older than twenty. Despite the sharp angles of his face that usually came later in life for boys, he had the lean build of late adolescence. His curly hair was short on the sides, but it added an extra three inches to his height.

Lenille was explaining how the lower level opened to Aquillo's personal garden when she paused and turned toward the young man. Without being called or excusing herself, she left them standing in the middle of the ballroom to go to him. Once close enough, she tilted her head down in a brief bow.

So he's a royal. The other royals weren't supposed to arrive until the summit began, three weeks from now. Maybe he was the king's younger brother—or his child. It hadn't occurred to Jaya that Aquillo may have children. He had no queen, and her grandfather said he was involved with the woman who disappeared. Of course, that didn't mean he wasn't married, but the invitation was from Aquillo alone.

The thought that the foreign king may have children who loved and depended on him, that she may be taking their father from them the same way that hers had been ripped from her, made Jaya's stomach revolt.

"Where's the restroom?" She turned towards Quielle. He was fixated on the two by the door, an expression of pure rage on his face. With a blink, it was gone. He took in Jaya's face and thankfully didn't ask questions.

"There's one this way."

They didn't bother telling Lenille before leaving the ballroom. Quielle led the way to the restroom, and Jaya burst in, shoving her face into one of the marble sinks.

She blindly turned the handles, hoping it was the one for cold water. The cool mist was an instant relief to her clammy hands and forehead. She splashed a few handfuls of water on her face, fanning off the excess and bringing the last bit of her emotions under control. With one more deep breath, Jaya walked towards the door. She paused when she heard voices on the other side.

"--wasn't feeling well."

"She's not sick, is she? I told Aquillo he should have sent a bolkin before bringing her here. Who knows what diseases they're carrying on that planet?"

"She's fine. Just overheated from the walk."

Jaya nudged the door open, not caring to hide that she had been eavesdropping. The young royal stood in the hallway with Quielle. Lenille was nowhere in sight.

"Are you okay?" he asked with fake concern.

"I'm fine," she replied shortly.

"This is Prince Nyro, Aquillo's most loyal pet. Shake hands, Nyro," Quielle said, smiling down at the prince.

At least she wasn't the only one who wanted to see him squirm. Nyro's cheeks hollowed as he ground his teeth, his eyes turning to emerald flames. His hands balled into fists but quickly relaxed at his side. He wouldn't stand a chance. Not because Quielle had at least thirty pounds on him. Jaya had faced similar odds before and came out on top. But something told her the prince wasn't a rumbler. No, his skill sets lie in drawing in his enemy, learning their secrets and the things they value most. All for a greater payoff when he burned their life to the ground.

He reminded her of Bas, a snake who gave you a warning rattle just to see the fear it evoked.

"A pleasure," she deadpanned.

"You know, in most civilized places, they bow to royalty. Is that not how it's done in your little village?"

Jaya's whole body stiffened. She'd be glad to show him what they do to weaklings like him in her little village.

Quielle's voice cut in smoothly, saving her from threatening the life of Dewar's prince on her first day. "Inestar is a small kingdom of its own, and she is the chief's granddaughter *by blood*, so you are the one who should be bowing."

Nyro found this incredibly amusing. Jaya wasn't sure what tickled him more, the implication that she was royalty or that he should treat her as such.

"Sure. Right this way, Princess Warrior. Aquillo's waiting on the terrace."

~

THE BRONZE DOORS of the elevator opened soundlessly to the rooftop. The ivory floors stretched to the maroon sky beyond until the sharp drop-off where the terrace ended. Columns etched in vines towered high overhead to the emerald and copper patterns of the ceiling.

In the center of the terrace, a man and woman stood from a round table. Jaya immediately recognized the king who had come to Inestar years ago on a rain of fire. He was much calmer today, his eyes glowing a warm, muted yellow that made her think of sunlight filtering through trees.

The woman next to him was younger. Fine-boned and elegant, like blown glass. A blinding smile broke free on her face when she spotted them, giving the impression that her roasted hazelnut skin was lit from within. Wind blew gently through the terrace, catching wisps of her silky black hair and making the soft waves dance around her face.

"Ms. Nideha, I'm glad you could make it." Aquillo enclosed Jaya's hand in both of his. They were big and surprisingly cool. Her mind flashed back to that day when the air in Inestar sizzled with his rage and power.

It was impossible to guess how old the king was. His beard and thick hair were trimmed short, but she could tell neither had any signs of gray. Fine threads- likely the best in all of Okew- were tailored to show off his sculpted arms and chest. Yet still, something about him felt ancient. He, or at least a part of him, had seen many lifetimes. She wondered how each one ended.

"Thank you for your kind invitation." She beamed while slipping her hand from his. "I'm humbled to be here."

Aquillo's smile was even more jarring than his anger. The lopsided grin he gave her was almost bashful and apologetic, but that couldn't be right. Even if it was, she tried not to assume too much from it.

"This is my daughter, Kalite." He gestured to the beautiful woman beside him. "And you've met my son Nyro and Prince Quielle."

Prince? Jaya looked at Quielle to see if there was a resemblance she had missed. He stood with his back against the elevator doors, effectively ignoring them even when everyone turned to look at him.

Aside from the varying shades of brown, they all looked nothing alike.

"Had I known you would be arriving, we would have waited to eat," Aquillo stated, drawing her attention back to him. Three empty glasses sat on the table next to plates, stacked neatly to one side to be collected. This was the meeting he couldn't leave, a family dinner?

"I couldn't eat a bite right now. The trip must have gotten to me," she said.

"Right, this has probably been a lot on you. Kalite can show you to your rooms, so you can rest. We'll talk tomorrow."

~

KALITE KEPT up a steady stream of chatter. Everything from Aquillo reviving his parents' universal coalition to the many empty rooms in the palace, left vacant by Aquillo's twenty-seven adopted children. *Twenty-seven.*

"Most of us have moved on, gotten jobs, or started families. It's just Nyro and me now. We couldn't bear to leave Aquillo here alone," she explained.

Jaya absorbed all this while noting the number of guards and the areas they guarded most heavily. There weren't nearly enough of them to secure a palace this big. She needed to find the weak zones and get an idea of their rotation schedule. There weren't any cameras that she could see, but she would make certain later on.

Aquillo's words came back to her as Kalite opened a set of double doors to her right. *Kalite can show you to your rooms.* The conjoining rooms together were larger than Bas's palace inside the mountain. A grand bed with teal sheets and a headboard framed in gold sat beyond two overstuffed chairs and a footrest that was big enough for Jaya to sleep on comfortably. The bathing area to the left had a massive tub and separate shower. Both had ornate fixtures, like the ones she'd seen in the ballroom. Recently polished, no doubt. Heavy drapes concealed the three glass doors behind the tub that opened to a balcony.

Jaya looked down at the private pond below. Its waters were clear enough for her to spot the colorful fish swimming from one floor up. To the right of the bedroom was a study, two closets, and another balcony. This one with stairs leading down to the southern garden. The doors swayed in the wind, stirring the faint smells of cleaning products and the bit of stuffiness that always lingered in old rooms.

"I could have someone get your things from Prince Quielle's ship, but I'm sure he'll want to bring them himself. He's very private. Doesn't like people in his space. And I get that. I do. He's probably used to having the ship to himself. He may not even come here again until the--." She paused mid-ramble, biting her bottom lip to keep more words from spilling out. "I'm, um, I'm going to see who is around that can get your clothes so you can get out of that dress. Not that there's anything wrong with it. It's a beautiful dress. I was just—I'm going to go."

She hurried out, closing the double doors behind her.

Jaya's breath rushed from her in a deflating gust. She needed to sweep the room for any devices or faulty locks. Jaya was on her hands and knees checking for loose tiles in the floor when a throat cleared behind her. Whirling around, she pulled her knife from her calf holster and brought it flush with Quielle's chest.

"Someone's on edge."

"No. I just don't like people sneaking up on me." She bent to re-sheath her knife.

"I'll try to make noise from now on." His eyes tracked her movement, briefly snagging on her breasts as she straightened up. "You probably couldn't hear me over you thumping the floor. What are you doing, anyway?"

"Nothing. Are those mine? You can leave them in here."

He sat the stuffed trunks down as if they weighed nothing, but instead of leaving, he leaned against the doorframe, shoving one hand in his pocket. "Have you thought about my offer?"

"I gave you my answer. I'm not trying to get mixed up in you and Aquillo's family rivalry."

"Family?" He grimaced. "Aquillo's no family of mine."

"But you're a prince. Unless you're one of the twenty-seven children he adopted and took into his palace."

"He should have. He's the one who orphaned them. But no, I'm not one of his *children* either."

"Are you a friend of the family?"

"No."

"Are you filling in until the real prince gets back from the restroom?"

"No."

"Then I'm not sure I understand your purpose here." She crossed her arms, a habit Bas had been trying to break since she was a little girl.

"Do you need to? I'm offering to help you. I know this place inside and out. I know for damn sure there aren't any boobie traps in your closet. And I've known Aquillo for a very long time."

"So why don't you just ask him about your friend?"

"It's not that simple."

"Well, that's a problem, isn't it? But not one I can help you with."

He pushed off from the door frame and dusted off his shirt.

"Okay," he said finally. Sparks flickered behind him as a shimmery doorway took up the closet entrance.

"Is that how you got in here?" Jaya asked in alarm. She knew she'd locked those doors when Kalite left.

"Yeah. With the right tools, doors aren't really a problem."

With that, he stepped back. The light from the portal closed around him, leaving behind a faint impression of him seconds after he and it had disappeared.

Jaya finished her sweep but skipped the final check on the locks. Instead, she peeled off the dress, changing into the pants and tunic she wore when she left Inestar.

She crawled across the enormous bed, taking pillows and arranging them beneath the sheets. Her arms barked in pain as she hauled one of the oversized chairs from the seating area to the corner near the double doors.

With her knife in hand and clear sight lines to the three entrances, Jaya settled in for a long night of watch duty.

PART II

KINGDOM OF RUST

9

The red and blue strips of light blazed along each loading dock, signaling and drawing in returning travelers. Ships docked above and below on the individual platforms of the Orb Center.

The OC was shaped like its namesake, a square building with a ring of open sky at the center. Ship maintenance and the processing facility were in the right half of the building. To the left was the rest of the compound: orb transit and production, the training compound, the Travel Committee, and the visitors center.

Quielle turned away from the column of windows across the way. He had no business over there today. Really, he had no business anywhere, and that was the problem. It was day three of him being grounded to the palace, and Quielle was feeling that urge to just go. Tension and boredom drove him here.

Several ships dotted the hangar, some barely recognizable as ships in their dismantled state. Rea stood off to the side of one of the finished crafts. Her honey locs were tied back loosely, with some escaping to swing around her wide hips. She wore blue coveralls like the maintenance workers. Aside from being a pain in his side, this was Rea's other full-time job: engineering and mission coordination.

Quielle took in the ship she was inspecting and whistled. It was the latest model. Still shaped like his, but smaller and much sleeker. His ship was meant to house a team, whereas this was probably for a single traveler. Luminescent steps led up to the door on the side. Jaya would appreciate that little feature.

It had been days since he had seen her too, but judging from what little he saw of her on their trip from Inestar, it was probably intentional on her part. It stung a little when he thought about it. He may not have been the most welcoming host, but he wasn't that bad, was he?

He might have pressed too much during that first conversation. And, yeah, he could have put some effort into gaining her trust first, but he needed to find Mia, and she was his only chance. The problem was he knew how he would have responded in that situation, the same as Jaya had.

Suspicion and distrust of her people ran deep in Okew. Quielle had been guilty of this too. People didn't know much about them, so they did what they could to relieve their fear- they speculated. Nyro wasn't the first person he had heard speak down on Inestar and its people. Sentiments towards them had turned even harsher in the past six years since the attacks. But the look on Jaya's face as he mocked her people made Quielle want to knock Nyro's entitled ass out.

So yeah, he understood her hesitation. It would be her greatest weapon in the next couple of months. Quielle's short time as prince had shown him that the Okew royals were like spiders weaving webs too close together. If you escaped one, another was waiting for the easy kill.

"Why are you here?" Rea's voice cut into his thoughts.

"I work here. Did you forget where you are again, MeMaw? You want me to help you find your way back home." he spoke slowly, earning a scowl.

"I'm younger than you, half-brain."

"So you say."

Finished with her external inspection, Rea walked up the stairs into the ship. Quielle followed, eager to see what upgrades they'd thrown inside.

Rea was irritating as hell, but she was good at her job. In the years since the Travel Committee decided to appoint someone with a pilot background to work in engineering, the ships had started to lean towards a more comfortable, less utilitarian design. One that would make the days, weeks, and months spent in space easier to handle.

The ship was indeed made for a single passenger. Rea and her team had packed it with every luxury: a tv with preloaded movies, games, a hologram station, a few art pieces, an herb garden, and even a workout area in the back.

"Please tell me these are going to be the standard models for DET."

"No. We don't want any more Deep Exploration travelers thinking it's safe to go on missions alone. It's not good for the mind."

"Okay, so what's the plan for these?"

"It's just a prototype right now, but if they are rolled out, it'll be for Okew travel only."

What a waste. The rulers of Dewar, Eroni, and Pati had industrialized travel enough that they didn't need ships to get around Okew. The other kingdoms chose to stick to the old ways where The Gifted sat high on their thrones and left their people to worry about things like producing energy and getting around. That was their problem.

"How's Tone doing with the install?" He asked.

"They reached Hanlar LVI last week. The install was quick."

Quielle tapped the scanner for the ship's control panel. He'd already been granted clearance as prince, so he could access the design feature. He scrolled through, checking out the different furniture pieces and activity zones.

"They'll be running checks for the next couple of days, then they should be heading back."

He hummed. They had a new weight set in inventory. His was still in good shape, but he was thinking about turning one of the empty rooms on his ship into a workout area.

Quielle swiped to check the dimensions, but he must have done something wrong because he ended up back on the add inventory screen. A section labeled 'Artillery' caught his attention. He tapped it.

Images of weapons filled the screen, many that were beneath the OC in the weapons lock up.

"What is this?"

"What is what" Rea responded, but she didn't look up from her screen pad.

"This."

He tapped the screen twice before scanning his hand. The hologram of a weapon Quielle had never seen before appeared on the floor. It was even more ominous in full scale. Two handles were anchored to the bottom of a metal box. Above it were illuminated rectangles. They branched out of the side of the box and sat parallel to one another. He couldn't find a trigger or any indicators of what this thing was capable of doing.

Quielle looked up when Rea didn't answer. Her green eyes squinted at him in suspicion. "I don't know what it does or how to use it. Not my department. But I'm going to say it's a weapon of some kind."

"And why is it in the craft's inventory?"

She continued to eye him for a moment before she answered. "The Travel Committee approved them for the DET models."

"Does Aquillo know about this? If travelers start showing up on these planets armed with bombs and whatever this is, the natives will see us as hostile, and they won't let us put our tech there. That's if they don't kill us."

"They said the approval came from up top. If it wasn't Aquillo, it had to have been one of you royals."

The implication was hard to miss.

"You think I approved this? This could lead to a massive amount of death. Not just the travelers, but Dewar civilians, if people from other planets go to war with us. I'd never approve no shit like this."

"It's no big deal right now. They haven't figured out how to create the weapons yet. Those are just models. The Committee assigned a team to research ways to weaponize the orbs, but the only thing orbs will form outside of fuel for the ships is a doorway."

"That's because they were designed that way. Aquillo and the others didn't want the destructive part of The Gift being used to harm or control people."

"Well, maybe our king isn't concerned about things like that anymore."

10

Cinega wasn't particularly fancy. The houses here were nothing like the mini replicas of the palace that were all over the southern borders and cozier than the small, industrial homes near the markets. Quielle and Tonure had saved every coin during their first years- he in craft maintenance, his brother working nights in the artsy village- to buy the house by the sea for their father. Lirhop never forgot to complain about his sons 'stashing him out in the middle of nowhere', but Quielle knew he appreciated the slower pace, even if he wouldn't admit it.

The door was propped open, and the smells from his childhood wafted out to greet him. Quielle walked in to find Lirhop wiping down the concrete countertop. His brother- or at least a holographic version of him- knelt in front of the fireplace, tinkering with an orb pod.

"I'm so ready to get off this damn planet. I'm freezing my balls off out here," Tone said, his voice quivering.

"Two minutes," Lirhop called from the kitchen.

If you didn't know better, you'd think Tonure was Lirhop's biological son. They both had the same lean, athletic build. Tone's from his love of swimming. Lirhop's from good genes. They were both lighter than Quielle and had the same pointy ears that tilted away from their heads like antennas. Quielle shared a short haircut and wide-set jawline with his dad and brother, but that was about it.

"What up?" he said.

Tone paused with his hands hovering above the exposed orb chamber to frown at him. "What up? I've been calling you nonstop. Why haven't you been answering your communicator?"

"Hey. Focus." Lirhop pulled a round serving platter down from the black cabinets. "You got two and a half minutes."

Quielle made a beeline for the stove. He lifted the lid before remembering to move his face. The steam and smell of hen and peppers soaked into his cream sweater. Two ovens, a full-size grill, a walk-in storage, and eight burners- all custom-made, yet Pop insisted on using the burner in the very back, to the right. He swore it seared and stewed better than the others.

"Sorry. I needed to focus while I was in Inestar, and after I picked up the soldier, I was... distracted."

Quielle added water to the pot along with some herbs he'd gotten from the royal garden and put the lid back on. Lirhop peaked over his shoulder. He turned away, but not before Quielle caught the glow in his wrinkled face.

Lirhop's favorite pastime when he was head culinarian for Queen Exia and King Ormiez was walking the gardens and finding inspiration for new recipes. Kabusha was a month away. Quielle usually stocked up on magic-infused herbs during that time. If Lirhop was going to see the age of one hundred and fifty, he would need some help.

"Times up, Tone. If it isn't ready, let somebody else come out and risk their toes for it."

"I got it up and running, Pop" Tone bounced to his feet, shaking warmth back into his limbs and fingers. The next second, he was back on the ship.

Quielle glared at his brother's crew mates as he walked by. Sinest had his back to them, whispering something in the female crew member's ear. She leaned away, giving him a look of downright disgust. He never learned. There'd be a summons for him from the Travel Committee when they got back. Juri was lounging on the sofa.

"Lazy bastards," Pop said, voicing Quielle's thoughts.

Juri spun around, mouth open and ready to say something ignorant, when he locked eyes with Quielle. The words stalled on his tongue. He faked a cough, turning back around to take a sip from his cup. Juri had been one of Quielle's team members before he joined Deep Exploration. He was also the reason Quielle worked alone now.

"What'd you do to Rea for her to stick you with them?" Quielle asked as Tone entered the room he shared with Loak, the only other member who didn't think they were on a party trip- and wasn't female.

"Who knows? Maybe she takes offense to being treated to lunch at her favorite place. It might be time for me to accept defeat." He pressed the wall scanner, and a recovery station materialized in the middle of the room. They were for travelers who had been severely burned, poisoned, or, in Tone's case, had mild hypothermia.

"You should have worn your suit," Quielle chastised.

"I was trying to hurry and get it done so I could get back and check on you," Tone bit back.

"Boy, don't you get naked in my—" Tone's pants hit the floor before Lirhop could get the warning out. His thermal and briefs followed. Naked, without a shred of self-consciousness, he grinned at them. Quielle shook his head. He only did it to fluster Pop. As a kid, Tone had a habit of running around the house in the buff. Lirhop put a stop to it after the meat incident.

They had been running around the kingdom all morning looking for silver helmet crab meat for a private dinner Lirhop had coming up. Maybe Tone thought Lirhop had touched the location for home on the portal map, but Quielle suspected his brother was just tired and ready to get home to play. When they'd stepped through the portal for Pati's western dock, Tonure came through last with nothing on but his shirt, tied around his neck like a cape. Lirhop was furious.

Tone stepped on the small circle on the floor, and the blue sheath molded from his feet to his neck like a wetsuit. He pulled a blanket off one of the beds, wrapped it around his head and shoulders like a cloak, and plopped down on the floor with his legs crossed.

"That's your problem there. You've been showing your business to all these girls, and now the one you want won't take you serious."

"I haven't been with anybody since I met her."

Quielle, who was spooning the food from the pot onto a serving tray, paused to check his math. Tone and Rea met over a year ago. If what he was saying was true, this had to be a record for his brother.

Even Lirhop looked shocked by the admission. "Well, son, if you want this woman, you'll have to do more than buy her things. I mean, I'm assuming she has money, right? They pay her at the Orb Center?"

"Yeah."

"So she can buy her own meal. You need to do something special for her. Cook for her instead of taking her out."

"Cooking is you and Elle's thing. You know I can't even mix salad."

"It's toss salad, boy. And it doesn't have to be food. Just find out what she likes and do that."

Quielle flopped onto the sofa. He tapped his foot against the hologram, making one-half of Tone glitch.

"And what about you?" Quielle turned towards Lirhop, who leaned against the center bar with his hands and feet crossed. "Where's Rea sending you next?"

"I'm here for the next two months. Aquillo wants all of us here for the Summit, including me."

"Mr. High Life here. You living in the palace now?" Tone asked.

"I'm staying on my ship, but I've been keeping close to the palace. Keeping an eye on the soldier."

A beat of silence passed through the room. Lirhop asked, "You think he's the guy who broke into Mia's?"

"No. She's a woman."

Another pause of silence, and then, "How she look?"

The question came from both ends of the room, but since his brother was on a self-imposed hiatus, he answered Pop instead. "Young enough to be your descendant."

Tone squawked loudly, nearly falling over into the empty fireplace.

"Hey, some women like their man seasoned. As a matter of fact, I took Gisete out to dinner last week and the week before that."

Ms. Gisete was eighty years old, but she was a young filly compared to his father's one hundred thirty-two years.

While Lirhop filled Tone in on the details of his date, Quielle's mind drifted to the memory it had been running circles around for the past couple of days: Jaya standing in his kitchen with water dripping from her hair down her back and into a sheer, nearly see-through dress. The thin fabric molded to the most glorious ass he had ever seen.

It was easy to see that she was beautiful when she first walked out into the desert. But seeing her first thing in the morning, before she had time to construct the Jaya she would present to the world, fresh-faced and looking like a sea goddess, messed with him. It made him consider things he shouldn't. She'd be gone in two months, back behind the reinforced wall of Inestar.

"Knock knock."

Three pairs of eyes swung to the front door as Ms. Gisete's dainty frame stepped through the door.

So that's why Pop is all dressed up.

Lirhop had thrown on a moss green blazer to complement his black dress shirt and khakis. He'd even matched his pocket square with the orange dress she had on. Obviously, this was no just-in-the-neighborhood visit.

"Yeah... Alright," Tone said out of nowhere. "Aye, Pop, they're getting ready to take off. I'll see you when I get back."

"Okay. Be careful and call Quielle if anything happens out there."

Maybe Ms. Gisete didn't realize she could hear everything on Tone's end, including if someone came in and told him they were preparing to leave. Quielle covered his mouth with his fist to hide his laugh. His view of Ms. Gisete was suddenly blocked by a tweed blazer at the end of the sofa. Lirhop pretended to arrange the pillows while staring at him intently.

"Damn, I don't even get to eat the meal I helped cook?" Quielle said low enough that only his pop could hear.

"Boy, you better get out my house," Lirhop whispered, brushing imaginary dust off the pillow.

Quielle stood and headed for the door. Ms. Gisete's tangerine sandals quickly shuffled to the side as he approached. She bowed her head, keeping her eyes on the ground. He stopped close enough that she could see his boots. When she still didn't look up, he tucked his finger beneath her chin, gently raising it up. Her brownish-blue eyes met his, and he gave her his most charming smile. Those saggy cheeks of hers flushed with color, and what was probably a dazzling set of dimples back in their prime peeked out at him.

Lirhop cleared his throat.

Quielle gave Ms. Gisete one more smile before leaving and closing the front door behind him since Pop obviously wasn't expecting any more visitors. He waited until he made it past the neatly trimmed lawn to crush the orb because of Lirhop's 'no teleporting in or out of my house' rule.

It wasn't until he was back in the palace garden that Quielle realized he really was hungry. A stew would be nice, but it was late, and he wasn't sure if he had everything he needed on his ship. Maybe he'd see what the royal staff cooked for Aquillo.

It was closing in on twilight, so the king would be going to the terrace soon to eat. Would Jaya be joining him up there? If the king invited her to his family dinner, would she go out of necessity? She had survived for six days on his ship with nothing but fruit and bread, and that was before she knew of his connection to Aquillo.

Maybe she was up there now, in another pretty dress, hair pulled tightly into a no-nonsense bun, smiling on cue and making Aquillo feel like he was the most interesting man in the universe. The prospect of seeing the performance for himself was almost enough for Quielle to make a trip up to the terrace.

He was debating the path to the kitchen versus the one straight ahead to the elevator when a shadowy figure slinked out of double doors on the second level of the palace. The person descended the stairs into the garden and quickly made their way to the cove that led to his ship.

Quielle followed, keeping his distance in case it was just one of the palace staff out on a supply run. No guards around, he noted. Whoever this was had timed their outing during the shift change. He made it to the cove just in time to see a familiar pair of gray pants turning out of the stairwell.

Where are you going, little fox?

Even more intrigued now, Quielle took the stairs two at a time. He came out at the bottom, turning right- the way that led to his ship and the rest of Dewar. There was no sign of her.

Everything slowed around him as a sinking realization took root in his mind. Turning away from his ship and society, Quielle faced the darkened archway to the left of the stairs. Dread swarmed inside him like a nest of angry stingmize. He wanted to believe she had taken another route, but there wasn't one. She must have gone into the archway that only led to one place.

The Sleeping Forest

11

The archway was smothered with overgrowth. Vines and flowers planted in remembrance of loved ones lost tangled within the metal frame, forming a barrier against the sun. Any grass on the pathway had long since withered away into the dry dirt path Quielle now walked.

He squinted into the blackness, hoping to find Jaya returning from the dead end. An impenetrable iron door blocked the only other exit. Aquillo had forged it with enough layers of shields that even a planet-shaking blast wouldn't dent the thing.

Still, he quieted his footsteps, walking as fast as the clattering rocks and dried petals from the wilted flowers would allow him. No sound of scurrying insects here. Even the most basic life could sense the shadow of death that haunted this space. The door should've been close. He still couldn't see well enough to gauge how far he had gone into the archway, but his instinct told him the threshold was near. Jaya should have been within reach by now.

The thought sent his heart racing into his throat. He sped up, digging his heels in as he went from a trot to a jog. Soon he was full-out sprinting down the pitch-black path. His lungs constricted, both from exertion and panic. Maybe he passed her on his way in. He was moving so fast that he could have blown right past her without noticing.

Quielle burst from the archway into a deadly stillness. His skin prickled. Not twelve feet away, thrumming with negative energy, was The Sleeping Forest.

The droning that emanated from within the forest snuffed out the calls of the usual nighttime creatures. Its black trees loomed high above, forming their own sky.

Delusions that Jaya had taken a path around the forest tried to force their way into his mind, but the twisting feeling in his gut was saying otherwise. He didn't have much time. Resolved, Quielle charged into the dark mass.

The droning was louder inside, sending tremors through his boots and into his spine. The leaves shivered in its echo. Quielle listened for Jaya in the seconds between each hum. Anything. The slightest hitch of her breath would be enough. He stopped, looking back to judge the distance from the archway to where he stood. He was a dangling carrot in here, blood in the water. If he didn't find her soon, they would both be trapped.

To his right, a twig snapped.

There, standing with her back to him, was Jaya.

Her hands were stretched out wide by her face, palms forward. What was she doing? It didn't matter. They needed to go before they caught the attention of something here, or the forest shifted, taking the path back out with it. They were in the worst type of maze. The forest was ever-changing: skies tilting sideways, lakes appearing out of nowhere. It screwed with the orbs. He couldn't risk accidentally teleporting them farther into the woods, so they would have to make it out on foot.

Quielle grabbed her hand and tugged, but she didn't move. Her eyes were fixed on the figure in front of them. Hovering near a thick, hollowed-out tree was a creature Quielle had hoped was a myth. The tattered cloak that covered its stained bones billowed in a breeze that didn't exist. Its silence and unnatural stillness provided the perfect camouflage within the forest, so it probably saw Jaya long before she saw it. Two spear-shaped horns jutted out of the ripped neck of the cloak where a head should be.

Krylvonhar.

The twig that Jaya must have stepped on crunched beneath her feet as she took another measured step back. Slowly, the Krylvonhar reached one bony hand out towards them, holding up a small bell-shaped object. Seeing the thing move caused alarms to go off inside Quielle. Some long-dormant animal instinct for survival kicked in and charged through his body with urgency. He jerked Jaya's hand hard enough that she stumbled back into him. She looked up at him, her pupils large and darting from side to side. He mouthed his next words. Although, if the legend behind this creature was true, that silence would be short-lived and useless.

"Run."

They turned just as it rang the bell. Jaya shot forward into the cluster of trees with Quielle on her heels. She skidded into the turn and fell forward, digging her fingers into the dirt to propel her forward. The bell's echo grew louder with each toll, forging with the forest's droning in a pulsing wave of sound.

Tree limbs tore at Quielle's skin as he barreled through the forest. He hit the turn, and his eyes darted left in time to catch a blur of movement. Whatever the Krylvonhar had summoned with its bell had caught up to them fast. Jaya bounded over a large stone, landing on quiet feet, and continued without breaking stride. They just needed to make it out of the forest. The edge stood twenty feet away. Jaya was halfway there.

The blur to his left sped up, moving at an angle to cut off her escape. Quielle shoved his hand into his pocket. Four orbs. He couldn't kill them, but he could send them back to whatever pit they crawled out of.

He cut between the bushes separating him from the creatures- two of them. They turned and charged at him immediately. Running on all fours, limbs folding forward over themselves. He waited and let them clear the distance. Their humanoid bodies pulled tight over bones that flexed and jutted beneath the skin as they hurtled toward him. Claws, long enough that they were probably feet, slashed forward next to their heads made of dripping fangs. The portal opened in front of them, blazing bright in the darkness, too close for either of them to dodge. It swallowed them and sealed shut quickly.

Quielle didn't waste time. Darting through the bushes, he caught sight of Jaya just as she raced past the barrier of the forest ten feet away. She had made it out.

He didn't know if there were more or how close they had gotten. If he made it to the edge, it wouldn't matter.

Six feet.

He dodged a dip in the ground, and a screech ripped through the air. It was like a thousand screams, human and none, wrapped into one.

Three feet.

The trees rippled once and then again, and out of the brush stalked three beasts. They were so close to the forest edge that their disjointed legs brushed against the invisible barrier. They paced, wavering in and out of the physical. He was trapped. The Krylvonhar appeared to the right of the beasts, sealing his fate.

Pine-scented air burned in his chest as he heaved. He staggered back, putting distance between himself and the monsters and freedom.

He pulled out an orb and crushed it, holding it tight in his fist. The beasts tightened their circle slowly, cautious of his next move but unwilling to let fresh prey slip away.

Focus.

In his mind, he pictured a grenade in his hand. He concentrated on its weight, the feel of the pin sliding free from the fuse, the explosive light consuming them. The orb contorted in his fist, battling between taking its usual form and the form Quielle was forcing it into. Sparks shot out, seeping into his blood, tasting and testing the essence of its wielder. The light shuttered, and Quielle feared it would shut down on him.

They stepped more confidently toward him. From its spot near the barrier, the Krylvonhar watched. Its featureless horns tilted to the side either in intrigue or amusement. The beast to Quielle's left- the closest of them- rocked back on its hind legs and prepared to attack when its head lunged forward and slammed into the ground. A dagger jutted from its skull, embedded to the hilt.

Jaya darted from the trees and leaped onto the beast, wrapping a wire around its fleshy neck before it could shake off the blow.

Light shot from Quielle's fist, elongating and sharpening into a sword. Not what he was going for, but it would have to do. The other two beasts charged, leaping over the few feet that separated them and Quielle. Gray fangs extended from their jaws to the base of their spines. He plunged the sword into one, catching it midair and slinging it into the other beast before they disappeared into the portal.

Jaya held on for dear life as the monster beneath her thrashed and screeched. Blood dripped from her lacerated hands onto its jagged flesh. It wouldn't be long before the scent caught the attention of the other predators of the forest.

"Let go," Quielle yelled.

Jaya's hand immediately released the wire, and the beast bucked, launching her backward. She landed hard on her shoulders, inches from the portal that opened to swallow the creature. Quielle ran for her.

A blow slammed into him from behind, sending him crashing to the hard ground. He only had time to turn before the third beast pounced on him. It had avoided his two-for-one trap, unlike the ones from before. One clawed foot pressed down on his arm. The other landed on his chest. Like the nightmare it was, the beast extended its mouth, and black tentacles spewed forth. Those writhing limbs coiled around his neck, tightening and pulling up with excruciating force. His veins throbbed in agony, and Quielle struggled to loosen its hold on him. His chest burned from lack of oxygen and the weight of the claws pressing down on his ribs.

Images of his approaching death flickered like photos through Quielle's mind, each one more gruesome than the last. He would either pass out, and the tentacles would strangle him to death, or the clawed foot would crack his ribs and crush his heart. Or- worst of all- the tentacles would pull his head off and carry it with them back into the beast's mouth.

Crack.

His neck popping snapped Quielle out of his induced terror. He fumbled into his pocket and palmed his last orb. The gray fangs of the monster drew closer. Its hot, sulfur-tinged breath coated his face. Just as he was close enough to see the black hole of the beast's throat, he shoved the orb into its mouth. It let out an ear-splitting shriek as light ruptured and spilled from its neck like heated ore.

Quielle scurried from beneath it, stumbling to his feet at the last moment to race for the forest barrier. He grabbed Jaya as he went, pulling her up from the ground and throwing her arm around his shoulder. They ran as fast as they could out of the forest, passing the Krylvonhar where it still stood near the bushes.

They didn't speak again until they were out of the archway and back in the palace garden. "I have some bandages on my ship. We should get your hands cleaned and wrapped up."

Quielle winced. His voice was ragged, so much so that even speaking was painful. Jaya's body grew heavier, and her head leaned against his. She was fighting the crash, but adrenaline was wearing off for both of them. It wouldn't be long before exhaustion took them. They passed the stairway to the palace, limping in sync with one another back to his ship.

Quielle carefully lifted Jaya's arm off his shoulder and made sure she was steady on her feet before walking around to the left flank of his ship. There were two emergency orbs in a side compartment of his ship. He took both, putting them in his pocket, before returning to Jaya. She was laid out in the grass with her bloody hands covering her face. Her eyes were closed, but her chest rose and fell quickly with panic, so she hadn't passed out yet.

"Come on." He opened the portal before reaching down to scoop her up and set her on her feet.

She kept her eyes closed but walked through the portal into the ship. She flopped into the nearest chair in the eating nook, and Quielle went to find the healing kit. It was in the main area beneath the sofa where he had left it. He grabbed it and went back to the table. "Let me see your hands."

She didn't move.

"Jaya?"

Quielle kneeled and gently pulled her hands towards him. He worked quickly, cleaning and sterilizing the open wounds before securing them with bandages.

Jaya's eyes were open and staring at him. Shadows swirled in them. "What were those things?"

"One of The Sleeping Forests' many nightmares. We don't have names for them because people that see them don't live to tell about it. The one with the bell, though, it's from an old Dewar legend. It's called the Krylvonhar- soul eater. My brother and I used to chase each other around when we were kids, pretending to be that thing. I never would have guessed that shit was real."

He opened the aerosol balm, tilting his head back to spray the soothing mist across his throat.

"The Sleeping Forest is a person? A being?"

"We think so. Can't say for sure. It was here long before we were." He got to his feet, dusting off his pants. "I need to restock on orbs. I can use my last one to take you back to your room in the palace, and I'll walk to The Orb Center."

He could use the palace's port station, but he needed time to calm down before anyone else saw him. When she didn't respond, Quielle looked down to find Jaya passed out.

12

Jaya rolled over and stretched. The muscles in her arms and legs jerked in protest, and her back throbbed like she had been bench-pressing boulders. She untangled the sheets from around her feet and kicked them onto the floor. A dull headache was building at her temples, and her mouth felt like it had been packed with gauze. She opened one eye, hoping the light didn't turn the mild headache into a full-blown situation. It was dim despite her earlier motion. The ship had learned her erratic sleeping habits early on and disabled it's usually sensitive motion lights.

Jaya rolled off the edge of the bed and slumped to her feet. She padded over to the door and pressed her hand to the scanner. The space immediately flooded with light, triggering a switch in her mind. She wasn't in the palace. The sterile white walls and the cube chair clued her into her current location. The normally white sheets were filthy with black dirt that also covered every part of her but her hands.

Scenes from the night before filtered in like sand through an hourglass. Spying to find out where Nyro had been sneaking off to, hoping to find something to use against the overprotective prince. Wandering past trees that oozed black sap. The Krylvonhar. Quielle coming to save her. Him nearly dying in the process.

If there was any doubt in her mind before, the events of last night confirmed that she was in incredible danger here. There was no wall to shield her from the predators that stalked the night. Not even her grandfather's title could protect her on this deadly planet.

Jaya dropped onto the rock-hard chair, thankful for the lack of palace staff and royals, as she folded her arms tightly around herself and cried. She thought of her mother back in Inestar, slaving for the rest of her life, all while grieving the loss of the only family she had left. Again, having nothing left of them to hold on to. Jaya didn't allow herself to think of her father. She feared that the well inside her would never dry up if she did.

This was her retribution, her punishment for a lifetime of bloodshed. It was only logical that she would die a violent death. Quielle didn't know her, the things she had done. He thought she was a bumbling spy. Someone with fuzzy morals but still worth saving. She wouldn't have been able to live with herself if he had given his life for hers.

Jaya stayed there, tears falling onto her grimy pants until her eyes stung from the room's clean air. She lifted herself up and went to the bathing room to rinse them and try to pull herself together. A worn backpack filled with a change of clothes- her white dress- and a toothbrush were on the vanity. At least she didn't have to wear the reminder of her stupidity all day.

She peeled off the dirty clothes and stepped under the showerhead. The soil clung to her like a spirit in need of a body. She scrubbed and scrubbed until the water ran clear. Even then, she couldn't bring herself to leave the shower and go back out into the world where everything felt too big and foreign.

Jaya tilted her face into the spray, letting the water rinse away her tears. She slowly began rebuilding the Jaya who stood between that world and the quivering mess she was now. When she was somewhat stable- only when she could say the words *Aquillo* and *forest* without her voice shaking- she shut off the shower.

Exiting the bathing area, she felt the weight settle back in stone by stone. The dirty sheets were still on the floor- a welcomed distraction. Jaya stripped the rest of the sheets from the bed and gathered them up, careful not to get dirt on her dress. Quielle was sitting on the sofa in the main room when she came out. "Hey. What should I do with these?"

He tilted his head back to look over his shoulder at her. His eyes roamed from her face to her bare toes, where he lingered on the bright red paint. Bas had called a beauty expert to Inestar to pluck, strip, and buff Jaya before the trip. She had insisted on painting her toes. Self-conscious for some reason, Jaya bent so the hem of her dress hid her feet.

Instead of answering, Quielle stood and came around to take the sheets from her. She opened her mouth to tell him she could carry them but paused when she realized how close he was. Close enough for her to make out the impression the tentacles had left on his neck. It was mostly healed, so the marks were barely visible on his dark skin, but his eyes were still red around the edges.

He was studying the towel she had wrapped around her head like it was a weird piece of art. Normally she would have opted for an old shirt, but the only one she had was in his hands.

"What?"

"You look comfortable."

What did that mean? Was he trying to say she had gotten too comfortable in his space? Kalite said he liked his things to himself. She should have showered in the palace. But he was the one who brought her clothes here. Warm fingers pinched the skin between her eyebrows. He laughed when Jaya reared back and swiped at his hand. "It's cool. Get comfortable. Come on, the chute's this way."

He turned to walk down one of the corridors. Jaya followed behind, confused by his light mood after last night's horror show.

At the end of the walkway was a pocket of drawer-lined walls. He turned to the one on the left, pulled the top chute open, and tossed the laundry in. A minute of awkward silence passed, then he opened the bottom chute and pulled the now clean sheets out.

"It doesn't fold them too? What kind of magic house is this?"

Quielle let out a surprised laugh. Jaya had never heard anything like it. He actually said 'haha' when he laughed. His voice was so deep and loud in the small space she could feel it in her body. It wasn't a bad feeling.

"You'll have to file your complaints to the Travel Committee. That's above my pay grade." He went back to the main room and tossed the sheets onto the sofa, flopping down next to them.

"What time is it?"

"A little after one in the morning, Dewar time," he replied with the certainty of that internal clock of his.

Feeling too rested, she asked, "How long was I asleep?"

"A day."

A day she was supposed to use to learn more about the head of Aquillo's royal guard. She hadn't seen Aquillo without the pock-faced mountain of a man since the first day. If she ever got past Nyro's persistent defense, she'd have a much bigger problem to deal with.

Jaya claimed the seat on the opposite end of the couch, tucking her foot under her. Quielle rested his head on the sofa and turned to examine her face. "You haven't been sleeping up there."

Not a question, but she clamped her lips together, anyway. He probably saw the pillows she'd put under the sheets when he went to get her clothes.

"Do you go out every night?"

Figuring this bit of information was safe, and he didn't seem inclined to tell Aquillo the things he had learned about her so far, she answered. "No."

He considered this for a minute, turning over her words and checking them for holes. Whatever conclusion he came to was obviously enough since he turned towards the ceiling and let his eyes drift shut. It wasn't long before his deep breaths signaled he was asleep. Jaya took the opportunity to openly stare at the prince. It was inappropriate, but she hadn't been able to do it since that day in the desert.

His cheekbones could cut glass. Fine hair that wasn't there three days ago shadowed his jaw and upper lip, and a few random strands dotted his cheeks. Jaya had never thought of a man as beautiful before- or even handsome. Devlon, her first and only boyfriend in Inestar, was cute, and his goofy nature always made her feel as if things weren't as bad as they seemed. His father, a noble who could move between tribes because of his skills as a welder, left Inestar right before Devlon turned eighteen and would be forced to enter the hexagon. She'd had crushes since then, but none of them looked like Quielle.

He had changed into a white t-shirt and relaxed cotton pants. One of his hands rested on the couch while the other sat in his lap, next to the outline of— she should go back to her room. Two days in the palace without sleep had weakened her senses and rationality. Had she not been delirious with exhaustion, she would have noticed something was off about the snoring forest before she went in.

Quielle's arm jerked, getting her attention again. His hands were balled into tight fists, and they were shaking. Was he dreaming? Jaya tentatively reached over to grab his arm. His pulse thumped wildly in his inner elbow. A nightmare. The Krylvonhar was probably stalking his dreams like it had hers, waiting at the edge of an arena for him to do battle so it could eat.

The drumming against her fingers shifted, slowing, then settling into a normal pace. His hands relaxed and rested on the cream sofa, so Jaya let go. As she scooted back to her end of the couch, she listened for changes in his breathing. Any sign of distress and she would wake him, pull him out of the nightmare just as he had done for her.

13

Of course, Kalite noticed Jaya was gone all day yesterday. She'd been popping up everywhere. Inviting Jaya to have breakfast and lunch with her. Kalite was nice, and under different circumstances, they might have been friends. But getting close to her would only complicate things when she killed Aquillo.

Jaya was strolling through the Kani temple in the north wing, pretending to marvel at the bronze walls and ornate ceiling while she noted the rooms with multiple servants coming in and out. She was just about to look into one she thought might be a bedroom when Kalite breezed in with Lenille, Aquillo, and the head of the royal guard.

"For the celebration of The Gift, I thought we could start here before we move to the courtyard for the- oh, Jaya, you're back. I hope we aren't interrupting."

Jaya smiled, moving away from the window that overlooked the guard barracks. "No. I was just looking around. I haven't seen this side of the palace."

"I have some time if her highness is finished with her summit brief. I can finish giving you the tour," Lenille said.

"I don't want to interfere with your planning, not with the summit coming so soon."

All eyes shifted to Kalite. Her heart-shaped face pinched with anxiety over being put on the spot.

"I can show Ms. Nideha around while you finish your brief, Kalite." Jaya wasn't expecting Aquillo to volunteer. Apparently, neither was his guard, whose head shot up from his position near the window Jaya had left.

"I believe I have all my assigned duties." He chuckled. "Brome can go over security, and Lenille will handle staff and decor. "

Kalite beamed at Aquillo. He turned, giving Jaya a reserved smile.

"Shall we?"

JAYA FOLDED her hands in front of her as Aquillo walked silently by her side. He didn't give the history of the royals who had lived here before or ramble on about how the stonework was done by Okew's most sought-after mason, as Lenille had. He seemed happy for the moment of peace to wander and take in the beauty of his home.

"This summit means a lot to Kalite. We haven't had so much company at the palace since she came here as a child. She wants everything to be perfect. She's like my mother in that way, a social butterfly."

They walked out into the courtyard and took the path around the long rectangular fountain that ran down the middle. The greenery here gave off a honey scent that drifted on the afternoon breeze and up four stories. Situated at the center of the palace, the courtyard's draped arches led to every wing, ballroom, and servants' quarter.

Jaya ran her hand over the waist-high hedges and glanced up at the second-floor windows. Just as she thought. Brome stood in one, glaring down at them. She almost waved at him, but refined emissaries didn't toy with the guards.

"My mother used to plan the summits each year. It's a pleasant irony that Kalite's carrying on the tradition. I never could have pulled it off myself."

"I'm sure you could have put together a great summit. Lenille would have made sure everything was to your specifics, down to the year of the wine."

His gold eyes flickered with amusement. "Lenille is very efficient at her job. My father used to say that Kani himself would have to schedule his Gift through her."

She would love to hear that.

"He always told me that The Gift was meant to bless others, not just the person it chose." Aquillo sighed. "It stuck with me because I've never been able to see this power as much of a gift. After losing my parents and then Tomi, I struggled to find any purpose in it. What's the point of having power if you can't protect the ones you love?"

Bas was almighty in Inestar. His word was law, but it wasn't enough to save his son from a gruesome death. Would things have been different if he had The Gift?

"I did everything I could to find Tomi. Brome and his men searched every building in Dewar and the surrounding kingdoms. By the second week, I was so desperate that I summoned the death gods."

His voice quieted on the last part as if he was admitting some great shame. Who was Tomi? More importantly, who were these death gods, and how could Aquillo summon them? What other gods could he summon? What if he sent them after her?

"There wasn't any other way. I thought I could get the soldier's name from your grandfather, but things didn't go as I'd planned."

"Is that why you retreated that day? You could have wiped out our entire army, but you left."

"Despite what history would tell you, I don't enjoy taking innocent lives. I needed to know." A look of despair crossed his face. "The death gods confirmed they took her that day, but they wouldn't tell me his name even though I begged and offered them my soul in exchange. They sent me back."

He paused near a tranquil fountain, staring at the checkered tiles at the bottom, his mind and heart years in the past. Aquillo cleared his throat, coming out of the trance. "I'm not sure why I'm telling you all this."

Jaya smiled, hoping to ease some of the king's embarrassment and mask her rising panic.

He laughed out of nowhere. "I expected your grandfather to burn my invitation. Had it not been virtual, I imagine he would have. When he agreed to attend the summit, I thought he would come himself or send his second in command."

The thought of Yido or her grandfather being here, dealing with Nyro's prejudice or the king's olive branch, made Jaya cringe internally. They would have spat in the face of both, and Inestar would be a smoldering crater by now.

"I'm glad it was you," Aquillo said.

"WHAT DO PEOPLE EAT IN INESTAR?" The question came from Kalite, who was researching food to serve at the opening banquet. The two were lounging on Jaya's terrace that overlooked the southern grounds of the palace.

"Usually whatever we grow in our garden. We don't have much livestock, so most of our meals are meatless."

She nodded, adding the information to the screen hovering in front of her. "And the livestock there, are they like the animals here, or are they more scaly and small?"

Was Kalite asking if they ate lizards?

"I'm sure whatever you serve will be fine, but I like red grains, and my favorite fruit is peaches."

"Red grains?"

"It's a rice dish that's cooked in vegeta—" Jaya's words and thoughts went up in a puff of steam as Quielle appeared on the staircase to their right. The sudden warm weather had Jaya in a good enough mood to invite Kalite to join her outside. It was probably also why Quielle had chosen the short-sleeve shirt that showed off his big arms and defined muscles.

Jaya looked up, blocking out everything below his jawline. That left sexy eyes, big lips, and two rows of perfect white teeth.

"Ladies. I'm heading to the pier market. Do you want me to bring you something back?"

"Mind if I come?" Jaya blurted out. She didn't know what was at the pier market, but as long as it wasn't the palace, she was fine with it.

"I'll come too," Kalite said. "I just need to find Brome and let him know I'm leaving the palace."

She shot up from the ivory chair and scurried off, her onyx hair fanning in the wind behind her. Jaya watched her disappear through her room door and down the hall, feeling a depressing kinship with the caged princess. She turned back to find Quielle's eyes glued to her rear end.

"I'm gonna regret saying this, but that dress- as good as it's fitting you- is a little too classy for the docks."

Jaya looked down at the plain emerald green satin she had cut from its layered animal teeth gown. The thin straps drew a lot of attention to her shoulders, which already looked bulbous whenever she stood next to Kalite. And the split was two inches away from showing her business, but it was okay for lounging on her terrace.

"Oh. Okay. I'll go change and meet you at the front of the palace in fifteen minutes?"

"Mmhmm," he said to her thigh. It took him a second to realize Jaya wasn't moving, and when he finally looked at her face, he smiled at being caught. "I'll be out front."

He turned and headed down the stairs, and Jaya dashed into the oversized closet. She threw her trunk open, tossing the pressed gowns out haphazardly. If she slowed down, she'd have to question her excitement. Then she might back out. So it took all of four minutes for Jaya to realize she had nothing to wear. Her gray pants were torn thanks to the mishap in the forest, and everything else made her stand out.

A knock on the bedroom door drew her attention to a man she had seen with Kalite a few times. He stood in the doorway, holding a stack of folded clothes in his left hand. The right sleeve of his dress shirt was folded over his arm, which was amputated up to his elbow. Based on his below-average height, at least a head shorter than Jaya, and slight build, he was definitely not a royal guard. Brome only surrounded himself with people who looked like him and were of the male species. This guy only had one of those going for him.

"Prince Quielle asked me to bring these up to you." His voice was a heavy baritone that sounded like it rattled the throat on its way out. Jaya hesitated, but eventually, she pushed her pride aside and took the stack from him.

"Thank you. We haven't met. I'm Jaya."

"Jondien, palace seamster." He smiled and bowed at the waist. "It is my absolute pleasure, Princess. If you need anything else, my room is right below this one." He winked, then turned to leave.

Jaya closed the door behind him, chuckling as she stripped out of the green gown. How many women had Jondien, palace seamster, charmed into, then out of their clothes, she wondered.

The outfits he picked out for her were warm and comfortable. She pulled on the black pants and soft sweater that hugged her shoulders and went to find Quielle.

14

They were spotted as soon as they entered the pier market. Word traveled fast, and soon, the wooden walkways were flooded with shop owners who had abandoned their customers for a bigger fish. It was interesting and unnerving to witness the twelve-foot barrier take shape around them. While eager, the shop owners knew better than to get too close to the princess.

Kalite wasn't oblivious to it. She struck up conversations with random peddlers, drawing them into their bubble, and commanded that all but one of her guards wait outside whenever she entered a shop. She had just gone into a bookstore when Jaya noticed the blue letters in a nearby window: *The Royal Treatment.*

The summit's opening banquet was in a week. Jaya had studied most of the palace and a few private rooms. She'd even come across a copy of Aquillo's daily schedule in Lenille's room since, unlike everyone else on this planet, Lenille preferred using pen and paper. But she had yet to figure out her escape plan.

"Can we look in there real quick?"

"Tour guides? Really?" Quielle looked like he was rethinking her cool factor.

"It's better than sitting in the palace for the next two months."

"If you say so." He shrugged. "But there's way more exciting things to do in Dewar than look at ugly paintings in a museum. I can show you."

"Show me? You want to be my tour guide?"

"Sure, but only for the fun stuff. Can't have you telling your friends back in Inestar that we're a bunch of boring, stuck-up aliens."

Jaya laughed because she'd thought just that when she was trapped in the white room. And what friends? The only people she spoke to casually were her mom and Durand whenever their watch shifts lined up. Yido would've loved the bit of gossip, but Jaya was still thinking about pushing him off the wall when she got back for choking her mom.

But she wanted to take Quielle up on his offer. More than he realized. And why shouldn't she? He could show her the more populated areas of Dewar, and she could learn to blend in with the people, which could come in handy later. So what if they had a little fun in between?

"Okay, how about this? You do your garden tours with them, and afterwards, I'll take you out and show you the real Dewar."

Jaya pretended to consider his new deal.

"Okay."

"Okay?" He ducked his head down to meet Jaya's eyes, giving her a goofy grin. She grinned back despite herself.

"Okay."

He rubbed his hands together like he was trying to start a fire, then gestured for her to lead the way to the shop. She didn't, of course, which only seemed to delight him more. He let out one of his boisterous 'haha' laughs, then walked ahead. The bell above the door rang when they came in.

"Here for the tours or piercings?" A woman called to them from behind a desk and a pair of thick-soled black boots.

"Tours," Quielle responded.

"You sure? I got my set up in the back. Did these today." She dropped her feet to the floor. Leaning forward, she pushed her turquoise hair behind her ears to show them the collage of piercings and the red algae charms that curved along both. Jaya was more focused on the two sets of gills on the sides of her neck.

"Those would look nice on you," Quielle said, following Jaya's line of sight.

The gills? Was he serious?

"Just the tours then," he said.

"Suit yourself." The tour guide drummed her pierced fingers on her blue and white desk, and a large screen appeared on the blank wall behind them. She stood up, strolling around to them with the grace of a cloud dancer. She wore a cropped shirt that showed off her willowy frame and two more sets of gills along her ribs.

"We have the one-week tour that takes you around Dewar. The Surf and Turf Tour, which goes from Dewar to the island kingdom of Eroni. Or there's The Royal Treatment. That takes you to four of the six kingdoms."

"Umm, I'd like the Dewar tour."

"Good choice. We can meet at The Hall of The Gifted tomorrow."

"A museum. Should be fun," Quielle said, giving Jaya a smug grin. "Send the schedule and bill to my communicator."

"Of course, Prince," the tour guide simpered, eyeing him like he was a rare and expensive cut of meat.

Quielle chuckled and gave her his communication ID. They left with a schedule and a map of the inner kingdom port stations.

"Do you know her?" Jaya asked when they were back on the dock.

"The tour guide? No, I've never seen her before."

"She seemed to know you, Prince. Or at least she wanted to."

"Uh oh. Is that a little jealousy, I hear?"

"No. I was just pointing it out since you didn't notice."

"Who says I didn't notice?"

"Oh *wow*. Okay." Jaya gave an exaggerated eye roll. "It must be nice having women throw themselves at you."

"Woman. There was only one in there besides you. Unless you were thinking about throwing yourself at me."

Jaya bit her lip, looking around at the busy shoppers. They passed closer to them whenever Kalite and her guards weren't around. Some waved or smiled at the prince, which he returned in kind, paying no attention to how the women lingered after they had caught his attention. At least she thought he wasn't paying attention.

"Hasn't crossed my mind," she replied.

"Ouch. Alright." He stepped closer, and she had to tilt her head back to see his face, "But trust me, Jaya, it would be much more than nice."

And with that fantasy now embedded in her psyche, Jaya changed the subject. "Are all the shop owners fish people?"

"No, and neither is she. It's body modification. A guy in outer Dewar does them. My friend Mia and I went into his shop once. She swore she was gonna get steel claws, but she backed out last minute."

It could be coincidence. Jaya hoped it was, but something told her that the Mia he spoke of, his friend who had disappeared six years ago, and the love Aquillo still mourned were all one and the same.

15

Jaya sneezed for the fifth time in twenty minutes. The dust in the old armoire was as thick and suffocating as the sandstorms that tore through Inestar in the hotter months. Her eyes burned from the dander and another night on watch. She was going on day two of no sleep, and she felt it even more now than before she slept on Quielle's ship. The rest was much needed, but it had weakened her.

She stood up from her crouched position, stretching her aching calves and back. There was enough room inside the closet for her to lie down and stretch her arms a bit, but she needed to be upright to stay awake and to see Aquillo through the jagged crack in the door.

She'd left her room before even the earliest risers of the palace staff were up and crept to her hiding place. Like all the other furniture in this room, the armoire was covered up. She had moved the sheet just enough to uncover the crack and for her to creep inside. From here, she had a good view of the king's private garden and the doors on the opposite side that led to his bedroom.

Aquillo stood up from the indigo plants he had been giving quiet words of encouragement and stretched his arms towards the sky. Jaya noticed the black images that covered them for the first time. She couldn't make out what they were from the distance, but they rose from his wrists and disappeared under his dirt-stained t-shirt. They didn't glow like the marks on the slaves in Inestar and were nowhere near as crude. His bronze skin stood out in between the areas of black ink, making him one with the art. And here it was art, not a mark of low class and inhumanity. There was no reason for the tightening she felt in her chest upon seeing them. Aquillo was no one's slave. He was free to grow pretty flowers in the morning and host month-long parties.

In Inestar, if it wasn't edible or used for medicine, it wasn't grown. Everything was for the sake of the community or Bas. Jaya could sense her grandfather, even millions of miles away, judging every misstep she had made so far, and calling her weak for longing for such useless privileges.

Aquillo stepped over a freshly planted bed of flowers, heading for his bedroom, likely to shower before his morning brief with the heads of the border patrols. The sun had risen shortly before he came out, and the pink gauze had since given way to a pleasant blue sky. Jaya would have to meet with Olivia soon. They wouldn't be outside today, but maybe she could find time to enjoy the crisp air a bit. The cool weather and daily showers were drying her skin out, but Jaya quietly cherished them. These were simple memories she could pull out and smile over after she returned to the desert.

She pushed aside the old clothes, reaching to open the heavy door of the armoire when the door to the bedroom creaked open. Kalite's head poked around the jamb before she sauntered inside. "Close the door behind you."

Nyro came in after her, a mug of morning elixir in one hand while his other held a container on his shoulder.

"If you want to get this done before the summit, we're going to need help," he said, placing his mug on a nearby surface so he could sit the container down. He tapped the keypad on the top of the box, and another identical container appeared next to it.

"I don't trust Lenille not to put it in one of her notebooks, or to tell Aquillo just to spite me. You know she doesn't like surprises." Kalite took a dust-clouded mirror down from the wall.

"I'm not sure I'm all the way on board with this one myself. If Aquillo wanted his parents' old bedroom where they were gruesomely murdered transformed into a gallery, he would have done it himself." He pulled a sheet off of a long dresser and began pulling clothes out and placing them inside his box.

"He told me himself he wanted to do something to honor his father's legacy. He has a lot of pictures of King Ormiez with the heirs of the original travelers from his exploration days. A lot of them reached out when Aquillo announced he was doing the kingdom summit this year. They said they'd come. Maybe they can bring something from their planets to honor the man who reunited our people."

Kalite put a matching set of lamps in the box, along with a jewelry box and a toy ship. Nyro pulled a sheet off another dresser, close enough for Jaya to see his throat bob as he swallowed more of his drink. She inched the old clothes to the left side of the armoire and tucked herself into a ball behind the locked half of the double doors.

"I'm not saying it isn't a good way to remember him, Kalite. I just don't want you to get your hopes up. Aquillo is dealing with their deaths in his own way, and if this doesn't fit into his plan... I just don't want you to get hurt."

"Aww... Nyro." Jaya caught a glimpse of Kalite through the crack as she passed by with two arms full of old books. She dropped them in the box before wrapping her arms around Nyro from behind, squeezing and rocking him from side to side.

"Quit it, or I'm going back to my room to lie down."

"Sorry." She grinned. "It still catches me off guard when you show emotion. I'm so used to the robot."

He didn't respond, and they continued to pack away the items in the room. A bead of sweat trickled down Jaya's spine as the room got emptier. Those damn containers must be bottomless. With any luck, they'd forget about the dusty coats hanging in the armoire.

"Have you ever thought about Jaya's people?"

Jaya flinched at the sound of her name, but Kalite was focused on a black stain on the patterned tiles. Identical to the stain she had found when she briefly uncovered the mattress. Obviously, no one had set foot in this room since that night, not even the servants.

"What about them?"

"Aquillo said that the groups Ormiez found had ended up all over the universe. They had adapted to their planets and formed different societies based on their circumstances."

"You think the Inestars are descendants of Xeonere?"

"They look like us, they speak like us for the most part, and their planet is next to ours."

"Ormiez would have found them first, then. Those savages are nothing like us." Nyro yawned.

Kalite stopped frowning at the black spot to survey her brother. "Another late night out? When are you going to bring her to meet us?"

"When you get that there is no her."

"So you'll bring her then.. or...? Anyway, I'm thinking of asking Quielle to be my date to the summit."

"That's a terrible idea."

"I knew you'd say that. There's nothing wrong with Quielle. He's a prince, he's kind to me, sort of, and he's nice to look at."

"Your standards concern me. One- Quielle's a prince because of his mommy issues, and two- you shouldn't have to ask him."

"He's shy. You know that. And we aren't exactly the perfect family ourselves."

"Right. Why invite more dysfunction? Quielle deserves someone just as messed up as he is, but that person doesn't have to be you."

"There's the Nyro I know and love."

"I'm just being honest. Would you rather I handle you with kid gloves like everyone else does?"

Kalite cleaned the dirt from under her nails. Her back was to Nyro, so he couldn't see the hurt his words caused her. "No, but it's better that I choose someone now than wait around and have some random guy show up to claim me as his."

"Maj chose to marry that guy. If she didn't want to, Aquillo would have sent him away."

"I know. She just... she couldn't let herself be happy here."

Nyro paused his cleaning and leaned against the damaged wall, closing his eyes.

"I think this is good for today. I can get Roland to take the furniture to the waste center to be destroyed," Kalite said, dusting off her pants. "I need another shower after this."

She left, taking the shortcut through the garden to her wing of the palace. Nyro stayed behind long enough to close the lids on the containers, which triggered them to compress into small cubes. He picked the two blocks up and left out the room door.

Jaya wasted no time getting out of the armoire and the room. Weeks of scouting to find this spying location wasted, and now she needed another shower.

THE MAP of Dewar filled the port station screen. On it, the stations twinkled like stars forming constellations across the kingdom. Jaya pressed the light east of the palace for the Hall of The Gifted. The gateway was an outline of a square, tilted to one side with one of the four points hidden underground. Blue light zipped around the gateway, and the portal shimmered into existence. Jaya stepped through.

It only took three seconds for her eyes to recover from the glare this time. Two months may not be long enough for her to get used to Dewar and all its technological advances, but at least she could get around on her own now.

The Hall of The Gifted was... interesting. The building was like most of the other buildings Jaya had seen in Dewar- white and oddly shaped- but the towering figure behind the hall was different. All she could tell was that the sculpture was male. Light bounced off of the head of the silver structure in every direction, giving the effect of looking directly into the sun. She couldn't see the face, but the hands that reached down to pour water into the fountains surrounding the hall looked masculine.

Olivia was lounging on the marble steps that led to the entrance, her knee propped up and head thrown back, bathing in the spray from the fountains. She gave the impression that land was, in fact, her second home, and she returned to an underwater apartment every night.

"Where's your friend?" she asked, standing up from the stairs.

"I don't know."

Olivia rubbed the water droplets into her neck and chest like a moisturizer. She was more covered today in a tight pair of pants and distressed sweater.

"I wouldn't exactly call him my friend."

Her hand paused on her neck, and a lascivious grin crept across her face. "*Nice*. How is he? Big? Thick? I get thick vibes from him."

She nodded, then laughed when she noticed the shell-shocked expression on Jaya's face. "I'm sorry. I sometimes forget that normal people don't talk about who they're fucking with strangers. Just us weirdos. Anyway, are you ready to start the tour?"

She didn't wait for a response. Jaya followed the sound of Olivia's combat boots up the stairs while trying to shake the images of a naked Quielle from her head.

The Hall was a large open space with little color outside of the paintings on the walls and the water flowing beneath the glass floors. There was a young couple near the back and an old woman kneeling before one of the paintings with her head bowed.

"Is this a temple?" Jaya whispered.

"No, but there aren't any temples devoted to The Gifted, so people who choose to pray to them sometimes come here."

"Are they gods, The Gifted?"

"The zealots in Mezanya will tell you Yehala is, but no. Anyone can receive The Gift. It just depends on who Kani chooses."

In the center of the Hall, encased in glass, was a painting of a man in his early thirties, maybe. The portrait had no background color or scenery, just the man. His eyes pulled in light from every direction. It was oddly hypnotizing.

"That's Xeonere. The first person on record to receive The Gift. He thought it made him a god, too."

"Did something happen to him?"

Olivia looked at her with both eyebrows raised. Was she supposed to know this story?

"I grew up sheltered, in the mountains. I don't know much about the world outside of my parent's home." It was enough truth that she wouldn't have to worry about keeping her lie straight, but vague enough not to give away too much. She was sure there were mountains in Dewar somewhere. Still, Olivia's eyes bugged as if she had told her she was raised by wild dogs.

"Okay, so this is a first for both of us. I've never had to give the guide speeches during my tours. Most people just want to be left alone to wander. This is good, though. I get to brush up on my monologues."

Olivia cleared her throat loudly, drawing the attention of the other patrons in the Hall. She stood tall and tested out a few different voices before landing on a snobbishly nasal one.

Jaya marveled at her ability to find the strangest people and things Dewar had to offer. She could make a career out of it if she planned to stick around.

"We've been around for millennia, but Okew wasn't our first planet. Long ago, our people lived… somewhere else in this vast galaxy?" She shrugged. "And were ruled by Xeonere, an asshole with a little man complex. You don't mind if I wing it a little, do you?"

Jaya watched the young couple storm toward the exit, shooting daggers at Olivia the whole way. The praying woman stayed, but she looked somewhat disturbed by Olivia's word choices.

"No," Jaya replied.

"Good, because it's hard keeping all the scripts together and doing the voice, you know? Xeonere was given The Gift to help his people. Instead, he used it as a weapon to force them into worshiping him. They built these massive shrines in his honor. It took years, and when they were finished with one, he'd order them to build another. He demanded more and more until there was nothing left. There wasn't enough food, the soil was dried up, the kids were illiterate, everyone's back hurt, and people had to live in the temples because they had no homes. The planet was plastered with his face, and it was pissed off. At that point, Xeonere decided it was time for them to move on. The Gift wasn't as powerful back then as it is today, so he could only take a small group of his most devoted followers with him. They went from planet to planet, trying to find one that was habitable. They were the first travelers. Eventually, they found Okew."

"What happened to the people from the old planet?" Jaya asked.

The question sobered Olivia. Her nasal voice slipped, and sadness crept in. "They never went back for them."

For once, Jaya agreed with Nyro. Her people were nothing like them. Bas was a tyrant, but he would never sacrifice his land and the livelihood of his people so that he could play god. "Is the statue outside of him?"

"It was until Ormiez blew its brains out. Now it's just a statue with half a head that blinds anyone who looks at it. A literal eyesore." She snorted.

Jaya took one last look at the megalomaniac king before she moved on.

16

Okew was a fairly young planet, evidenced by the handful of rulers it's had so far. The paintings were in chronological order, so they came to the one the woman had been kneeling at last. It was between three other paintings, closer together than the others in the hall. There were small gold plaques beneath each, identifying the person depicted.

Ormiez: 402- 459, The Unifier
Exia: - 459, Kabusha
Yehala: 378-459, Kani Sent
Fadiern: 390-459, The Curse

Aquillo may have been able to pass for his father's twin in the face, but his tall stature and air of life and death in human form came from his mother. The deceased queen kneeled on the ground in the painting, her brown hand knitting into the dirt. Iridescent plants bloomed in the path of her bark-like fingers. In the near-black background of the painting, a giant creature stood guard behind her. One of its four legs extended forward into the light, showing its leathery skin. Two of the three horns triangulated on the creature's head peaked out of the shadow, along with a bony crown that matched the gold headdress on the queen's head. Two beings from different eras bonded by some unimaginable force.

The artist had captured every fissure in the horns and the flow of the petals. The painting was so lifelike that Jaya found herself unconsciously putting space between her and it.

"These are Aquillo's parents?"

"Yeah. Another sad story. King Ormiez held an annual kingdom summit. He'd invite royals from around the planet to come and celebrate the holiday at the palace. Fadiern, Aoeja's king, he hated Ormiez. Envied the way the other royals glorified him and Exia. So he murdered them in their bed the night before Kabusha."

The painting of Fadiern was yellowed and peeling. Whoever preserved the art in the hall had been severely neglecting this one. The former king stood tall in the painting, but the angle was from above, like the painter was looking down on the king as he immortalized him.

The painting next to Fadiern's was the only headshot among the group. In it, the male gave a simple and warmhearted smile. His marine blue eyes glowed like a backlit ocean. He looked like someone who had better things to do than sit for a picture, but he was being a good sport about it.

"What happened to him?"

"Yehala. His kingdom bordered Aoeja. They had been at war ever since Fadiern seduced Yehala's sister so his men could gain access to Mezanya's trading docks. He took her virginity, then the docks, and never spoke to her again. Yehala led the hunt for Fadiern when the royals were found dead. Chased him all the way to The Sleeping Forest, where they faced off. Fadiern killed him and ran into the forest. He never came back out."

So much bloodshed in one night. No wonder Aquillo tried to forget the room and the summit afterward.

"What do these titles mean?"

"The Orej Zans are given by the people of the kingdom. It's a way of giving them some power over The Gifted. They get to decide on their legacy. How they'll be remembered. Fadiern will be remembered as a murdering piece of shit and a coward. Ormiez as the king who unified his people across the galaxy. And Exia, the foreign queen who brought new life to our planet."

"What about Yehala?"

Olivia tilted her head, making her silky bob sway. She squinted at Jaya. "You've never been to Mezanya?"

"No. Dewar's the first place I've traveled to."

"Ever?"

Jaya cleared her throat, uncomfortable with the way Olivia was looking at her- like she had been dropped on her doorstep.

"Yes."

"Yikes," she muttered, though Jaya still heard her. "It's not too late to switch to The Royal Treatment package. I can send your 'not a friend' the adjusted bill, and we can go there next."

"No. I couldn't ask him to do that."

"I'm sure you could ask him to paint the sky fizzy, and he'd do it for you."

"You assume a lot. Is this another weirdo habit?"

"Maybe, but I think I'm right here. If you hadn't been stuck on that mountain your whole life, you'd know that the prince is not what we call a people person. It's rare to see him around the kingdom, much less playing escort and handing over his comPay ID with an ear-to-ear grin. That man is smitten."

"I'm not focused on dating right now," Jaya replied, refusing to get swept up in Olivia's crazy fantasies. Even if she believed Quielle was interested in her that way, it couldn't go anywhere. She wasn't about to set herself up for that kind of disappointment.

"What are you focused on?"

Jaya hesitated. *A little more truth. Just to keep the lie easy.*

"Getting free from the mountain."

Olivia's mood shifted yet again. She examined Jaya, possibly for the first time. Her ombre lips spread into a half smile, and she nodded. She said nothing more about Quielle for the rest of the day.

"Mezanya's one of those places you have to see to believe. It's beautiful on the inside. As the story goes, before Yehala met his end, he gathered all his power and flung it across Okew. It went over Dewar, Aoeja, and the Turbid Sea to Mezanya, where it formed a physical power grid over the entire kingdom. Instead of using his energy to survive Fadiern's attack, he used it to shield and liberate his people."

Olivia checked the time on her itinerary. "It's almost time for the lunch break in the tour. Your meals are included in the package. There's a place not far from here that serves really good ice cream. Their food's decent too. Wanna try it out."

Jaya chuckled. "Sure."

17

Fun must mean something else in Dewar, like 'prince' and 'forest'. So far, Quielle's idea of fun had been one near heart attack after another. Yesterday, he took her to an outdoor torture chamber.

It seemed innocuous at first, almost serene. Hundreds of bubbles in a field of red and orange wildflowers. So Jaya didn't think anything of it when one of the larger bubbles split in half, and they were told to climb in and find a seat. The little woman managing the field checked their straps and gave Jaya a wide smile before the bubble sealed shut.

Without warning, they were launched into the air. Her stomach had just climbed out of her shoes when the bubble switched direction, plunging so fast it felt like they were about to travel through time.

As the landscape of Dewar came into stark detail, they started to slow down, more and more, until they were drifting. Relief flooded Jaya to the point where she was lightheaded. The frosted glass exterior transitioned, and they were given a clear view of the land as they floated over lakes, crops, and herds of wild animals. It was one of the most beautiful things she had ever seen.

Now, as Jaya stood frowning at a teal seat cushion, she debated if getting another breathtaking view of Dewar was worth the stress. This ride would be much fuller than the one from yesterday. She counted thirty seats next to theirs and at least forty rows above them. They were filled with people of every age and size, some with white robes tied around their chubby necks.

Quielle took his seat while Jaya tried to calculate their collective weight. All this fun was giving her a headache, so she gave up and plopped down in her seat. The sky was clear, aside from one threatening cloud. If it rained, they'd have to cancel the ride.

Something moved up above. A bird, maybe, but birds didn't wave, and they sure didn't wear face shields.

Six figures appeared in the sky, standing on a hovering platform. They wore strange outfits- white bodysuits with flaps of fabric that connected the space between their arms and feet. The crowd below exploded with cheers as they came into full view. At the same time, three men walked out to the patch of dirt at the center of all the seats. They wore face shields and form fitting suits as well. Their arms and calves were exposed, and their outfits were more stylish, with rust-colored backpacks and fingerless gloves that matched the spotted pattern on their right sleeve.

Was this some kind of fashion show?

Before Jaya could ask, a booming voice filled the arena, speaking fast and in a foreign language. She leaned close to Quielle's ear but still had to scream over the amplified voice and roaring crowd. "What is he saying?"

"He's introducing today's lineup for the skytes," he pointed up at the wing-suited men, "and the dregards." He pointed down at the stylish men who were now spaced out on the arena's floor, three points of a triangle. The tallest of them, a bronzed man with white hair with a pattern of circles down one side, had an intense scowl on his face. He didn't look up at the crowd, not even when the arena lights zeroed in on him and the applause went from loud to ear-splitting.

"We're in the outer kingdom. People speak Enid, the old language, here. They're about to start the first round."

The border of the arena floor sunk, nearly swallowing the dregards where they stood, and a band of light rose from the trench. It rotated around the arena floor, faster and faster until it was one blur of light.

"Is that a port station?" Jaya asked.

"Yeah. The skytes go there if they can't reach the ground."

"Why—" Jaya's seat tilted back suddenly, and her heart stopped. She threw her hands out, clutching the nearest thing, but nothing happened.

They weren't shot in the air. She was still safe on the ground.

Quielle's lower lip was tucked between his teeth when she opened her eyes. He smiled and motioned for her to come closer. Jaya shifted in her seat, focusing on the curve of his lashes instead of how close their faces were.

"The seats adjust so you can see the air show," he said.

There were people in her world who had the skill of saying one thing and making it mean something else. Jaya had never been good at this. It was all in the tone, and her tone was always flat and disinterested, according to some of the other soldiers. Quielle had the tone in spades. She wasn't sure if anyone else noticed it. It begged whoever he was talking to slap that grin off his face- or lick it.

"Can I have my arm back now?" he asked.

Jaya released her grip and slouched in her seat, giving her attention to the men in the sky instead of the frustrating one beside her.

The first of the skytes stepped forward and dove head-first off the platform. He fell like a meteor until a cloud swallowed him up. Two more men followed suit. They all emerged, gliding in opposite directions, only the expanded wings of their suits visible against the afternoon sky. They sailed past one another, elegant now that they had come out of their death drop, but one was coming in faster than the others. His arms were close to his side, hands clenched into tight fists.

Wait, she could see his hands.

He was close enough that Jaya could make out parts of his face behind the shield, and he wasn't slowing down.

Dewar and its people had a funny relationship with gravity. At some point, one had clearly agreed to stay out of the other's way, but this was different. He was plummeting, out of control, and headed right for the center of the three-man triangle. Were the dregards supposed to catch him? They were running now, towards him. Or at least two of them were. The white-haired player stayed planted in his spot, glaring up at the skytes on the platform. As the dregards closed in, something sparked in their hands. A silver speck of matter formed between their gloves and quickly grew to the size of a boulder.

They skidded to a stop on the dirt field and chucked the silver balls, one after the other, at the falling skyte. He banked left, dodging one, and tucked his left arm in at the last moment to avoid being hit by the other. The move sent him spiraling.

He spun out of control for one heart-stopping second before his back slammed into the thick plastic barricade surrounding the top of the arena. The audience behind the shield jumped to their feet and celebrated as the man fell limp down into the port station below.

The other two skytes were just now closing in on the ground. Like the man before, they seemed to be targeting the hard center of the field instead of the safety of the port station. A volley of silver spheres whizzed from behind them. These were smaller than the two boulders from before and lightning fast. Four crashed into one of the winged men, shattering on impact and leaving behind a silver goop that clung to his suit like tar.

A boulder-sized sphere hit the other skyte square in the chest, and silver goop went flying everywhere. It stuck to the barricades and covered the skyte from his head down to his feet. The once graceful flier was now a flopping mud pile. His teammate managed to get to the port station, but he flailed like a baby bird on his first flight, weighed down by the viscous substance coating his body.

Finally, a portal opened beneath him, summoned by someone off the field. The man reluctantly dropped into it and out of the arena. Jaya barely had time to process the chaotic scene before the next round of skytes dove off the platform.

Every floating screen in the market toggled between major moments of the game. You didn't need to speak Enid to know that the skytes lost, and it was all everyone was talking about. So many people had dyed their hair and eyebrows white to match the star of the dregards.

"If they didn't have him, the skytes would have landed a lot more," Jaya said.

She sidestepped a teenager before he could bump into her. He continued without noticing her, reenacting a moment in the game when a skyte ran over a dregard standing in the way of his landing. The boy hooked one arm beneath his neck and fanned the other, falling backward onto the ground.

"He has a brother who's a skyte. Guy is phenomenal. The arena's gonna be packed for the match between those two."

She couldn't help asking. "When is it?"

"Nine weeks from now."

Just as she thought. She'd be back in Inestar by then.

They crossed a wide bridge that led out of the busy arena district into a small square. The sound of celebrating fans drifted away, replaced with soft music from a man who sat outside a small shop, flicking at silver pieces of metal that hung on strings. The lights weren't as bright in this part of the outer kingdom. They twinkled within reach and chased off the chill from the night. "Well, hopefully, you all don't go overboard with the white hair. Not everybody can pull off that look."

"Don't tell me you're a skytes fan." Quielle laughed.

She shrugged. "They put up a good fight. All except for that guy who slammed into the wall."

"Ponchie. He's a first year. Always comes in too fast."

"I hear a lot of first-timers have that problem." Jaya eyed him pointedly.

"I wouldn't know. I've always been great."

"And humble too," Jaya said, rolling her eyes.

Quielle found an empty table for two and dusted off a few leaves that had fallen on it. He pulled a chair out and leaned against its back, causing his biceps to flex beneath his long-sleeved shirt. "Is that what you want? A humble man?"

"What do you mean?"

"I mean, what does Jaya Nideha of Inestar look for in a man?"

What a direct question. One she hadn't thought of until now. What did she look for in a man? Her relationship with Devlon had mostly been them sneaking into the wheat fields to have sex. Fueled by teenage hormones more than anything else. Her father had died a year later, and Jaya's world became much more complicated. Partners were for sex. She wouldn't risk anything more.

If she had to guess, though, she'd probably want someone who made her feel safe and wild at the same time. Someone with strong hands and kind eyes. Dark brown eyes that got all squinty when he smiled.

Quielle's fresh scent clouded her senses as he moved closer.

"What do you want, Jaya?"

Her mind was too fuzzy to come up with a response. As Quielle's fingertips trailed up her arm, her muscles clenched, and a swarm of butterflies took flight in her stomach. His lips were so close. They were moist, smooth, inviting.

Quielle jerked away suddenly. He cleared his throat, straightening to his full height and taking a big step back. Like a shade being snatched from a window, everything around them came back into bright focus, and a wave of embarrassment washed over Jaya.

"I forgot to grab some orbs before we left," he said, shoving his hands in his pocket. "I'm out, but there's a shop over there that has an orb pod. I'll be right back. Okay?"

He turned and cut across the square before the words were fully out of his mouth. He reached the other side of the eating area in no time and disappeared into an alley next to the odds and ends shop.

"You enjoy the game?"

Paole, Brome's second in command, leaned against the building drinking from a novelty cup shaped like a skytes uniform. The silly straw- equipped with a little face shield- was ridiculously long. It looped and twirled his neon-colored drink up to his mouth.

"Would have enjoyed it better if the skytes didn't suck."

"They disappointed a lot of people tonight." Jaya was sitting at the table, looking in his direction. "We're going to hang around here for a while, probably get a meal. You want to join us?"

"You know I can't. Not while on duty." Paole tapped his royal guard crest with the brim of his cup. He was still in uniform, and his weapons were in full view. He stuck out like a sore thumb among the cape-wearing fans of the outer kingdom.

"Yeah. About that. How long are you gonna keep this up?"

"As long as she's outside of the palace, she has to have an escort. That's the law for any non-native."

Since when did they have laws for non-natives? Jaya was the first foreigner since Queen Exia to spend time on Okew.

"She's been with me this whole time. Aquillo appointed *me* to be her chaperone."

"Is that what you're doing? I don't know. It just feels a little less official than that. I'm not judging. To each his own. But keep in mind we're way outside of the inner kingdom boundaries."

"So?"

"So, there are less eyes out here, Prince. You need me here watching your back in case she decides to stab you in it and run off with her buddy from Inestar."

Quielle wanted to defend Jaya. He wanted to tell Paole that he didn't know what he was talking about and he should focus on teaching his men how to stand in the rain without drowning instead of playing seeker.

But the problem was, he wasn't sure.

Jaya was clearly keeping secrets. Deadly secrets that made her do things like walk into the Sleeping Forest in the middle of the night. But that didn't mean she was working with the soldier. There hadn't been one sighting of him since the day at Mia's. If he was smart, he would have left Okew long before now.

"I appreciate the warning, but I can handle myself."

Paole sighed. "Alright then, Prince."

"Chill with the prince stuff. We grew up next door to each other." Quielle turned to leave. "And you need to work on your stealth skills. I've spotted you every day. It's only a matter of time before she does. You wanna be the one responsible for insulting a foreign royal?"

Paole took another sip from his silly straw. He said nothing, but took three steps back into the alley's shadows.

Jaya had moved to a table closer to the musician and was swaying and staring off at the nearby stream when he came back. She sprung to her feet as soon as he reached the table, proving she wasn't that distracted. "Did you get the orb? It's getting late, and I need to get back to the palace."

Quielle pulled one of the orbs from his pocket and held it up. "Got it. I got something else for you, too."

He pulled the cape from behind his back and fanned it out with a flourish. Jaya looked at the white cloak with the teal lining and finger hooks like it was a worm.

"If you're going to side with the losers, you have to look the part."

Quielle swooped the cape over her head, moving closer to fasten the pearl button at her neck, then leaned back to study his work. She looked ridiculous, but she was smiling, at least. Maybe Paole hadn't completely ruined tonight.

Paole passed behind Jaya at that moment, close enough to reach out and tap her on the shoulder. He locked eyes with Quielle, his warning from earlier bouncing between them.

18

Quielle grew up in a house where food was spoken of like rowdy family members.

"Son," Lirhop would say, "be careful putting those two together. You'll either end up with a nice meal or in a fistfight."

So he loved it when other people could share his passion for it. And Jaya was about as passionate as they came.

"This is the best thing I've ever had in my mouth," she said.

"You said that about the last one."

"Mmm." She took a moment to swallow. "That was before this one."

He had brought Jaya to Rind because it was where most of Dewar's best cuisines could be found. Culinarians came here to test new recipes or make a quick living doing what they love for a day. For a hefty charge, guests got to try the latest and best food in Dewar. Quielle's first job was working as a server here for Pop.

He smirked, sliding the bowl with the rest of Jaya's now second-best meal toward him. He took a spoonful of the Ofrran soup, looking up just in time to see her eyes pass over. It wasn't the first time it'd happened. In fact, Jaya had been doing a good job of avoiding looking at him since he picked her up from the palace.

Things had changed since yesterday. They'd taken a few steps back, or at least she had. She still cracked jokes occasionally, but the Jaya who lounged on his couch with her head wrapped in a towel was gone. She was now more like the guarded woman who had boarded his ship in Inestar.

He reached across the table and took Jaya's hand in his. She stilled, and for a moment, he thought she would pull away, but she turned her hand and linked her fingers with his. The next round of dishes was sent out, and Quielle plucked two off a server's tray as she passed by.

"I'm going to bust out of this dress if I keep it up." Jaya laughed, rubbing her flat stomach.

Today's dress was only a shade lighter than Jaya's earthy skin, and it was tight enough that he didn't have to work too hard to imagine what little was underneath.

"Quielle."

"Huh?"

Caught red-handed. Jaya shook her head but didn't call him out for staring at her breasts. "It's an interesting name. What does it mean?"

"Enid for honor is his strength. It was Lenille's great-grandfather's name."

Her hand jerked in his. "*Lenille* is your mother?"

"You're surprised?"

"No." She sat back in her chair. "Yes. I honestly wouldn't have guessed if you hadn't told me. Huh."

She turned his palm face up to explore the lines.

"What is that look for?"

"Nothing. I think I just figured something out."

"And what's that?"

"You. The deals. Why you like making them with me. You have a huge ship, but you're the only one on it. I haven't seen anyone come there since we landed, which tells me that's normal. You're a loner, and you like it that way. No one to depend on you, and you don't have to depend on anyone else. If you need something and you can't get it yourself, you're going to make sure that there's an even exchange. Nothing owed. No lingering debts."

She made him sound like a bridge troll. He leaned forward, staring at his palm with wide eyes. "What else do you see in there?"

Jaya rolled her eyes and continued. "You got that from Lenille. She's very intelligent, but she sticks to herself. And the palace doesn't function without her. For her services, I bet she demanded something equally valuable. Like a crown for her only son."

Jaya paused, meeting his gaze straight on for the first time today. "How'd I do?"

He took a moment to enjoy the close-up view of her mouth set in a satisfied smirk.

"Not even close. Princes don't wear crowns here. I have a dad and a brother. Even a few friends, believe it or not. And I make deals with you because I like messing with your careful plans. You got some things right, though. Lenille is devoted to her job. It's her life's work. She gave me up when I was seven so she could move into the palace full-time. I went to live with my pop, a retired culinarian, and his other adopted son. She didn't intend for it to be permanent, but just while she worked turned into just a few days. After a bunch of missed visits and too many apologies, I started finding other places to be when she came around. Pop wasn't happy about me dodging her, but he let me make that choice."

Jaya had stopped drumming her fingers on the table during his confession and was now gaping at him. "I'm... I'm sorry."

He shrugged. "It was a long time ago, and I got a father and brother out of it, so I'm fine."

The noise of the pavilion was the only sound that existed between them for the next few minutes. Jaya was deep in thought, so Quielle cleared her pudding bowl from the table.

"Wow," Jaya said, shaking her head. "I've never been that wrong before."

He burst out laughing. "Glad I could be your first."

"I mean, I really thought I had finally figured you out. So, how did you become a prince?"

He picked up his fork and dug into his spicy smoked fish. It was just how he liked it. You couldn't grow up in Lirhop's house and not be able to take spicy food.

"You're not going to tell me?" Jaya asked.

"It's more fun hearing you guess."

She grumbled while reaching over to steal a piece of fish off his plate.

"I got one for you, too. It's that plate right there that you haven't touched." He pointed at the identical dish in front of her.

"It's more fun taking yours."

19

Jaya ran as fast as her legs could carry her. Her ankles ached from twisting in the soft ground, but she pushed herself to run faster. She made it to the edge of the crowd when the smell hit her, and her stomach heaved from the familiar scent. So many voices. Their screams blurred, echoing around her.

As she worked her way into the crowd, breathing raggedly from her two-mile sprint here, the mass of shoulders and arms closed in, getting tighter the farther into the crowd she got. A wail rose above the people, then broke into a sob. Jaya had never heard that sound come from her before, but she knew it was her mother.

It can't be her. The summit hasn't started. I still have time.

She pushed harder on the bodies in front of her, forcing them to part. The heat inside the crowd was unbearable. It felt like she was being burned alive, but the smell of burning flesh that clogged the air wasn't hers.

"Move!"

Jaya shoved a small woman who stood motionless, listening to her mother scream for help and doing nothing. The woman felt like a stone. Jaya shoved again, ramming her elbow and full weight into her when a fist slammed into her face. Jaya fell back into the rigid wall of people, but there was no time to find who had thrown the punch. She staggered forward and continued to push.

Her mother's sobs had turned to pleas for mercy. This time Jaya saw the kick to her ribs coming. Not in time to dodge it, though. She fought to catch her breath, gulping down as much putrid air as possible. Looking up from her bruised side, she was met with hate-filled eyes.

"Dwayne?"

Jaya tried to straighten up to face him, but her head was pushed forward, and she stumbled toward Dwayne. Vinjin's arrogant smirk was there when she turned around, blocking out all the other faces in the crowd. His jaw wasn't hanging off like it was the last time she'd seen him. Jaya took a couple of steps back so she could see both of her former opponents.

A pair of small arms wrapped around her neck from behind and dragged her down. She bucked and kicked wildly at the person behind her as her mother's screams became garbled. Vinjin and Dwayne stalked closer still. Their eyes glinted with bloodlust and anticipation for their revenge.

One by one, people in the crowd turned toward her. Their eyes held the same feverish spark as Dwayne's and Vinjin's. As they got closer, Jaya recognized their faces and recalled their deaths at her hands in the hexagon. She tried to speak, to plead with them to let her save her mother. They could do whatever they wanted to her afterward, but she needed to save her.

"Plea–" The first blow rammed into the side of her head, silencing her before she could get a word out. Another came on its heels and another. Jaya jerked awake, spinning around, looking for the next punch or kick.

"Not the nose! My piercing's still healing." Olivia cupped her hands over her mouth and nose and tucked her long legs into her chest.

Jaya lowered her fist and took in her real surroundings. They sat in a small and mostly vacant room. At the center of a bunch of plexiglass desks was a holographic man talking them through the process of orb manufacturing.

Still on high alert, Jaya scanned the room again, this time looking for Vinjin and Dwayne. They could have run outside. Maybe they were hiding in the hills behind The Orb Center. Her eyes landed on Olivia, who was still shielding her body. Jaya's face burned with humiliation.

"I'm sorry."

"It's alright. The Orb Center videos are boring as shit. I was nodding off too, until you started throwing hands." Olivia's boots came into view as she set them back on the floor.

Just when Jaya thought this moment couldn't get any worse, Olivia shouted, "I'm hit!"

She flapped the drool-stained shoulder of her sweater while Jaya, mortified, wiped slobber from her face and chin. "I'm sorry."

"You don't have to keep saying that. A little fluid never killed anyone. Come on." Olivia bounced up from her clear chair and stretched. The hologram continued on with his presentation as they left.

Jaya followed her to the first-floor corridor of The Orb Center. Four elevators were on the left, and to their right were port stations. They took the elevator to the rooftop, where Olivia steered them toward the tables along the edge.

The height and shape of the building made it so the bit of land before the ocean was hidden. The open-air and illusion of being on a floating island brought an unexpected calm to Jaya. She closed her eyes and let the chilly breeze wash away the lingering heat from her dream.

"You want to talk about it?"

Jaya bit down on her lip to keep the words in. She didn't talk about her nightmares with anyone. Her mother knew she had them, but she didn't know the details. She didn't need that guilt.

Olivia meant well, and over the past few days, Jaya had come to like and even trust her due to what she called her 'weirdo candidness'. She lived her life with a freedom and openness that Jaya both envied and thought was highly dangerous.

She reminded her of Aquillo that day in the palace and his unguarded honesty about losing his loved ones. Maybe there was freedom in talking about these things with someone who doesn't know you or the people involved. They can't hurt you.

"I dreamt my mother was in danger, and I couldn't help her because... I was trapped."

"Trapped how?"

"I was being held down by people."

"Did you know them- the people?"

"Yes."

Olivia picked at a loose thread on her pants while Jaya tried to clear her mind by focusing on the distant sound of the crashing waves.

Olivia's voice soon breached the stillness, quiet and unsure in a way Jaya had never heard it. "I grew up in Mezanya. My mom, dad, and me lived in a nice house near the palace. My father made instruments. His specialty was horns. I remember the day the grid came down. I was outside playing when this shadow covered everything. I thought it was a storm cloud, so I started picking up my toys to go inside. That's when I saw this flash, like lightning. It was miles away, but I could see the borders of the grid falling down around us, closing us in. It seemed like everyone was outside that day. I witnessed grown people fully lose their shit for the first time: crying, screaming, passing out. Some just started running and tried to make it out before the grid closed. They were willing to leave everything behind in an instant if it meant not being trapped inside.

My mother grabbed me and carried me into the house. She locked the doors and huddled in a corner with me. We didn't move until my dad knocked on the door an hour later. His face and hands were all scraped up, and he was out of breath from running.

Word that Yehala was dead had reached Mezanya, but The Gift hadn't. There was no new king or queen to stop this thing from closing us in. My mom was cleaning my dad up in the other room, and I heard him tell her we couldn't leave the house. It wasn't safe. People were going crazy. It was the end of the world, so, of course. Some of them tried to burn a hole in the grid. They took things from businesses and homes to add to the fire and nearly burned down the south Atlien district.

We stayed in our house with the lights off for three weeks, praying to Kani that the people we heard shouting and breaking into homes didn't come to ours. I felt powerless and terrified every second of every day. The Kingdom Council had a few trackers stuck inside since Yehala never told them about his plan for the grid. They did a house-to-house search for The Gift. All the royal guards were needed for the search, so the terror and bodies in the streets were overlooked for the time being."

Olivia sucked in a quick breath, turning to give Jaya a carefree smile that wasn't as convincing as the ones she had seen before.

"It took years of the Council badgering the other kings and queens to send port stations to Mezanya. When Mezanyans could come and go again, many didn't want to. They had accepted the changes that came with the grid, some they even liked. Yes, they were poor and trapped under a net, but what was outside of Mezanya but the old ways that had killed their king and nearly ended them? You've done the hardest part, Jaya. You left. That makes you stronger than most people. Don't let anyone convince you otherwise."

"But I didn't leave. Not really. I can't leave her."

"Your mom? Where is she?"

Too much.

Jaya had been toeing this line, blending lies with truth, for days now, and she may have finally fallen on her face. Olivia was smart, and it was obvious she had been piecing together a backstory from the bits Jaya had given her, one that had nothing to do with her being raised in the Dewar mountains.

If anyone could understand Jaya's desperation to free her mom, it would probably be Olivia. But she couldn't risk exposing herself to anyone. Secretly- stupidly- she had grown attached to Olivia and Quielle. They were the closest things she had to friends here, which meant she had to keep them as far away from this mess with the king as possible. Knowledge of the royals and their kingdoms. That's all she needed. Friendship was a distraction. One that would get them all killed.

"Do your parents live here?" Jaya deflected, trying to climb out of the pit her thoughts had cast her into.

"Another sad story, I'm afraid. We're getting a strong drink after this, agreed?"

Jaya nodded.

"Cool."

Olivia pulled a gold trinket from her pocket. Her spiked nails traced the lines of the small turtle's shell, making its head and legs bob up and down.

"My parents still live in Mezanya. I haven't seen them in years. Relations between Dewar and Mezanya became hostile after the royal assassinations."

"I thought you said Yehala helped kill Fadiern for killing Aquillo's parents."

"He did it for his own revenge, for his sister. After the assassinations, Aquillo's army tore through most of Aeoja in retaliation. The parts they left standing became Dewar territory. Yehala's army wasn't happy with the power grab since they were technically still at war with Aeoja, and the land he seized bordered theirs. But Aquillo had the power of The Gifted on his side, so there was nothing they could do about it."

"Can't your parents come here?"

"Sure. They'd need approval from Dewar's Travel Committee and the leaders in Mezanya first. It's a lot of work just to see me."

Jaya had become adept at putting pieces together too. It was obvious that it wasn't just the feuding kingdoms that kept Olivia and her parents apart for all these years, but she didn't seem inclined to share, and Jaya wouldn't push, not when she had so many secrets herself.

"The piercings and gills may look a little crazy, but they remind me that I'm strong and in control. You are too." She handed Jaya the gold turtle. "Remember that when you go back for her."

20

Jaya stumbled through the portal to the palace. It was a little after midday, and she was beyond drunk. Belisa's makeshift wine back in Inestar was water compared to the drinks at the bar Olivia had taken them to. Jaya had two drinks to Olivia's four. Yet, somehow she was the one who ended up being escorted to the nearest port station with her arm slung over Olivia's shoulders and her face buried in turquoise hair.

She'd had enough sense to select a random station on the map instead of going directly to the palace. It was the only good decision she'd made today.

Jaya took the long way around the palace to the stairway of her balcony. Once she was in her room, she flopped backward onto the bed and waited for everything to stop spinning. The teal tiles on the ceiling blurred in and out of focus like chameleons. Their bronze diamonds shifted, morphing into brown circles.

"What are you looking at?"

Stupid, judgy chameleons. She rolled on her stomach so she wouldn't have to look at them anymore. He probably brought them in here. *Come look at the drunk savage.* Like she gave a damn what he thought, what any of them thought of her.

Jaya starfished on the bed, rubbing the smooth sheets between her fingers. Her thoughts trickled in slowly. She reached out, trying to touch both sides of the enormous mattress, when it hit her, like an animal that had scented its predator nearing. Ice crowded in her veins, acid in her lungs. She wasn't sure where it came from, the knowing, but it was undeniable.

Someone was in her room.

And it wasn't the first time. She had sensed them before, watching her. She thought it was paranoia, but now the pounding in her chest was proof her instincts were right. Jaya sat up, casting her eyes from the patterned ceilings to the floor. Entrance to exit. There was no one there, and still, she felt the air stir as they moved closer.

Forget this. She pulled her dagger, ready to slice her way from corner to corner until she hit flesh. *No. Save your energy.* Her warrior's mind was functioning even if her body had descended into chaos. Whoever this was would come to her. In the past, they had watched passively, but today the clouds darkened in anticipation of a coming conflict, filling the room with charged ether. She would meet her enemy today.

"Come out, kitten. I know you're in here."

A slur, brief and muttered, told her a lot. It was a male, and he was somewhere near the bathroom. She turned and cursed herself for being so stupid. The room seesawed for half a second before settling into a blurry-edged illusion. This was what she got for wanting more. He had probably seen her drunken stumble in and decided today was the day.

"I've been called worse, kitten." She said, taking a step towards the bedroom doors.

"I'm going to enjoy killing you."

She felt the air bristle as he moved. She panned left with him, breathing deeply to pick up his scent. The room's stuffy smell made her stomach slosh like an overflowing cup. "I wish I could say the same, but I don't even know who you are."

"That's never been a problem for your kind before, killing a stranger. That's all you people do- kill and infest the planet with more like you." The voice was in front of the doors now, blocking her escape. She wouldn't run, not when she had finally drawn him out. "I told Aquillo he should've wiped that filthy planet away six years ago. No one would've cared. Just like they won't care when I kill you."

"Tough talk, sweetheart. You sound hurt. Wanna come out here and tell me about it?"

The wall splintered across from her like someone had thrown a mallet through it. A crack spread down the stone and tile, dividing the room. Jaya's feet folded, sending her careening sideways towards the shattered floor. She threw her hand out and bounced back up in time to see Brome's hulking figure step out of the black abyss of the crack.

Darkness gathered closely around him, coiling and writhing like a pit of snakes. They moved in and out of his face, ear, and eyes. Horror filled Jaya past the point of being hidden.

"Where's all that talk now?" His battered cheeks pulled back into a sinister grin.

She had never heard Brome's voice before, but she knew it wasn't this. This voice wasn't even the same from seconds ago, before the room had split in two. Despite his cocky words, he struggled to get them out, like something inside him was being strangled to death.

"What was that? I couldn't hear you."

His smile dropped, and his serpent eyes filled with glass shards. He lunged. Jaya parried, nearly falling when her feet caught on the uneven floor. The raised pieces of tile were a minefield, but Brome moved through them effortlessly. His snakes coiled around the shards, surrounding them in darkness and clearing a path for their master.

Jaya waited until he got closer, then punched out with her dagger. The blade missed his thick neck by a hair. She bounded back, wishing for the hundredth time she had just returned to the palace instead of going to the bar.

His movements were quick, but the attacks weren't. His enormous fist moved toward her in slow motion. If her aim and senses weren't impaired, this would've been an easy fight.

He grabbed for her throat, muscles straining like he was punching through brick. Jaya thanked the skies for the slight advantage and charged. She easily ducked his hands and jerked her dagger across his gut. Darkness closed around them, ghosting him away.

For one disorienting moment, Jaya stood alone in the rubble. In the next, Brome was there, breathing hard in her face. She got off two stabs, one to his shoulder and collar, before his fist slammed into her stomach with blinding force.

Jaya fell to the floor, hacking and gasping. Bile lurched up her throat and spilled into the void beside her knees. Brome staggered back as the snakes coiled around his wounds, sealing them. They pulled away to reveal smooth skin.

What the hell?!

He got to his feet slowly, sneering. Swimming through mud might have taken less effort, but he wasn't giving up. He would use his last drop of energy to kill her.

Jaya blinked away her tears and tried to ignore the pain as she stood up. Light-headed and outmatched, she pulled her last dagger from the holster beneath her sweater and squared up.

Brome sprinted, moving faster than she would have thought him capable. It caught her off guard enough that she blanked, throwing a wild punch instead of her knife at him. He absorbed the blow to his eye and returned with a punch to her head. It would have knocked her unconscious had it landed, but it didn't.

Something held Brome captive. His arm stood frozen, extended in midair, halted by a cloud of blackness. It moved, engulfing his fist, bicep, then shoulder. Jaya watched in shock as it enfolded him and the void sealed shut with Brome inside. She fell to her knees, staring aimlessly at the floor that was now mended and back to normal, aside from a pool of vomit.

She wasn't sure when he came, but Quielle was standing in her room. He must have come up the stairs since the balcony doors were open. His arms hung defenseless at his sides, but his fingers were spread out in an odd way.

"Are you going to put the knife down, or is this your way of telling me we're not going out today?"

What knife? Jaya blinked and realized there was a knife in her hand. She didn't even remember picking it back up. Gods, even unconscious, she was a killer. Jaya lowered the dagger gently and deliberately, more than a little shaken by her revelation.

It had been a while since she'd had a blackout. She had them all the time during her first years in the hexagon. Her spirit would leave her body, carrying all her fear and humanity with it, while she was left behind to slaughter. She needed to be alone. She could keep it together for a few seconds to convince Quielle everything was alright, but any more time and she was going to fall apart in front of him.

Jaya was trying to get up off the floor without making it obvious that she'd just been gut punched when a spark caught her eye. A symbol was on the wall next to the room doors, where Brome had first stepped out of the void. It was a combination of images and sharp lines, and they were arranged vertically. A language, maybe? Quielle was familiar with the old languages of Dewar, but he looked just as confused by the symbol as she was- and furious.

When he finally stopped glaring at the wall long enough to look at her, it was with an expression she had never seen on his face before. Hatred.

21

Her skin had lost all its warmth, and there was dried vomit on her chin, but Quielle couldn't let himself be distracted by that. That's how he had missed all the signs before. Paole was right. She'd been playing him this whole time, meeting with the soldier in the palace under everyone's nose.

"Where is he?"

"Who?"

"*Who*? You're going to act like I can't see that over there. I'm not stupid, Jaya. Where is he?"

She looked at the symbols, then off to the side. That mind of hers was working, trying to come up with a story he'd buy, another way to manipulate him. He wasn't having it this time.

"You don't want to hand him over to me, fine." He pulled out his communicator and took a picture of Jaya standing in front of the symbol. "I'll give you an hour's head start before I send this out to all the guards, seekers, and contract workers in Dewar."

He sat on the bed and pulled up the projection so she could see her face and the countdown as the seconds ticked away. "You better get going."

"I don't know how he got in here or where he went. I thought it was strange that there weren't any cameras in this palace, but now I see why. They wouldn't matter. He's been watching me for weeks, and I had no idea until now when he just tried to kill me."

Quielle raised one eyebrow. "Is that it?"

Jaya was quiet for three whole seconds, according to the countdown, then she grabbed the hem of her shirt and tugged it over her head. She stood before him naked, besides a black bra, from the waist up. A bruise the size of a fist colored the area between her ribs red. She had a few other scars, but this one was fresh.

"He came through the wall, right where the symbol is now. I don't know if Aquillo sent him. Maybe the magic he was using came from him."

"Aquillo? Wait. Who tried to kill you?"

"Brome."

THE SYMBOL PULSED across the room from where Quielle sat on Jaya's bed, waiting for the shower to cut off. It was just as bright as the first time he had seen it on the soldier's neck. Brome looked nothing like the man who had attacked him that day, but they had the same build. It was possible whatever power he used to stalk Jaya could have changed his features. But how did Brome get that kind of power?

Quielle had experimented with orbs in every way possible. He was probably just as familiar with Aquillo's power and its capability as Aquillo was. There was no way that Brome used an orb to do the things Jaya had described.

The water shut off in the bathroom, and soon after, Jaya padded out in an orange sweater dress and bare feet. She stepped carefully around the spot where she'd vomited, even though the mess was long gone, swallowed up by an orb. Not even an odor remained. She went over to the symbol. Her hand hovered over the white lines, tracing the details.

"Do you know what it means?" he asked.

"I was going to ask you the same thing. I thought maybe it was an old Dewar symbol."

"You've never seen it before?" Quielle watched her closely. He would know if she lied.

"No. How would I?"

"The soldier who attacked my friend had a tattoo like that on his neck."

Her hand paused. "That's weird. Did it glow like this?"

"Exactly like that. Why is that weird?"

"We don't have tattoos in Inestar. We have brands. The slaves are marked above their eyebrows with them."

"So you don't think the soldier got his tattoos in Inestar?"

"No. And honestly, no soldier would willingly take a slave mark. Besides Bas and Yido, soldiers are the highest-ranking people in Inestar. Even the livestock are more valued than the slaves. And the symbol would be red if it came from Inestar. Our brand is infused with Syntia. When it comes in contact with blood, it gives a red shade. Like a wound that never heals."

The situation with the soldier kept getting more and more confusing. What Jaya said made sense. He had seen a red tint on the soldier's knife the day of the attack. The guards had packed the market that day. He shouldn't have been able to slip past without one of them seeing him. Unless someone helped him leave, like the head of the royal guard. But what reason would Brome have for taking Mia?

"Did your friend know Aquillo? Personally, I mean," Jaya asked.

"They were dating. They might have been in love, or at least she was. After she disappeared, Aquillo did, too, into this palace. He called off the search for her after three weeks and said nothing else about it. No announcement, no one punished. He probably didn't even question his guards."

"He came to Inestar. I saw him. It was the first time I had ever seen my grandfather afraid. I would have been glad he came, for that reason alone, had he not set our crops on fire and erased one of our soldiers." She took a few deep breaths, bracing herself before she spoke her next words. "Maybe he felt guilty about it because he told me about Mia when I got here. He never stopped looking for her. I didn't tell you about it before because I wasn't sure if you two were talking about the same woman, and I didn't want to tell you unless I was sure."

"Tell me what?" Quielle asked over the loud static that was filling his head. His heart was beating too fast, and he was starting to feel nauseous. Jaya looked at him with so much pain and sadness.

"She died that day. The soldier killed her."

Jaya's words sunk into him like a brick, echoing through the hollow places he thought had healed after all this time. Six years. So long. A lifetime of hope. He had told himself over and over that Mia was still out there somewhere. He just had to keep looking. If he kept looking, he would find her eventually. She'd be safe. She didn't deserve to be forgotten. Mia cared about him making it home, even when he didn't.

Shame over the many times he had caused her to worry came in like a tornado. If he hadn't wrecked his communication system on his solo trips, he wouldn't have had to go to The Orb Center that day. He would have been there with her when the soldier broke in. He could have saved her.

"It's my fault. I failed her."

The bed dipped slightly as Jaya sat down next to him. She wrapped her arms around him.

"I'm so sorry."

Why was she apologizing? He was the one who had abandoned his friend when she needed him. Jaya's arms tightened around his torso, squeezing, holding him together. She didn't say anything else as time passed, and the world around them darkened with nightfall.

THE ROOMS on the ship were shielded against teleportation. You could only get in if you were programmed into the scanner.

"It's intended to give the crew some privacy," Quielle said. "You can sleep in my bed tonight. I'll take the couch."

He'd recommended they stay on his ship until they could figure out how to break through Brome's invisibility cover. It was the first thing he had said in hours. Jaya thought he had fallen asleep when his face leaned on her head. His arm hadn't loosened around her since she'd grappled him into a bear hug, but that didn't mean anything. Maybe he felt just as awkward as she did about how much their relationship had changed. She was about to try to maneuver his big body into a comfortable sleeping position when he suggested she stay on his ship.

Jaya took in Quielle's room for the first time. His bed wasn't much different from the one in her old room on the ship, but everything else was. Large panels took up the walls behind the bed. On them were night-time images of a purple and magenta river flowing peacefully into a sea of stars. It looked so real like she was staring out a window into the cosmos. Across from the bed was a round alcove.

"That's my trophy room," Quielle said.

"Trophies?"

"Things I found on my trips." He flopped down on the light gray sofa and leaned forward to unlace his boots.

Jaya wandered over to the alcove, climbing one step into its white interior. There was only one box on a pedestal, like the box Jaya had seen Nyro and Kalite packing furniture into. Small items floated around under the translucent lid. One shuffled to the top every two seconds: a green crystal, old books, a toy moon, a bottle of oil, a three-pointed crown with orange clay caked on it, a long turquoise feather, a tiny claw. Each item was as obscure as the last. Nothing Jaya would consider a trophy.

She slipped off her shoes at the foot of the bed and climbed beneath the sheets. They were warm and smelled like their owner. Quielle's head and arm rested against the back of the sofa. His eyes were closed, but he was obviously still awake and troubled. He had taken the news of Mia as hard as any friend would. He blamed himself, even though he had done everything in his power to find her. It just went to show the kind of person he was.

"You and Mia had years of good memories, I'm sure. There must have been times when you came through for her like no one else could. Don't let the one time you couldn't be the only one you remember."

"That was the time that mattered."

"You think that, but would you trade all your good moments if it meant you could change that one?"

His brows pinched, and his lips twitched to one side. She had gone too far. You could always count on Jaya to say the wrong thing. She was terrible with words, and it was Bas's fault. He always told her words won't help in battle. Jaya had been preparing for battle her entire life. She didn't know what she'd do if she ever got peace. She wasn't persuasive or charming. She couldn't even console a friend. She was as useful as a sledgehammer.

"I don't know," Quielle said. He turned away, tucking his boots beside the sofa, so she wouldn't see the guilt that little admission caused. "So what kind of friend does that make me?"

Jaya waited for him to turn back to her. She needed his full attention, and he needed to hear this. "You are a great friend."

"How do you know?"

"Experience. You've saved me more times than you know, and you never stopped to question if I'm worth it. You're not just a good friend. You're a great person. Anyone would be beyond lucky to have you in their life."

Jaya closed her eyes and pulled the covers around her nose. The room dimmed, and the projection's calm waters began to babble. Quielle's quiet words carried in the darkness.

"You'll always be worth it to me, Jaya."

22

Rando's ass was always late. Quielle should have known better than to schedule a meet-up with him. When he sent the message to his communicator that he was back in Dewar, he should have just popped up on him and got his stuff.

Now he was stuck here waiting on this fool instead of taking Jaya across the pier to the pre-Kabusha festival. She was over by the docks, checking out the trade ships that sailed in. There were plenty of them coming and going because of the holiday.

Inestar was nowhere near an ocean. Considering everything he'd learned about Jaya, this might be her first time seeing a boat in real life. He had started forming an idea of Jaya's life on her home planet, and it wasn't one he liked. It was how her face lit up at the most mundane things. Even though it was a beautiful sight and he was growing addicted to the sound of her laugh, those moments also made him feel uneasy and violent. He hadn't been able to pinpoint where the conflicting emotions were coming from until their conversations confirmed what he suspected. Jaya was a prisoner.

Those stone walls surrounding Inestar kept outsiders out and her people in. Obviously, some were allowed to leave since the report he'd gotten on her before his trip to Inestar said her father was a traveler. But

Jaya wasn't one of those people. If she returned to Inestar, he'd never see her again.

"Prince Quielle. Long time."

Quielle had drifted off into his thoughts while looking at Jaya, so he missed the man coming to sit on the bench facing the ocean. "Do I know you?"

"That's right, we've never met in person. I have to maintain a certain level of secrecy, but I keep a close eye on all my travelers- you especially. I can't tell you how satisfying it's been to watch you grow from that young man, fresh out of flight training, wanting to make a little money on the side, to this- *royalty*. You've made me proud."

He had the outfit of a high-end dealer, but if anyone had asked Quielle to describe The Collector, he wouldn't have pictured this slim, old man.

"Look, you must be mistaking me for one of your grandkids. I don't know you or what you're talking about."

The Collector smiled at the lie. He wasn't convinced, but the key to a successful lie was knowing when to shut up. Quielle had come too far to be taken down for the things he did almost ten years ago. Even his royal status wouldn't save him from being hauled off to Gudarin if he admitted to stealing and trading extra-planetary goods. It didn't matter how long he had been out of the business.

"Anrand had to leave on a last-minute trip, so he asked one of my men to deliver this." He grabbed a square box from the bench and held it out.

"I don't get many requests for these. Can I ask what it's for?" His gray eyes drifted over to Jaya, who was making her way over to them with a concerned look. "Or who?"

Instead of answering, Quielle took the box and checked to make sure Rando got the right thing. Cool air blasted out when he opened the lid. He closed it, then pulled the coin pouch from his pocket and handed it over.

The Collector set the pouch on the bench without verifying the amount and folded his hands over his crossed legs. "You could have gotten these yourself. Would have saved you a lot of gold."

"I didn't have time to make the trip," Quielle hedged, keeping an eye on Jaya. "Are we done here?"

JAYA WALKED UP JUST in time to hear Quielle's clipped question. She'd read the tension in his shoulders from across the pier. The man he was speaking to, however, showed no outward aggression. He stood as she approached, pulling his long gray coat together before extending a deep brown and heavily inked hand to her. His grip was strong, belying his appearance.

"I hope you don't mind me saying this, but I've never seen anyone so beautiful in all of Okew. I'm a collector of rare things," he waved his other hand dismissively, "so when I spot something beautiful, I can't help but let it be known."

Now she understood Quielle's tense posture. There was something wrong about this man. He spoke of her like she was a rose beneath a glass case instead of a living, breathing human being. He finally let go of her hand. At the same time, she felt Quielle's hand land on her back. His thumb stroked lazily down her spine and came to a rest at the lower curve. Calm and assured, as if he touched her like this all the time. He gave her two light taps, signaling that it was time for them to go. He didn't have to tell her twice.

"I hear your brother is traveling. Tell him to come see me when he gets back."

Quielle stilled. With his free hand, he pulled an orb from his pocket and handed it to Jaya. "Wait for me on the ship?"

Jaya gave the old man a parting smile and turned to face Quielle. She ran her hand down his stomach slowly- a lover's promise for later- while she assessed the six men standing at the shops behind them. At first, they seemed like everyday window shoppers, but they'd been drawing closer during this conversation. She closed her hand around Quielle's and the orb. Meeting his eyes, she imperceptibly shook her head. The odds were not in their favor.

He either misunderstood her message, or he ignored it because he let go of her and closed the space between him and the old man. "I'm not telling him shit, and you better stay away from him and me. You understand?"

It was like a flare signal shot in the air. The *shoppers* took off running towards them. Three more came from wherever they had been hiding, weapons drawn. Jaya was about to pull her dagger when she noticed the orb in her hand. She grabbed a handful of Quielle's sweater and rubbed it. Were there words she was supposed to say to get the magic started?

The armed men suddenly came to a stop. One by one, they all tucked their weapons behind them and folded their hands at their waists. The old man lowered his fist and cleared his throat. "You obviously do not know how good I've been to you, so I will forgive your ignorance."

Quielle laughed in his face. They were going to die today.

"I don't remember you being there when I was out putting my life, my traveler's license, and my freedom on the line. Don't act like you've done me any favors."

"I paid you well for your finds, Quielle. And when the seeker went missing, I used every connection I had to find her, despite her trying to cut in on my business."

"I don't give a damn what you did six years ago. I'm telling you *now*, if you send anyone for my brother, they're coming back in pieces."

A tense second passed between them. The gunmen shifted like gargoyles coming back to life. Jaya shook the orb. *Work dammit.* The old man let out a smooth chuckle. "Little brother is off limits. Got it. Would you consider coming back instead? You wouldn't have to make the trips yourself anymore. Just train the new recruits and give my travelers intel on the planets you've visited. Zero risk to you."

He turned the grab a pouch off of the bench. "Be a part of building an empire instead of being Aquillo's puppet."

Jaya clenched the orb harder. It shattered in her palm, and a sudden blaze of light made her eyes snap shut. She pictured the photo she'd woken up to for the last few days in her mind. It was still sitting on the table beside Quielle's bed. In it, Quielle looked as handsome as ever in a black suit with a teal sash coming out of his suit jacket and wrapping around one of his shoulders. His father stood beside him with his arm around him, smiling from ear to ear.

The sounds of the busy shops were replaced by chirping birds and the intoxicating aroma of food on the ocean breeze. Jaya whirled on Quielle. "Have you lost your mind? They could have killed us!"

"They weren't going to kill us."

"Oh, so they had their weapons out just because?"

"No." He took both of her hands in his and brought them down between them. "I found some things for The Collector back when I first started traveling. He has been trying to get me to work with him ever since I got appointed prince. I'm too valuable for him to hurt me, and he knows I'll never work with him if he hurts anyone close to me."

He stepped backwards as he spoke, distracting her with his confession while leading her to his family home. The double doors were open, and chatter filtered out from somewhere in the house. They approached the three steps leading up to the house, and Jaya dug her feet in. "I didn't bring anything."

"You didn't have to bring anything," he assured her. The coffee brown in his eyes warmed with amusement. He put his hands on her waist to hold her in place. Was it that obvious she was ready to bolt? She needed to get her game face together before she went in here.

Their hostile encounter from moments ago was all but forgotten for him. It was unfathomable because Jaya was still on edge. Her hands were slick with sweat and humidity, and her heart was ready to sprint out of her chest. "But you brought something."

Quielle opened the lid to the mystery box. Inside were a dozen ripe peaches. "I was going to save these for after dinner, but if you want to go back to the ship..."

"Sir, are you bribing me with peaches?"

"Yes. Unless there's something else you want? All you have to do is ask."

He was serious. He looked her straight in the eyes, leaving no room for guessing. She'd spent the past four nights in his bed, breathing in his scent, aching for release. And now he was offering it- in front of his father's house. Her body didn't care where they were. It clenched a rhythmic yes. Yes, we want whatever he is offering. Everything. All the things.

"Hi, *friends*." Olivia's voice had never been grating before, but hearing it now made Jaya's teeth grind.

"Hey. Glad you could make it." Quielle greeted her when it was clear Jaya wasn't going to.

"Am I too early?" she asked, looking from Jaya to Quielle and back. "I can find something else to do for a while. Give you two some time. "

Quielle's hand crept under Jaya's hair. His thumb circled the groove of her neck while his other fingers trailed up her ear. Her body went loose. She bit down on her lip and tried to maintain composure. Olivia and Quielle smiled like twin imps who had just sat the contract of a lifetime in front of her.

"No," Jaya said. "You're on time. We were about to go in."

"Okay. I brought wine." She held up the bottle.

Jaya cut her eyes at Quielle as they walked up the stairs. He grinned back. *This isn't over*.

23

Tone kept shooting goofy looks at their father that he thought no one could see. Pop was no better, asking Jaya questions like, 'Did you and Quielle meet during a trip' and then turning to ask Olivia the same question word-for-word. They were having dinner out on the terrace, so they wouldn't miss the Moon Run, the highlight of Kabusha.

Olivia sat to his left. Jaya told him she was from Mezanya, which explained her sky blue hair and deep purple lipstick- her kingdom's colors. Everyone wore their kingdom colors on Kabusha or white. Jaya had gone with white. She sat to his right, and it was a struggle not to ignore everyone else at the table. She was a fantasy come to life in white. This dress had more coverage than the one she wore on his ship (thank Kani), but her shoulders and the soft curve of her breasts were right in his line of sight.

"Me and Jaya were just there the other day. Do you work on the manufacturing side?" Olivia asked in response to Rea telling her she worked at the OC.

"No. I oversee orb pod missions."

"She's our boss," Tone interjected from his seat next to Jaya.

"That's badass," Olivia said, giving Rea a nod of approval.

Quielle sucked his teeth loudly, just to be a jerk. Rea sat forward and folded her hands under her chin. The knife she held coincidently pointed in his direction. "Do you have something to say, Quielle?"

Her locs, as usual, hung in curls down her back. She wore a teal blouse that was see-through in places beneath a white blazer and pants. The rust-colored makeup made her green eyes more intense, but his brother probably didn't notice since his eyes hadn't made it past her breasts.

"Not at all."

"You work in tourism?" Lirhop asked.

He sat at the opposite end of the table between Tone and Ms. Gisete. His hand hadn't left hers since they sat down to eat. Quielle couldn't think of any other way to describe them, but *cute* kept coming to mind. Pop's gray cardigan was the same color as hers. The same went for his white shirt and blue jeans.

"Yeah, but piercings are my passion. I like making people shine. My hope is it'll make its way in with time."

She capped that odd statement off with a grin. Quielle didn't really get what she meant by that, but Jaya obviously did since she nodded along. They had formed a fast friendship, but the bond ran deep from what he could tell. He hadn't expected Olivia to respond to his last-minute dinner invite, but thankfully she did. This was Jaya's first Kabusha, and he wanted it to be special.

Celebrating the holiday with friends and family always brought him peace, which is why he always made it home for Kabusha.

"Jaya's new to Dewar," Quielle offered before Pop could ask Jaya what she did for a living. "Olivia's been showing her around. This is her first holiday here."

Tone snorted. "And you brought her here to Geriatric Junction?"

"What my simple son is trying to say is there are a lot of festivals and parties for you young folks in the inner kingdom," Lirhop clarified.

"I actually like it out here. The view is amazing." Jaya said. The sun had mostly disappeared, but the ocean glowed with iridescent lifeforms. The first moon of the night appeared in the sky, and cheers went up from the shore down below. They cranked the music up, signaling the official start of the new year.

“What is Kabusha?” Jaya asked.

“It means renewal. We call it that because the planet literally renews itself. It’s the many lives of this planet converging and sharing energy for one night,” Tone replied.

“Not just the planet." Olivia tilted her head back towards Jaya, causing the gills on her neck to stretch open. Her chair faced the ocean so she’d have a better view of the moons as they surfaced and faded in different parts of the sky. "Some people have said they’ve met another version of themselves on Kabusha. Sometimes they come to give a warning or tell a secret that they can’t tell anyone in their world.”

Jaya smiled politely, but she clearly wasn’t buying it. Quielle had heard this legend before too, and his reaction was about the same.

“It’s true,” Rea said.

All eyes swung in her direction.

“And you know this how? Ran into yourself at the market?” Quielle joked.

“My house. Four years ago."

“Did she come to warn you or tell you a secret?” Olivia asked without nearly enough sarcasm.

“Neither. She just wanted to talk. She was in love with a man from her world. It wasn’t a secret. She told everyone how she felt, including him."

“And?”

“He didn’t feel the same." Rea went back to eating her food, ignoring Tonure and his attempts to get her attention.

Pop cleared his throat and stood to his feet, keeping his hold of Ms. Gisete’s hand. “My boys and I always have dinner together on Kabusha. This year is our first year with a full table. I’d like to think that it’s a sign of things to come, that our family is expanding.”

Quielle locked eyes with Tone behind Jaya’s back. No way was Pop about to announce that he had gotten his eighty-year-old girlfriend pregnant. Tone shrugged, but he looked panicked.

"Gisete and I both come from small families, but this morning," he smiled down at her, "we made vows to share everything we have, including our love and family, with each other."

Quielle sighed and fell back in his chair. That was a close one. Lirhop was active for his age, but he was well past his child-raising years. A piece of lettuce hit Quielle in the chest. Rea glared at him across the table and tilted her head towards Ms. Gisete. Oh, right. He stood and joined his brother in front of Ms. Gisete.

"Congratulations. You got two sons now, and we'll split anybody's head over you and Pop," Tone said, clapping his hand with his fist.

Quielle shoved him out of the way, taking her hands in his and giving her a quick kiss on the cheek. "He means welcome to the family, Ma."

Tears gathered in her eyes, and she smiled. "Thank you both."

Lirhop disappeared into the house and returned holding a ciaré tray. He set the gold teapot and its ivory tray in the center of the table and removed the six lids from the square trays surrounding the teapot. The smell of spices wafted up. Their earthiness blended with the salty mist of the Bobinsii. Two ivory tea cups sat on the outer edge of the tray with gold strips of metal down the center of each. Quielle and Tone took their seats as Lirhop finished the presentation.

"These spices represent a union between people. In life, you taste a bit of everything, from the bitter nutro to the sweet pume. But with love and the support of the ones around you, they blend together to create a rich experience."

He lifted the gold metal strip from one of the cups and pulled it apart, revealing a tiny spoon. He took a spoonful of each spice for his cup, then handed it to Ms. Gisete. She followed suit, dumping a heaping spoonful of the yellow pume spice in her cup. She passed her spoon to Rea, and another went to Tonure. They both reached for deep purple fifta spice.

"What does that one represent," Jaya whispered in his ear.

She leaned back, and he found himself coming to terms with gravity. This unseeable force that could make you feel like you were floating and falling. He had traveled to the deepest parts of space but never truly felt it until now.

Jaya touched his knee beneath the table. Her brows pinched together as she waited for his answer.

"Devotion."

Olivia passed Quielle the spoon, and he pulled himself away long enough to wish his father many years of wedded happiness and a spoonful of security. Jaya hesitated before dumping two scoops of red jomora into both cups. Olivia snorted, and Rea turned her head away to hide her laughter.

"What?" Jaya looked back and forth between them. "Is that one of the bad ones? Can I take it out?"

"It's in there now, girl. Might as well enjoy it," Olivia said.

Quielle took sympathy on Jaya since, clearly, no one else was going to. "That represents intimacy. You just wished them a long and very active sex life."

"I'll drink to that!" Lirhop said, pouring hot tea into the cups.

24

The ambush came as soon as they were alone in the kitchen. Quielle had been preparing himself for it but was still caught off guard when it came.

"Which one of those girls is yours?" Lirhop asked. "I'm tired of trying to guess."

Tonure burst through the door and hopped up on the counter between them. His ears were practically vibrating from the oncoming drama.

"Neither," Quielle said. "They're good friends with each other."

Lirhop stopped pulling wine bottles from the refrigerator to look at him. Quielle hadn't seen that look since he was sixteen and came home blackout drunk. He had tried to sneak into the house but ended up vomiting on the doorknob and in Lirhop's garden boots.

"You're trying to be a third wheel?"

Tone snorted. His face had turned bright red from holding in his laughter.

"I don't know what you laughing at," Lirhop said. "How'd you get Rea to come here? She better not be here against her will."

"She's here because she wants to be, Pop. And I offered to model for one of her painting parties if she came."

Lirhop shook his head at both of them.

“Hey. Try these out.” Quielle grabbed a peach from the cooler and handed it to Lirhop. He prodded the skin of the fruit before slicing off a piece. He frowned over the intense sweetness, then took another slice with him to the closet, where he began rummaging for ingredients.

Tone picked up the leftover peach from the counter and took a bite. “Where’d you get this?”

“Old associate. Has anyone asked you to take or bring something back from a trip?”

Tone frowned. “Something like what?”

“Just random stuff. Things that aren’t for the OC."

Quielle had done a good job of keeping that part of his life far away from his family, but Tone was no idiot, and neither was Pop.

“I’m not trying to lose my freedom over some foreign junk, and neither should you,” Tone said, handing the half-eaten peach to him. "This shit is gross.”

“Quielle, go upstairs and get my black smock. This white one’s filthy,” Lirhop called from the closet.

The black stairs creaked as Quielle made his way up to his old room. He’d sometimes wear his father’s old smock when he served at Rind. His room was mostly unchanged since his days in flight training when he came home more frequently. The bed was bare. Lirhop had probably taken the sheets off to wash but didn’t have the energy to put them back on.

Quielle opened the dresser drawer, tossing unfolded clothes around, when his finger bumped against something sharp. He swore, pulling his hand out.

At the back of the drawer, jammed in between the creases, was the Inestar soldier’s knife.

Quielle jerked it out, watching his blood coat the blade. He had stolen it from the palace when it was clear that the search for Mia was over. He’d been so pissed off he’d thrown the knife in his drawer with enough force to embed it in the wood. Now he had his answers for what happened that day.

Six Years Earlier

THE STILLNESS of the market was the first clue something was off. At the corner of the market was a multi-level building that was both business and home to Mia. The dark tinted windows wrapped around the outside of the first level, protecting the privacy of her clients and giving the impression that the place was abandoned. Beside the door was a hologram button for guests to announce themselves.

Quielle tried the front door, but it didn't budge. Mia's was almost always open because she rarely ever left, not even for lunch. She was a workaholic like him. Quielle touched the scanner below the guest button and waited for the lock to disengage. The lights were on, and voices were coming from the back.

Guess she closed for lunch today. Chuckling at his own paranoia, Quielle pushed her office door open. He had a split second to take in Mia's assistant's bloody face before a dark figure vaulted over her desk. Black boots landed with a wood splintering boom and came charging at Quielle. Next came the hard thump of a knife lodging into the wall near his head, so close he could still feel the warmth from the intruder's hand on the blade.

Quielle recovered quickly but not in enough time to catch his attacker. He jerked the knife from the wall and raced to the hall in time to catch the flash of the symbol on the intruder's neck as he threw the front door open and vanished into the market.

"Please... I need help."

A groan and wet cough came from within the office. Mia's assistant. He lay in a heap behind his boss's desk. His left eye was swollen shut, and blood leaked from a cut on his brow into the slit. He focused momentarily as Quielle crouched down over him, then his eyes rolled back in his head and shut. Most of the blood came from a gash on the side of his neck, from a knife being pressed too hard. The same knife Quielle held.

He fished his communicator from his backpack and called for a mend unit.

"Hinton." His brain supplied the boy's name out of nowhere. "Hinton, wake up. Where is Mia?"

"Mia," he whispered.

"Yes. Mia. Where is she?"

"Mia. No. Don't hurt her."

Hurt her? That monster was here for *Mia*?

Quielle was on his feet and halfway to the office door before he realized it.

He paused.

Hinton. Shit.

It wouldn't take the unit long to get there. The healing center was in the market. Quielle snatched a scarf off Mia's chair and made a quick compress before grabbing the knife and running out the back door.

He had never climbed stairs so fast in his life. He was on the fifth floor, the floor to Mia's apartment, in no time. His heart thundered in his throat as he struggled to get the right fingers on the keypad for her apartment. It was dark and quiet inside. Quielle barreled through, checking every room twice.

She wasn't here.

Everything was neat and untouched. She couldn't have been here lately.

Hinton was unconscious when he got back to the office, and there was still no sign of Mia.

"Do you know this young man?" A mender stopped Quielle before he could enter the office.

"Yes, he works here. His name's Hinton."

"Do you own this place?"

Quielle was jostled to the side by another mender as he entered, followed by a bolkin. The tips of the creature's sloped ears brushed Quielle's thigh as it passed. Maybe by accident, but more likely, it was checking him for unseen wounds. It glided in on a white mist, the same color as its sleek body, making its way directly to where Hinton lay sprawled at the base of Mia's desk.

"No. My friend Mia owns it."

"You're friends with the owner?"

"YES. Yes." Didn't he just say that?

The bolkin was having a conversation with its partner. The slits on the edge of its round skull fanned open and shut as it spoke. Without his translator, Quielle only heard teetering chirps mingled with whooping noises. Menders, however, were trained in bolkin communication, so he understood what the creature wanted. He reached over to remove the blue mender's cloak that matched his own uniform from around its serpentine body. He then removed Quielle's hasty compress from Hinton's neck. The mist at the bottom of the bolkin rose, dispersing its form into a white cloud that settled over Hinton's head and shoulders. Crimson filtered in, momentarily turning the cloud red before it returned to its translucent color.

"Sir, I need you to speak with the guard out front."

HE SMEARED the blood across the blade as the red words took shape.

Humanity After War

"It should be in the closet. I cleaned it not too long ago." Lirhop paused in the doorway. "Is that what I think it is?"

Quielle nodded absently. Lirhop squeezed behind him and went into his bathroom. He came back with a wet cloth and bandages.

"Let me have that." Lirhop coaxed the knife from his hand, laying it on the dresser with the words face down.

Quielle kept his eyes on it while his father cleaned and bandaged his bleeding finger. The inscription lingered in his vision, stark with red definition.

"Son, I know it was hard for you, both the day it happened and when they called off the search. Mia was a wonderful woman and a good friend to you. And you did all you could–"

"She's dead, Pop. He killed her."

Lirhop let out a harsh breath and dropped onto the bed. "Come sit down, son."

"I'm fine. Go check on everybody."

"They can wait. Come sit down." He waited until Quielle sat beside him before asking, "Are you sure?"

"I always knew. I just didn't want to know. Her uncle moved away. There were less and less guards searching every day, and Aquillo had locked himself in that palace. I just felt like someone needed to be looking for her. It wasn't right for everyone to give up like that."

"I don't like asking about people's personal business in the bedroom, but did you and Mia ever—"

"No. She was too happy being Aquillo's secret to consider being with me."

Lirhop grunted. "You can't force anybody to be with you, Quielle."

"I know. I didn't mean that. I'm just upset."

"Hmm. Did you love her?"

"Yes," Quielle answered without hesitation.

"What I meant to ask was, were you *in love* with her?"

Quielle pressed his nail into the bandage, agitating and drawing fresh blood from his wound. It wasn't a difficult question, nor was it one he hadn't thought about before. He cared for Mia deeply. There wasn't much he wouldn't do for her. With time and some hope from her end, the feelings would have matured.

"We never got there, Pop. She didn't want that."

Lirhop shook his head. "I don't think you would have ever gotten there. I've known you your whole life, son. And your whole life, you've had a vengeful streak to you. It's not a judgment, just an observation."

"What does that have to do with Mia and me?"

Lirhop grimaced. He swiped his hand down the front of his shirt several times, weighing his next words. Quielle had picked up the habit from him, so he was already wary of whatever his father was about to say.

"I don't think it's a coincidence that this older woman, who is nothing like any of the girls I've seen you with before, just so happens to be a good friend of Lenille's."

"Lenille doesn't have anything to do with this."

"I think she does. I think you wanted to show Mia off and throw it in Lenille's face that somebody wanted you."

His words hit like poison, burning through Quielle's chest.

"That didn't come out right. What I meant to say was–"

"No. I-I get it. It's true. I busted my ass, Pop. Getting back from trips for her birthdays, bringing her gifts from all over the galaxy like a fool, and none of it meant a thing to her. She wanted to be the next collector. Lenille wanted to run the palace. They didn't want me. All that other shit meant more to them. Everything meant more to them than me."

The tears fell now, hot with anger and bitter on his lips. As soon as he wiped one away, another came on its trail. He was pathetic, sitting here crying over these women. One who left him twenty-one years ago and the other who never wanted him to begin with. He'd taken Mia's pitying smiles just as he had waited for Lenille to visit. Bending and shaping their minor gestures to fit into this collage of love he'd made for himself.

"Lenille made her choice, and while I hate that it hurt you, I can't wish it any other way. It brought you to me. You and Tonure mean everything to me, son. And I'm sorry if I didn't make that clear enough to you growing up."

Quielle wrapped his arms around his father, wishing he could take back the things he'd just said. He couldn't, and that made his shame all the worse. "You've been an amazing father, Pop. You did everything for us. I don't want to think about where I'd be without you."

Lirhop sat back, wiping his tears with the back of his hand. Laughter from outside the window broke the silence in the room. Quielle easily singled out Jaya's from the group, quiet as it was.

"The one you brought here. She's the woman from Inestar, isn't she?"

He considered lying, but he was done lying to himself and to his father.

Lirhop sighed. "You and your brother sure know how to pick 'em. If I remember correctly, she's only here for another month, right? Then she's going back to her planet."

"Yes."

"So why'd you bring her here? Why are you spending all this time with her? I didn't raise you boys to play with people's hearts."

"I know. I just... I can't stay away from her."

"You're going to have to. Give her space to figure out if she feels the same, and give yourself time to figure out if these feelings of yours are genuine."

Quielle winced. His heart ached at the thought of being away from Jaya, but maybe Lirhop was right. Of course, he was right. But that didn't mean Quielle could bring himself to take his advice. He wasn't sure how much time he had left with Jaya. If he couldn't convince her to stay, he didn't want to waste a day away from her.

"And, son... whatever resentment you're holding onto towards Lenille, you have to let it go. If you want a chance at finding true happiness, you're gonna have to."

25

Quielle walked out to the balcony, balancing two cups of peach ice cream in one hand and a blanket in the other. "Where'd everybody go?"

Ms. Gisete looked up at him from her seat. "They went down to the shore for the party."

He squeezed her shoulder and headed for the stairs. Lirhop came out, blanket in hand, and sat in the lounge chair next to his wife.

Quielle maneuvered through the drunken revelers on the beach, keeping the chilled cups above the mass of sweaty bodies. He found Jaya and Olivia near the sound system, dancing with big goofy grins on their faces. They weren't drunk, but they definitely looked high on life. Jaya's knee-length dress had hiked up to mid-thigh, and she was barefoot. You could tell she had natural rhythm, even though she didn't move much.

Quielle snuck up behind her and wrapped his arms around her waist. Surprisingly, she didn't elbow him in the face. Her body molded to his as she continued to roll her hips. He tucked his nose into the curve of her neck, nudging some of her hair aside to place a kiss there.

"I brought you something." He held the cups up, letting Jaya choose one and handing the other to Olivia.

"Mmm. This is really good. You should try it," Jaya said, dropping her head back onto his shoulder.

"That was the plan. You're sharing, right?"

She side-eyed him while sneaking another larger spoonful.

"*Wow.*"

"Okay. I'll share, I guess. Since you brought it down here."

"How generous of you."

Olivia was smiling at them with a dreamy look on her face.

"You love to see it," she said. "Anyway, I'm going to go check out the nude beach. Thanks for the ice cream, Prince."

She danced away before Quielle could tell her this wasn't a nude beach. "She's going to give these old men a heart attack,"

Jaya pressed her face against his and laughed. A breeze swept by, and he pulled her closer, breathing in her sweet scent by the lungful. "Come sit by the water with me."

He steered them across the sandy dance floor to the water's edge. The tide was still high because of the Moon Run. The wave crashed on the shore and grazed the edge of the blanket Quielle laid out. He sat down and patted the empty space between his legs. Once Jaya was comfortable, he folded the other half of the blanket over them.

She was quiet for a long while, happily eating- and not sharing- her ice cream while a sequence of moons raced across the sky. They transitioned from orange to blue, full to a quarter, and back.

Quielle toyed with a coiled strand of her hair, extending it to its full length, then letting it bounce back to her neck. It had been over a month since his last mission. Usually, he'd be pacing the hangar floors by now.

"They seem happy, your dad and Gisete," Jaya said.

"Yeah. They met when he moved here eight years ago. Took him six years to get up the courage to ask her out."

"That's sweet. Were you there for the vows?"

"No. Vow exchanges are sacred in Dewar. Only the two people are allowed in. The pledges they make to one another are their secret to keep. They can have something made to commemorate it. Rings or gold strips for their noses. I've even seen people get the tip of their finger encased in gold."

"I can't see Lirhop or Gisete walking around with gold fingers."

"Nah. Pop would never. He needs all his fingers in the kitchen. It seems like they've settled on dressing alike for the rest of their lives."

"Okay, I got it." Jaya bounced up and turned to face him, bringing her breast dangerously close to his lips. "Aquillo made you prince, but only if you agreed to marry the princess he was arranged to marry."

She grinned triumphantly.

"You are adorable and still wrong. You're putting too much thought into this. It's just a title. It means nothing outside of the palace. It guarantees even less. The next king or queen is Kani's choice, not Aquillo's."

"I wouldn't have to think about it if you'd just. tell. me." She emphasized her words with little jabs to his chest.

He wrapped his hand around her wrist, keeping her hand where it landed over his heart. "You're violent for someone with such tiny fists."

"Tell me, or I'm gonna hit you again."

Quielle laughed and pulled her down onto his lap. She stretched her long legs across his and turned to him expectantly. "*Alright*. It's because I'm in Deep Exploration. Travelers are looked up to by our people. To some, we're more important than The Gifted."

"Why?"

"Fear. The first of our people died with their planet. We weren't about to have a repeat. Kabusha helps, but it gets weaker every year without Exia, so everyone relies on us to scout for new homes. Ormiez excluded, I've traveled the farthest."

"And stole things along the way."

"I didn't hear any judgment while you were inhaling that ice cream."

She bit down on her spoon and chuckled.

"Aquillo's never been able to live up to his parent's legacy. So he does stuff like raising his victim's children and appointing a traveler as prince, hoping it'll at least save his reputation."

"I get that. I mean, not the children, but I can understand wanting your people to remember you as a good person."

"Yeah, but all the princes in Okew aren't going to bring back the lives he's taken. I think he knows that."

Jaya's smile faltered. She shifted away, turning to stare at the ocean.

"Hey. What's wrong? What'd I say?" Her hair was blocking her face. Initially, he was happy to see it out of the bun, but now she was using it to hide from him. Her shoulders were hunched, and little bumps ran along the back of her arms. "You're cold. Come back under the blanket."

She leaned back and let him wrap the blanket around her shoulders, but her mood had visibly taken a dive. He held her close and rubbed her arms to help her warm up.

"So, no arranged marriage then?" she asked after a few minutes.

"No." She nestled into his neck, and her lips accidentally brushed against the side of his Adam's apple. When they did it again, this time against his jaw, he knew it was no accident. Her lips trailed up his jawline, brushing against his skin but not kissing. When she reached the base of his ear, she stopped.

"You want to head back up?" he asked, ignoring his raging hard-on. He wasn't an animal, so he wouldn't push her to do something she didn't want to. But he needed an answer soon so he could walk her back to the house and go to his room to jerk off.

"No." She turned to face him. The full moon cast a purple glow over her skin and haloed her curly hair. She was exquisite, beyond anything he would have imagined himself experiencing in real life. The chilled scent of peaches crested over his face, blending with her scent as she leaned in and pressed her lips to his.

Kissing was never for Quielle. He did it for the women he was with, and because not enjoying it made him feel like an asshole. But kissing Jaya was a different experience. His whole body responded to it, not just the parts below his belt. It was like a riot was happening inside him, chaotic and red hot. His skin tingled, and his heart felt like it was going to jump out of his chest. He buried his hand in her hair, pulling her closer, needing more of this feeling.

Her off-the-shoulder dress had fallen slightly, revealing more of her breasts and flushed skin. He paused to run a finger across her collarbone.

If collarbone fetish was a thing, he was in trouble. Jaya turned to straddle his lap, and her immediately resumed their kiss. Maybe she was just as hooked as he was. She bunched his sweater in one hand while her other reached underneath to run up his stomach. She was driving him crazy. Rationality was fading fast, and he needed to get it together before he blew this. Jaya must have felt the change in him because she pulled back. "What's wrong? Did I—"

"No." He kissed her lips one final time, then another. "Nothing's wrong, but if you keep it up, Olivia's not the only one who's going to be put on a show tonight."

She smiled and pressed her forehead to his. Her fingers lazily traced his abs, while rubbed her back.

Stay with me. It was on the tip of his tongue, but his father's words were in the back of his mind.

PART III

FIRESTORM

26

It's feature day at First Note. Outside on the sidewalk, an all-female band played for a small crowd. The musicians were in the middle of a complex breakdown while their lead singer, a raspy-voiced songstress, danced with a little girl.

First Note always had live music once a month. It was the one constant that remained amongst the many changes the central market had gone through. They were imperceptible to some, but Quielle noticed every one of them. Shop signs had been updated. Some had new names and owners.

The general store hadn't changed much. Quielle went down the aisles, tapping the screen of things Pops was running low on. It was the least he could do. He and Tone had been at their father's house for the past five days. It took them no time to get Ma's things moved in, so for three days, they'd been doing nothing but eating them out of house and home.

He missed Jaya. If he'd been thinking, he would have given her his communicator so she could call him. If he'd really been thinking, he wouldn't have gone along with this stupid distance plan in the first place. He needed to be near her. What if Brome showed up? She could protect herself, but that wasn't the point. Truthfully, he was starting to regret their kiss. Now that he had gotten a taste of her, every day he didn't get to do it felt like slow torture.

Quielle paid the young girl behind the counter, then exited back onto the boisterous streets of the market. The things he purchased would be delivered to Lirhop's, so he could hang back and listen to the live music. He needed something to clear his head, or his next trip would be to the palace.

On instinct, he looked down the street to Mia's old building. The blacked-out windows were gone. Now there was a metal sign over the door that read *Best Buds*.

Walking through the bright orange door again felt like a dream, a strange one that might end with him realizing he wasn't wearing pants.

Inside, floral scents mixed with herbals that were so potent you could practically taste them. Mia's small, sectioned-off offices were gone, replaced with open space to accommodate the massive shelves and all the flowers. They flowed from pots on the wall and sprung out of sculptures. He walked past a glass enclosure that used to be Mia's consultation area. He could still see the tiny desk and second-hand chairs she had spent hours arranging, then rearranging the day she had her first big client meeting. Now the room looked like a meadow.

"Welcome to Buds." A man greeted Quielle as he climbed down from a short ladder, balancing a watering can in one hand. He wore an orange apron, and his circular glasses matched the gold strip on his nose. "Can I help you find something?"

"Yeah, um. Some flowers?"

He looked around at the mountain of flowers and smiled. "I think I can help you with that. We have an excess because of the holiday that just passed, but if you tell me a little about who they're for, I can narrow down the search."

"She likes unique stuff. Something that catches the eye, but it's still simple."

"Say no more." He set off, plucking flowers from the shelves as he passed.

Quielle waited half a second, then headed for the back. The room where Mia's mini fridge and safe used to be had a door now. He quickly looked over his shoulder at the shop owner, who was still walking through the shelves, before turning the doorknob. Just a quick look inside to see what else had changed. The last thing he expected to see was Hinton sitting behind a desk. His eyes shot up before Quielle could mumble an excuse about looking for the restroom and close the door.

"Prince Quielle."

"Hinton?"

He stood from his chair and straightened his Best Bud t-shirt. On the right side of his desk, facing Quielle at an angle, the shop owner moved around the store on a screen. There were two more visuals of the front and back of the store.

"Can't be too careful," Hinton said, noticing his line of sight.

Quielle shoved his hands in his pockets while he tried to think of something to say. He hadn't seen Hinton since that day. He assumed he had moved away. What a surprise to find he was right here this whole time.

"Thank you." Hinton came around the desk. He paused a foot away and appeared to weigh his next words. "I never got to say it that day, and afterward, I didn't want to bring it to you because I wasn't sure if it was something you wanted to be reminded of. I figured you had your own stuff to deal with, you know?"

He stretched his hand out. The feeling Quielle had when he walked through the door came back stronger. He shouldn't have come here. Hinton was trying to move on. He had worked with Mia for years. Most of his teenage years were spent here, helping her with every case. And when the soldier came, he protected her with his life. They had a bond. One Quielle hadn't considered until now.

Hinton rocked back and lowered his hand. Quielle quickly grabbed it, pulling him in at the last second for a hug.

"Babe," a voice called from the front. Hinton pulled away first, playfully shaking off the heaviness of the moment. He walked with him back to the front. The other man was tying a string around a bouquet of tropical flowers. "Oh, I thought you left."

"Asaya, this is Quielle, prince of Dewar."

He smiled and bowed his head.

"Asaya isn't from here. We met when I went to Ziep for a week."

They were a perfect pair, from the slight height difference that put Asaya's head at Hinton's shoulder to their matching cinnamon skin tones. The gold stripes on their noses were identical in length and width and came from the same source.

"What do you think of these?" Asaya held up the bouquet.

"I think they're better than anything I could have picked out," Quielle replied.

He shrugged and nodded. While he sent the comPay request, Hinton disappeared into the back and came back with a backpack. "These were left in her apartment. I thought you might want them."

Jaya wasn't in his room when he returned, but he could tell she had been there recently. Her white slip dress lay on the bed's rumpled sheets, and the room smelled like her soap. She had made herself at home here while he was gone.

He put the flowers on the side table next to Pop's picture before going to his trophy room. There was just enough space in the compression box for Mia's things.

Quielle removed the items from his old, worn backpack and put them in the box. Her sketchbook, a charm bracelet from a family she'd helped with the date Mia found their daughter on it, two orbs (which he put in his pocket), and different forms of currency she'd been collecting. The last thing was the skeleton of a small animal. The sharp end of the bone snagged on the tattered threads of the sack as he pulled it out. Hard to tell, but it looked like a skull. Seven holes, intricately sized and spaced apart, ran along the underside. The ivory-colored bone was smooth and polished. Why would she keep this? It could have been from one of her big cases. Hopefully, it wasn't from a human.

Jaya's arms wrapped around his waist, and she rested her head on his back. He hadn't heard her come in. Her grip tightened as he pulled away momentarily to sit the bone and backpack down. He turned in the small space she gave him and cupped her face in his hand. "Hi."

Instead of responding, she pulled him down for a kiss.

His hand tangled in her hair, pulling her closer while the other ran up her spine. Jaya slid her hands beneath his shirt, feeling the hard, warm skin there. She hadn't gotten to explore enough last time. She wanted to feel every part of him. Not pressing against her beneath layers of clothes. Skin to skin.

Quielle broke their kiss and let her take his shirt off. She stood on her tiptoes, struggling to get it off his big arms. He took over and shed the shirt in one smooth movement. It hit the floor, and she immediately went for his belt. The strap was thick, and the clasp was being difficult. She tugged it hard, and it popped from the belt hole. Quielle grabbed her wrist, pulling her hand away before she could unbutton his jeans.

"What's your rush?" He chuckled, teasing her with short pecks beside her lips. "Hmm?"

He tilted her chin up, bringing her attention to his face and away from his pants. Damn, he was fine.

"I asked you a question."

"What was it?"

He nudged the strap of her dress down and kissed from her neck to her shoulder. She leaned back, willing him to go lower. He still had her wrist, held a safe distance from his pants, but her other hand was free.

"Jaya, I asked why you're trying to rip my clothes off."

"I don't know," she said, pulling on the waistband of his jeans.

"You don't know?" He grazed her ribs, then brushed his thumb along the side of her breast. "Well, let's do this. I'll catch you up on my the last five days, and then maybe you can answer me."

He pinched her nipple, and Jaya jolted like a puppet that had its strings tugged. "How's that sound?"

"Okay."

"Alright. So I woke up and pictured you in the bed next to me. I showered, and I smelled your shampoo even though it wasn't there." He kissed her lips. "I ate breakfast, and I tasted you. Then, again at lunch."

He brought her hand down to the bulge in his pants. "I've never tasted anything so delicious in my fucking life."

Jaya pulled him down for a hard kiss. She grabbed as much of him as she could through his jeans and squeezed. Quielle's answering growl made her head swim.

Suddenly, she was airborne. Lifted off her feet and spun around. He sat her down on his trophy box and dropped to his knees. His touch was frantic now, no more teasing. He gripped her hips and pulled her forward. His breath warmed her thighs and her already heated center.

Sprawled out on the box, legs spread open, Jaya was the picture of lust. She was desperate for him, and he knew it. He took his time pulling her panties down, stopping halfway to work a sensitive spot on her thigh with his tongue before pulling them off.

Now that he had removed every barrier, physical and mental, Quielle dove in. The sounds he made as he feasted on her were deliciously obscene. Jaya's head pitched back. Her hands struggled to find something to hold on to. They settled on his shoulder and head. She pulled him closer and tried not to be swallowed up by the wave of sensations wracking her body.

Quielle was a man on a mission, determined to find every hidden pleasure in her and making it bow to him. Jaya's vision blurred as electricity shot from her toes to her heart, then back to where they were connected.

"I missed you so much," Jaya gasped.

The words slipped out unbidden. Thinking it was bad enough, but actually letting those incriminating words leave her mouth? She may as well have added that today was the first day she'd left this room. That she'd only gone to the palace to show her face, and came right back here to be surrounded by his things since she couldn't have him.

"I missed you too, baby." His muffled response came from between her legs, spoken directly into her. The vibration from his guttural voice sent Jaya over the edge. Her lip parted on a silent scream as pleasure coiled tight in her belly, then detonated, blazing through her, frying her senses.

Quielle kept pace, making long, savoring passes, charging the energy that reverberated through her until she was a twitching mess.

Jaya clung to him as he gently lifted her from the box and moved them to the bed. He took his time undressing her before doing the same himself.

Quielle was perfection, as she knew he would be. A masterful balance of hard and soft.

This would be another step towards her undoing. He'd find that last key to her heart and stroll right in. It was what he'd been doing since he met her, working through every obstruction and steel wall to get her here. And she had allowed it. She couldn't have stopped it if she had tried.

Jaya had grown up in a house with two soul mates. She'd heard her mother's story about falling in love despite everything that told her not to plenty of times. So deep down, she knew what was happening when she ran back into the Sleeping Forest for him. She knew it was a losing battle. At least, she should have. Yet here she was, fighting to convince herself that this was just sex and she could have this piece of him without giving away too much of herself.

"We need to be careful," she said. This might be an excuse to end things here because there was no way she was going back to Inestar pregnant.

Quielle pointed to a small chocolate circle on his abdomen. "Contraception patch. Good for at least six months."

Thank the skies. The bed groaned under his weight as he came to hover over her. His heavy length bobbed between them.

"I'll only do what you want me to." He spoke calmly, despite the passion she sensed warring beneath the surface.

He covered her bare breast with his hand, teasing her nipple until it stiffened. The cool air of the room on her overheated skin heightened every sensation. He worked his way down slowly, feeling the curve of her waist, brushing his thumb over her slightly protruding belly button. He explored and cataloged every piece of character on her body. Her hips lifted towards him when he dropped his weight onto his elbows, but he didn't come closer. Instead, he doubled back to trace the faint scar at her hairline.

"Tell me what you want. I need to hear you say it." His eyes met hers, guarded and uncertain. His entire body had gone still as a photograph. He was so tense the veins stood out on his forearms. She ran her thumb up and down his jaw until it relaxed.

Her hands were trembling. She hadn't noticed until Quielle turned and kissed her fingers.

"I want you, Quielle. Only you."

That smile, it made her heart ache and soar at the same time.

She pulled him closer and felt him press into her. His girth and soul-seeking kisses worked in tandem to take her breath away. She broke away from his lips to anchor herself on his broad shoulders while he worked his way fully into her. Once there, he paused. Something was stirring in those warm eyes of his, and she couldn't let it be spoken out loud.

Jaya lifted her hips, urging him to move. He pulled out and sunk back in slowly. Again, then again. A sweet, slow torture meant to break the last resolve she was holding on to for dear life.

"You have me, Jaya. Every part of me is yours."

That was it. Words she hadn't wanted to hear, but they filled her with overwhelming joy. All the emotions she was supposed to be burying for this moment of good sex came spilling out faster than she could contain them. He'd done exactly what she thought he would, and she was stupid to think this would end any other way. That she could hide this part of her heart from the person it was always meant for.

He continued to feed the storm. Touching her as if he had already known and loved her. Holding her as if she were his salvation. It was too much. Tears welled in her eyes. Quielle's kisses caught them before they could hit the sheets. He drove deeper into her. Faster. His arms circled her, and his hands gripped her shoulder and ass, melding their slick bodies together and keeping her in place. Chest to chest, their hearts thundered against one another. She held his head, gasping. "Ahh. I'm–."

Her words were cut off by his lips. The war between mind and heart gave way to a flood of ecstasy. She threw her head back as the world around her momentarily phased out. Blurred shapes and images slowly came back, the first being Quielle, holding onto her, her name falling from his lips. He thrust into her a final time, and his large body shuddered. Jaya wrapped her arms around him, holding on as tight as she could, not caring about his weight.

Be thankful you got this. There weren't many epic stories in Inestar. She had traveled farther than anyone she knew in her village and met the love of her life all in one month. She wouldn't let this steer her off her path and wouldn't begrudge her mom for the sacrifice when she returned. Happy endings didn't last anyway, especially not for people who had done nothing to deserve them in the first place.

27

Jaya Nideha, Princess of Inestar.

The name tag sat there, taunting her. *You don't know what you're doing. You know it, and soon they'll know it. You spent all this time playing spy and didn't think to prepare for this.* She didn't think. What was a summit but a gathering for leaders to discuss and hash out their issues? It wasn't just a party for royals, although the welcome banquet would take place right after this meeting.

What was she going to say when they brought up Mia and the soldier? That had to be why Aquillo invited her here, to pressure her to give up the soldier's name. By now, she was sure that the man who attacked Mia was not from Inestar, but she couldn't tell them that. Not without proof to back it up. The glowing tattoo wasn't enough. Plus, the symbols from Brome's attack on her had inconveniently vanished.

She went to take her assigned seat as the others filtered in. Kabusha marked the start of the hot season in Dewar, so Jaya wasn't sure if her sweaty armpits were from the shift in climate or nerves. Who was she kidding? Dewar's hottest days were a tepid bath compared to Inestar. Her body was still very much aware of who she was and where she was from.

The meeting room was divided in two by a sunken floor. A silver round table sat at the center, surrounded by ten chairs. The drastic change in aesthetics- dark blue walls in place of cream stucco and a brown ceiling with no intricate mosaics- made this room feel more severe than the rest of the palace. Stepping down onto the blue and white tile felt like crossing over the weather-worn barrier of the hexagon.

Aquillo was the first royal to come in. He was talking with another king near the side doors that led to his wing of the palace. They lingered out of earshot in the shadow of one of the floor-to-ceiling drapes. She could guess what they were likely talking about.

The other king fiddled with the cuffs of his suit jacket, giving the impression that he was only half listening. This had to be Rore. Olivia described the king of Eroni as "an ego on three legs".

One of her many careers was as a lighthouse attendant on the island kingdom. Olivia had an admittedly perverse weakness for sailors. When she came across the king preparing for a trip on his private boat, she was intrigued. He invited her to join him on a three-day sail. After the first day, she said she wanted to throw him overboard, but then she couldn't enjoy his best feature anymore. Once they docked, she said her goodbyes and left his kingdom altogether to avoid being tempted back into his bed.

Everything from the bright tribal patterns that adorned the scarf around his shoulders to the crown on his head said that this man was used to being admired. The white crown molded seamlessly to his head, casting a soft blue light into his hair like the airglow around a planet. In all the time Jaya had been here, she had never seen Aquillo wear a crown, including now. His hair was neatly trimmed and unadorned. He wore a simple teal suit with rust-colored buttons slanting diagonally up the front of his suit jacket. His body language was relaxed, but he carried most of the conversation. Jaya pretended to read the other name tags on the table while she strained to pick up bits of their conversation.

"This is us. No shock, they separated themselves."

To Jaya's left, a woman sat in the chair her pudgy, middle-aged companion held out for her.

"It's a round table, Oji," she replied, tucking the hem of her champagne-colored gown beneath the white tablecloth.

"And we're clearly on the powerless side."

"You're being overly sensitive."

She turned, giving Jaya's nametag a cursory glance. Her neat brows rose. While Oji continued to mutter about the seating arrangement, she extended a hand toward Jaya. "Samorah."

Umbress of Mezanya. She was stunning in an alien sort of way. Her slanted eyes and light dusting of hair were the same shade as her mahogany skin. Based on the nature of Mezanya, with its people being split between worshiping Kani and praising Yehala, Jaya had expected their elected leader to look more like a priestess. Or at least someone more demure than the woman sitting beside her draped in enough jewels to fund a small rebellion.

"Jaya."

They shook hands as the rest of the royals came in to take their seats. Aquillo sat to Jaya's right, giving her one of his aloof smiles. Next to him was Rore. Samorah's companion visibly bristled as he took in the array of glowing eyes on the other half of the table.

The woman with no name tag in front of her seat stood and made her way around the table, handing out small devices. "You all can cast your votes on this at any time. Once you've voted on every proposal made today, your device will automatically come to us at the Center of Okew Relations. "

Jaya stared at the unassuming device, feeling like the sweet, freckle-faced woman had just handed her a bomb. She didn't know anything about Okew relations aside from bits of gossip from Olivia. They couldn't really be okay with an outsider deciding on their official matters, could they?

"It's just a preliminary meeting. A way for us to voice some things, so we can hopefully find solutions during the summit. We haven't been unanimous in the past, so we figured new input might help this time." Aquillo's whispered assurance was anything but. What was he trying to do here? She had been living in his home this whole time. He could have mentioned this before now.

"First up is the proposal for a memorial in the east Dewar land now known as the ruins."

Jaya snatched a glass of water from a servant before he could get away. The ice water sloshed over the crystal rim, soaking his white cuffs and Jaya's hand.

"Sorry."

"It's okay. Here." He pulled a napkin from beneath his serving tray and handed it to her before moving on to the rest of the ballroom.

Her frustration must be messing with her depth perception. Kalite had no way of knowing how poorly timed this welcome banquet was. Jaya had spent the last five hours in a room with the Okew royals, discussing everything from tree removals to resources for newly released Gudarin prisoners. The last thing she wanted to do was spend more time with them.

Discussed was an exaggeration. Really, Jaya sat quietly for most of the meeting, only speaking when Aquillo asked for her opinion on potential interplanetary trade of food items.

"You did well." Samorah appeared beside her, plucking a glass of wine from the bar table. "Looked like you were about to pee yourself, but you hung in there. I'm guessing Aquillo didn't tell you about the meeting before today?"

"No."

"That figures. Aquillo's never been the most socially aware person. How long have you been here, in Okew, if I might ask?"

"A while."

Jaya cast a look around the ballroom. A sea of people milled and mingled, one barely distinguishable from the other. Kalite was by the stage where the musicians were playing. She was in the middle of some animated story. Her hands fluttered about as she captivated the people around her with whatever tale she was spinning. This was the Kalite she had been trying to show her. Had Jaya accepted any of those lunch or breakfast invites, she would have been just as enchanted as these people were with the princess.

Aquillo was across the room, deep in conversation with the queen,

Mavin. Probably continuing their discussion from the meeting on the small forestation numbers this year, something that seemed to worry the otherwise stoic queen. She spoke with a lot of scientific terms that Jaya didn't understand, but she said it with so much passion that, at times, her olive eyes glowed a vivid jade and her pale skin flushed pink. Her proposal to label the balm valley calf as inedible wildlife was met with mixed opinions.

Jaya's right knee started acting up. She shifted her weight onto her left leg, but the tingling sensation intensified, moving up to her shoulder.

"Shoo. Run on back to your boyfriend." Samorah flicked her fingers at the small white creature at Jaya's waist. Its long ears twitched, brushing against her arm. The tingling sensation returned, and Jaya quickly took a step back. The bolkin's depthless eyes followed her. She hadn't seen one up close until now. Mist swirled beneath its translucent skin, and its pupils took up most of the eye sockets. More like obsidian cutouts in an otherwise featureless face.

"Tacius's pet bolkin. I can't believe he actually brought it here. Mavin's going to have a fit. Months of negotiations to keep those two from wiping each other off the map over his kink, and he blows it in one night."

Sure enough, Aquillo and the queen had frozen in shock, watching the bolkin float back to Tacius's side. It wore a silver collar and an emerald velvet cloak. The design on the collar was identical to the one on Tacius's crown.

"They feed off of healing. Mavin and her kingdom prefer a more medicinal approach to things. They don't think it's wise to be willing food. I can't say I disagree."

Jaya knew the history between the two rival kingdoms that bordered each other. Olivia had laughed herself to tears when she told her about the stories she's heard from women who had been invited to Tacius's private estate. Room after room filled with whips, flogs, and bondage devices of every kind that Tacius expected them to use on him while his bolkin waited nearby to treat his wounds.

"It's taken an interest in you. May I be so rude as to ask why?"

"No."

Jaya slammed her empty glass on the bar table and squeezed past the happy partygoers to find the nearest exit. She'd had enough of the royals' drama and Samorah for the day.

28

The gurgle of the wall's ocean projection filtered in from the timed sound system, waking Jaya. She propped her chin on her hand and looked down at Quielle's sleeping face.

He hadn't been back to the palace or to any of the morning summit meetings. She didn't blame him for staying away. After yesterday's near bloodbath between Aquillo and Samorah over the Aoeja territory, she was having a hard time not abandoning the summit herself. She could stay here, being served food and spine-curling orgasms for the rest of the day. It was an appealing thought. One she had no business thinking.

The rest of the summit attendees would be arriving today. Her window of opportunity was quickly closing. She had come too far, and her mother's freedom was so close.

Jaya fell back on the pillow, peeking sideways at Quielle through her bushy hair. His eyebrows were naturally neat, and so was his low haircut. If it weren't for his hooded eyes being heavier first thing in the morning, you'd never know he just rolled out of bed. It was kind of unfair. The only physical flaw she'd found on him was a small chunk of skin missing from his right ear, courtesy of a close call with an Elupian who didn't take kindly to travelers coming to his planet.

"Creep."

Another unfair advantage. His voice was extremely sexy first thing in the morning, even if he was calling her out for watching him sleep.

"If you put some clothes on, I wouldn't look."

"Who sleeps with clothes on besides you?"

"People. People sleep with clothes on." She bounced up on her knees, untangling Quielle's shirt from around her stomach and pulling it off. "Better?"

He pounced, pulling her on top of him. "Much."

His hand ran through her coils, pushing them to one side of her face. "What's on your mind?"

"You. This." She straddled his hips and came down with a moan as he filled her to near discomfort.

Quielle held her steady. His fingers gripped her waist and drew her closer as his teeth grazed her ear.

"Damn, Jaya," he groaned.

It was just what she needed to relieve that last bit of discomfort. She sat back, sinking further onto him and into the sheer pleasure he provided.

"Not that I'm complaining, but you never have to think that hard about this. What's really on your mind?"

This man saw everything. Jaya picked up her pace, throwing in a few squeezes to get him off her trail. It worked for a while. Quielle's face pinched in concentration as more curse words stumbled from his thick lips.

"Talk to me," he said, running his hand up her neck to trace her lips. "What's wrong?"

"I was... thinking. About the royals. The ban-quet. Tonight."

His hips drove up, meeting her on the downward stroke. Jaya pitched forward, trying to retreat from the area he had just tapped into, but he wasn't having it. He sat them back up, honing in that spot and working it until she was incoherent and babbling disjointed words about science queens and bed food. Quielle let out a growl, biting down on Jaya's collarbone hard enough for her to see stars. He soothed the soreness with a handful of kisses.

Jaya slogged sideways onto the bed, hitting it like a sack of clay. She watched the rise and fall of Quielle's chest as he regained his composure.

"Okay, I didn't get most of that last part, but as for the banquet. What about it?"

"The banquet isn't so bad. It's the meetings before it that are working my nerves. By the time I get to the banquet, I'm drained from trying to keep up, so I don't make a fool of myself and Inestar."

"I hear those meetings can get intense. Some have come to blows in the past."

"Have you seen any end like that?"

"No. This is my first summit as prince, and I'm not invited to those meetings. I'm here as a pretty face, not a decision-maker."

Quielle massaged her calf that lay across his thighs while she considered his words. "Does it bother you that Aquillo's using you and your work to salvage his reputation?"

"Yes, and no. On the one hand, I feel like if he wants to be seen as a good king, he should get out there and put in the work of rebuilding trust with his people instead of trying to gain trust by association. But, on the other hand, I can't say for sure what I would've done in his situation. If anything were to happen to Ma and Pops, or Tone, or you... I couldn't come back from that. I'd probably be just as lost as he is."

She hadn't known Aquillo before his parents' and Mia's deaths, but she imagined lost was a good description for him. He stalked the palace walls like a ghost, closer to his departed loved ones than the people he lived with.

"You're stronger than anyone I've ever met, Jaya, me and Aquillo included. And you're just as smart as the science queen." Jaya covered her face to hide her embarrassment. "Aquillo knows it, too. So, in true Aquillo fashion, he's trying to benefit from it by inviting you to these meetings and getting your take on things."

Was that his plan? Not to pressure her for information on Mia's killer, but to use her as a royal consultant? "I've been next to him at every one of these meetings, and I never thought that was the reason."

"Once you spend a couple of years around him, you'll see how predictable he is too." Quielle rested his arm over his eyes and drifted back to sleep.

They wouldn't have a couple more years.

Jaya crawled over and tucked her head between his neck and shoulder. His skin was warm against hers, or maybe *her* face was hot. *Breathe. Breathe.* She knew this moment was coming. She'd accepted it. It was now or never. She couldn't put it off anymore.

"My mother isn't missing."

"Mm," Quielle mumbled, half asleep.

"When we first met, you said you couldn't find any information on her. That's because we don't keep records of people who are marked. Once that brand hits their skin, they're as good as gone."

His eyes were open, and that quick mind of his was piecing together what she had just hinted at.

"My father was a kind man. He thought everyone deserved an opportunity to write their own history. That people shouldn't be judged by the actions of others. A long time ago, my people lived alongside the Carye in Gretznia. It was a beautiful place, much like Dewar, I imagine. The Carye are brutal people, but they have a knack for building cities. There was near-constant conflict between our two people, and a lot of blood was shed over unwarranted hatred. The Carye decided that fighting wasn't getting them anywhere. They were the natives of Gretznia, so they issued a mandate. All non-Carye were to leave or be hunted down like prey. My people were tired of the constant fighting, and people had already started disappearing, so they took their chances in exile. They broke off into different tribes. One of those tribes was led by my ancestor. He established Inestar."

She had never told this story to anyone. Had never had to since it was well known in Inestar.

"My father felt that time had tempered whatever issues existed between the Carye and our people. He said, 'with new life comes new views and the opportunity to start over'. There was no reason we couldn't at least establish communication. After months of unanswered messages, my father got a letter from the Carye leader inviting him to have a one-on-one. I don't know if he ever got to meet the leader."

Quielle had stopped breathing.

"He was burned alive. They cut his body up and dropped the pieces outside our walls. Someone on tower duty found him. There were a larger amount of buzzards hanging around than normal."

Tears blurred her vision, making it harder to tell if she was on a ship a billion miles away or back in the desert that day, with the smell of her father's dead body in the air.

"Bas was furious. He blamed my mother for filling my dad's head with soft-hearted ideas of world peace. He dragged her out in front of the people still gathered near the wall and marked her with his hunting knife."

Jaya got out of bed to find her clothes. She mechanically dressed while she tried to rein in her emotions. Maybe she shouldn't have told the whole story about her father, just what he needed to know to understand her decision. Quielle sat up, watching her with a look of confusion.

"My grandfather was vicious towards outsiders long before my dad died, but grief changed him. It made us all outsiders to him. He had no son, so he had no granddaughter. He wouldn't go so far as enslaving me. That part of his humanity remained at least." She bent down to grab her hair tie off the floor. "I can hear your mind working. You're thinking of a way to get in Inestar, get past the forty guards on the wall, and find my mother, who you've never seen before."

"You'd have to describe her surroundings in detail so I can direct my teleportation. Do you have a picture of her?"

Of course, he wanted to help. That was never a question in her mind. In fact, it was what she struggled with most. How could she stop him? Jaya shook her head, pushing down another wave of tears. "I didn't tell you this so you could save her. I told you so you would understand why I can't stay."

There. She'd gotten it out. Now she just needed to leave before he realized how much she wanted to take it back. *Where are my shoes?*

"Can't stay," he repeated her words with a sour look like they tasted bad coming out. "Wait. Where are you going? Shit, I need to wake up. Jaya, just give me a minute. I'll get up and make us something to eat, and we can come up with a plan."

"No. We don't need a plan. I already worked out a deal with Bas for her freedom. Now I just need to do my part and bring him what he asked for." She dropped to her knees, pulling one of her shoes from beneath the bed.

"Okay. Then I'll go back with you." Quielle started putting on his pants.

"*No*." Jaya almost screamed. "You can *never* come to Inestar. They'd put you in the hexagon. They'd kill you if they knew about us."

He scrubbed his hand over his head, looking more frustrated than fearful. "What's going on here, Jaya? What are you trying to say?"

"I can't stay with you. I never said I'd stay. I-I'm out of place here, Quielle. Dewar is your home, not mine."

"*You* are my home, Jaya. I'll go wherever you need me to go, wherever you are. You just... you just have to tell me what to do. Just tell me what to do. Whatever it is, I'll do it. I promise."

Something in her was shattering. She should have gone back to her room last night. This wasn't working. Quielle continued to stare into her, his face pleading.

"I talked to Rea when we were at Lirhop's house. She already agreed to assign someone to take me back."

He reared back like he'd been slapped.

"Was this before you came to the beach with me?"

She wanted to say no. She wanted to go back and do everything differently. It wouldn't have changed how she felt for him in the least, but at least she wouldn't end up here. "I didn't want to hurt you,"

He chuckled. "No, you just wanted to use me. When do you leave?"

"Tomorrow."

He nodded, then grabbed his t-shirt off the bed.

"You know the way out."

He brushed past her, leaving the room and the ship, and Jaya.

29

Someone was knocking. She had just made it back to the palace after spending the last hour clearing every trace of herself out of Quielle's ship. She'd only had time to dump her stuff in the closet and plop down amongst the mess before whoever was at the door started knocking. She should get that. Jaya pulled herself up off the floor and trudged to the door. She opened it without looking to see who came in.

"Good morning, gorgeous." Jondien entered, carrying a stack of gowns. He dropped the pile on the bed and started arranging them side by side.

Jaya curled up on the footrest while he worked. She wrapped her arms around her legs and rested her head on her knees. Today was going to be a long day. The sun was barely in the sky, and she already wanted to call it quits and try again tomorrow. Jondien cursed softly. It carried thanks to his deep voice.

"I'm sorry, Princess. Please excuse my language." He inspected the rip he'd just made in one of the dresses. Light flickered off the shiny metal of his prosthetic as he flexed his fingers.

"This one's out, but," He gestured to the other gowns, "what do you think?"

"They're beautiful," Jaya said, forcing a smile. The dresses differed in color and material, but they all fit a certain theme. She chose the nearest one. It was a long-sleeved dress that was fitted down to the thighs, where it flared out. The fabric was sheer but dark, and jewels covered the areas she didn't want everyone looking at.

"I was hoping you'd pick that one. Siren, my enchantress. You're going to be the center of everyone's attention tonight."

He was probably talking to the dress, but Jaya didn't care.

Jondien gathered the rest of the dresses up, draping them over his arm. "You and Queen Exia would have gotten along well. She's the only person beside you who could carry this look. Same natural grace and big heart. I look at you sometimes and—are you okay?"

"Yes." Jaya bit down on her bottom lip hard enough to draw blood.

"Are you sure?"

"Yes. I need to get dressed before the meeting." She stood and grabbed the dress off the bed. Jondien winced as she yanked his masterpiece up by its collar.

"Oh. Okay."

He left without another word. Jaya stripped and went to the bathing area to take a quick shower. She needed to get going. The others weren't scheduled to arrive for another two hours. That gave her enough time to sneak in and put her name tag next to Samorah's.

Initially, Jaya had planned to kill Aquillo and slip away during the chaos, but she would be the first person they suspected. She needed someone to take the fall. If Samorah stuck to her usual grand fashion, she wouldn't notice a missing jewel or piece of thread. Not until it showed up near Aquillo's body.

Jaya pulled on the dress and black heels, wetting her hair and pulling it back into a low bun before rushing out of the room.

The palace was busier than she had ever seen it. People bustled through the hallways, nearly colliding with one another in their rush to get where they were going. Jaya followed behind a servant carrying a bin of polished silverware. She slipped into the meeting room and stopped short.

Twelve guards searched the room from corner to corner, including

Brome, who stopped barking orders to scowl at her. All the other guards watched her too, but Jaya kept her eyes on Brome as she crossed the room. Kalite was hunched over the round table, propping name tags into their bronze holders. She gave Jaya a bright smile when she noticed her. "Wow! You look amazing! Is this from Inestar?"

"No. Jondien made it."

Brome turned to one of the guards and whispered something in his ear. Whatever he said did not sit well with the barrel-chested man, but after a few more harshly whispered words from Brome, he nodded and left out the side door for Aquillo's wing.

"It's so sexy. I hope he has something like that for me. I've been swimming in the stuff he's putting me in, and the guys at the banquet look at me like I'm wearing my mom's shoes."

"He showed me a few others. They're my size, though, so he might have to take it in some for you. If you tell him now, he could probably have it ready in time for the banquet."

Kalite tapped the name tags against the table, looking around at the blank holders.

"I can do this while you go find him."

"Okay. I put them in order for how they *have* to be assigned. Kani help us all if Mavin and Tacius end up next to each other."

Jaya nodded, reaching for the name tags.

"The other royal guards should arrive any minute to do their security sweep. Lenille will take care of them when she gets here. There she is." Kalite waved to get Lenille's attention with the name tags still in her hand.

Lenille walked over, accidentally bumping into a guard on her way. Jaya didn't know what all went into putting together a summit. But- from the stampede of servants in the halls, Kalite's possessiveness over name tags, and Lenille's thousand-yard stare- you could tell it was taking a heavy toll on the people involved.

Kalite handed Jaya the name tags and rounded the table to give Lenille her assignment. Samorah's name tag had already been placed in its holder next to Wren and Everett, the twin royals of Ziep. She picked up the placeholder, swapping it with Rore's, when a stifled cry came from behind.

The room tilted at an odd angle as Kalite dropped to her knees, clutching her chest. Lenille stood over her with a bloody knife raised above her head. She brought it down, aiming for Kalite's face. One of the guards caught her wrist, twisting until she dropped the knife, and tackled her to the floor.

The room continued to pitch until Jaya's face smashed into the cold tile. Brome's arm pressed into her shoulders. He bore down with all his weight, pinning her against the floor. People rushed in. Mender uniforms replaced royal armor. The whole time, Kalite laid motionless in the entryway in a pool of her own blood. Brome was really yelling now. His booming voice made the walls shake. He kept leaning down to snarl at her, telling her she would pay for this.

Jaya took it all in, including Lenille's lifeless eyes. They stared through the four people that crowded around the princess, working to save her life.

They saw nothing. They felt nothing.

30

The room cleared out after the mend unit teleported away with an unconscious and pale Kalite. That left Lenille- bound to a chair and muttering- and Jaya on the floor with Brome's sword pressed between her shoulder blades. The bastard hadn't stopped gloating since his people left. He was trying his best to scare her.

"That rat trap you call home is nothing compared to Gudarin."... "You won't last a week there."... "I should volunteer to transport you. Throw you overboard and see if you're a natural swimmer."

And they called her a savage. Jaya blocked him out and focused on Lenille. Her lips hadn't stopped moving since she came in, but Jaya couldn't understand what she was saying. It didn't help that she had to crane her neck up to see her.

The hallway went still and silent. Without a hundred servants bustling through, it felt eerie. Shadows coiled in the darkened doorway, and the smell of ash crept into the room. Aquillo emerged from the darkness. Like the Krylvonhar, he gave no warning. One minute you were alone, and the next, death was staring you down from three yards away. Smoke billowed around him like an aura. It was an extension of him, no different from his fingers and legs.

He must have been getting ready when they told him about Kalite.

His arms were exposed. Until now, he had kept his ink covered unless he was working in his garden. He had on a plain white t-shirt and suit pants. Both were covered in some kind of debris. Bits of emerald and blue sparkled in the cream powder substance like glitter- or a mosaic.

Are those the tiles?

The first trace of fear seeped into Jaya as Aquillo pulled out a chair and sat down ramrod straight. He didn't pay her any attention or order Brome to let her up. Instead, he leaned towards Lenille. His face was barely an inch from hers, and he stared into her eyes, unblinking. Lenille continued to ramble. She didn't pause even when Aquillo's face suddenly twisted with anger and steam rose from the floor.

Jaya shifted as much as she could under Brome's sword as the tiles beneath her heated. A dome closed in around them. It passed over Kalite's blood near the door, and Jaya watched in horror as red bubbles swelled from the stain and boiled.

Aquillo and Lenille sat unfazed in the eye of the storm, locked in their stare-off. Brome shifted his sword to his left hand so he could wipe the sweat from his eyes. No one was looking at her. Jaya's knife was strapped to her calf. She could reach it, but it might alert Brome and cost her her left shoulder, so she needed to be quick. She lifted her leg, keeping her eyes on the two at the table as she hiked her dress up. Before she could grab the hilt, Brome snatched her up off the floor.

Plan B, then.

She threw her head back, slamming it into Brome's face. The sound of his nose cracking was pure satisfaction until he grabbed her wrist and twisted it behind her back with blinding force. Jaya's vision went white. She fought to breathe through the pain as his sweaty arm wrapped around her throat and squeezed.

"I'm not going to kill you just yet. Wouldn't want you to miss this," he sneered in her ear.

He turned them towards the table just as the flames erupted around Lenille. They consumed her in milliseconds like she had been dipped in oil. Jaya's body went slack. Her knees crumbled like wet sand beneath her, but Brome held her up by her neck. His chest rumbled with laughter against her back. This had to be some kind of nightmare. There was no way that Aquillo had just killed Lenille. He wouldn't do that.

The fire dissolved in mid-air, leaving behind the white chair- pristine, with no indication that Lenille was ever there.

She hadn't even screamed.

"Have your men prepare another room for today's meeting. Tacius's guards are here. Let them know the location has changed and watch them while they do their security check." Aquillo spouted off the order while standing from his seat and turning to leave.

Brome released Jaya, and she fell to her hands and knees, convulsing. She tasted blood. He followed Aquillo through a path in the steam, turning at the last minute to smirk at her. Jaya pressed her forehead to the warm floor. She didn't need to look to know the path left with them, locking her in with the empty chair and the memory of Aquillo killing the woman who gave up everything, including her son, to care for him.

"BREAK, DAMMIT."

Jaya scooted forward on the floor, positioning her foot closer to the top of the chair's cushion. She drew her leg up to her chest and rammed into it with all her strength. Solid wood crashing into the dome sounded like anvils being thrown together. She tried again and again until her hips throbbed with pain. Not even a scratch.

Hammering into the dome did no good, either. All she got from that was a bent dagger and a broken high heel. Hurling chairs at it was an even worse idea, but that was before Jaya's anger had had time to deteriorate into hopelessness.

The damn thing was impenetrable.

The light filtering through the mist had changed from a soft early morning glow to the blinding sunlight of midday. No one had come for her. She could hear passing conversations from the palace's guests- amplified in the sensory chamber- but they were always decreasing in volume, going further away instead of towards her.

Jaya took a deep breath and lined her other foot up with the cushion.

"That won't help. Your bones will break before this shield does."

She swallowed her terror and scrambled to her feet, turning to face Aquillo. He had changed his suit. His arms were now covered by a light gray jacket, and he wore a black sash over one shoulder. The mist in the dome cloaked him, so Jaya could only see his glowing eyes.

"Why am I even here?" She tried to force some steel into her voice. "You know I didn't hurt Kalite."

Aquillo came forward. He picked up one of the chairs from the floor, noting the slight wobble it now had, before sitting down and folding his hands in his lap.

"Right. It was Lenille who tried to kill my daughter?"

He waited for her answer. Waited for her to accuse the woman who had served the royal family for two generations and probably raised the orphans Aquillo took in of attempting to kill one of them.

Brome was behind this. He had to be. *That* Lenille was not the stern, acute woman Jaya had met her first day here. She was blank. Hollow. Like all of her had been scooped out and replaced with someone else.

Maybe it had.

"I don't think she knew what she was doing." Jaya paused. How could she say this without coming off as someone making wild excuses to get out of her cage? "Someone was controlling her."

It was a slight movement, just a tilt of his head, but that tick said it all.

"You don't believe me, and I don't know what to say to get you to see that I'm telling you the truth." She sighed. "Is what I'm saying that far-fetched? I mean, your entire kingdom runs on magic. Maybe someone is using that magic to harm the people close to you?"

Aquillo's eyes flared. Around them, the once still mist climbed the dome like souls crawling out of a pit. Jaya mentally backtracked. But what had she said to set him off?

"If someone was using my power to hurt anyone I care about," he spat the word between his bared teeth, "I'd know it, and they'd be dead by now."

Jaya raised her hands in surrender.

"I'm sorry. I didn't mean to imply anything. I don't fully understand how things work around here. I know that. But I've seen this illusion magic before. Someone used it to attack me in my room."

Careful, Jaya. She was walking a fine line. Aquillo was already skeptical of her story. If she accused the head of his guard without proof, he'd leave her here to rot—or worse.

Aquillo rocked back in his chair. Another tic, but this one made Jaya see red.

"You knew about Brome stalking me?"

"Not at first. He told me about it this morning when I left for the meeting. He said he didn't want me to know that he had disobeyed my order to give you space and to treat you as we would any other guest."

So he didn't order the attack on her. He knew about it now, though, and he hadn't brought Brome with him. Maybe he torched him to oblivion for going against his order. Jaya could only hope.

"He also said that he had never been so afraid. Tell me, you're about average weight for a woman, a little more muscular than most, but still. How did you beat my best guard, who is twice your size, and leave him tainted with fear? How does someone like you manage to do that?"

He was watching her every expression. The mist drew closer, leaning into the dome to hear her response. Lying wouldn't help, and neither would the truth. Brome had set the perfect trap, one she had no hope of getting out of.

"He's lying. He used some kind of power to conceal himself, but it wouldn't let him kill me. I don't know why, but check his body for the white mark. It should look like a symbol, like an old language."

"And where should I look?"

"*I don't know*, but it has to be on him or in this room somewhere. He used it to control Lenille! Probably because he couldn't kill Kalite himself."

"Isn't it common practice in Inestar to mark your victims after a battle?"

It was, but saying yes would confirm much more to Aquillo. Accusation and disbelief were plain and clear on his face. He thought she did this. Like Quielle had that day in her room, he assumed the marks were from Syntia. How was it they knew about the marks but not what they represented?

Aquillo rested his elbow on his knee and rubbed his forehead. "I'm out of moves and alternatives here, Jaya, so I'm just going to be forward and ask you. Where is the man who killed Tomi?"

"I don't–" Movement caught Jaya's eye, stalling the words in her throat. The bolkin glided from the shadows of the dome. Its emerald cloak billowed in the mist that served as its feet. How long had it been in here?

"I'd choose my next words carefully if I were you," Aquillo said.

The bolkin's long ears raised and tilted towards Jaya as it came to stand by Aquillo. Those black, cut-out eyes closed, and she had the unsettling image of it inhaling her scent, savoring what was to come.

She took a step back. Her dinged-up dagger was on the floor next to the chair. She stepped on the blade, expecting the sting of jagged metal against her bare feet, but something slippery squished between her toes. Jaya stared down in disbelief at the puddle of steel and leather. Her destroyed weapon dissolved into a yellow light before disappearing altogether.

Aquillo's right hand continued to glow with the power he'd used to disarm her, still rubbing at his temple. "I invited you into my home, treated you like my equal, and you have done nothing but lie and sneak around my palace."

Okay. Think, Jaya. She'd been in desperate situations before. Maybe not this desperate, but she could survive if she kept her wits.

"You're right. I haven't been fair to you, but this... this isn't you, Aquillo. You are a good man. You wouldn't–"

"Stop lying to me. You don't believe that. You couldn't even look me in my eyes when you said it." He sneered. "You're just like your grandfather. You'll say anything to save your skin. He tried flattering me, too, when I came for the soldier. Even gave me some story about his son being killed. He claimed he would never give that pain to someone else."

"Do not talk about my father," Jaya seethed. Shock and rage rose within her so fast it made her hands and voice rattle.

"I actually felt sorry for him," he went on, ignoring the threat of violence in her voice, "an old man crying over his lost child."

Jaya wanted blood. Aquillo's. She'd paint this dome with it. How dare he talk about her father? As if he knew him, the kind of man he was. It didn't matter if she was stuck in here. She'd spend the rest of her life in here, carving up Aquillo's bones.

"I spared him, thinking he had suffered enough. Now I see you all for what you really are. *Vicious* and *untrustworthy* people with no loyalty to anyone. You never wanted peace with my people. All you and your grandfather want is to slaughter. If I had known, you never would have gotten near my daughter."

"*She's not your fucking daughter!* She had parents! You killed them, remember?" Jaya panted, her breath hot in her lungs. She was beyond the point of caring about Aquillo, the dome, or the bolkin. She was *done* being compared to Bas and listening to him talk about her father's murder like it was some convenient lie they had made up.

"You sit here judging like you aren't covered in the blood of your people. At least I left the families of the people I've killed to mourn in peace. I didn't try to make their children forgive me or love me. I didn't try to replace them. I may be a monster. I might even deserve everything you're about to do to me. But the only reason you trusted me so much is because I was familiar. You knew who I was, but you wanted to believe I was something better- just like y–."

The blast swept her off her feet. Her head smacked the floor before she was flung back into the dome. Phantom hands clawed through the dome, grabbing Jaya and dragging her high above the ground where Aquillo stood. His dark fists were nearly white and pulsing with power. Chairs flew into the dome like they were being pulled by a magnet, shattering on impact.

Only the ears of the bolkin remained intact. The rest of its body had dissolved into a cloud and hovered above its cloak and collar. Aquillo's power pressed in on her chest, forcing the air from her lungs. Jaya gasped as her heart struggled to beat.

This is it. You failed.

The smell of burned flesh flooded her senses just before she passed out.

31

Death was painful. You'd think that when the mind dies, so do the senses, but every part of Jaya hurt. Every muscle felt like it had been torn apart, then stitched back together. Even her tongue hurt. That bright light wasn't helping. Where was it coming from, anyway? Was she supposed to go towards it?

Jaya risked opening her eyes. The white light hovered just above her face. At least she didn't have far to go. Feeling was returning to her legs, and they were saying they weren't up for a long journey. The light began to pull away.

No. Come back.

Speed had always been her gift. She was the fastest runner in Inestar. Of course, it would abandon her now when she needed it most. Her legs felt like clay bricks being dragged from a river. She sat up and tucked her feet under her, stopping midway to catch her breath. At least the light had stopped moving. It came to a rest on the floor next to a pair of burnished shoes.

"Rise and shine, Princess."

The voice was unfamiliar, but she had seen those blood-red eyes before. Watching her across the table, anticipating her every fumble, glowing with laughter at her expense. She wasn't dead. Jaya sighed in equal parts relief and frustration.

"Where's Aquillo?"

Rore chuckled, his canines gleaming in the low light. "The first person you ask for is Aquillo? I thought you'd be much happier to see me."

"As you can see, he and I were in the middle of a conversation." She waved to the scattered rubble and the destroyed meeting room.

Rore glanced around at the broken furniture surrounding Jaya and, for once, didn't crack a smile. "Aquillo's always been the emotional type, even when we were kids. If he so much as scraped his knee, he'd sob into Exia's bosom for the rest of the day."

Aquillo, wrathful king and semi-god, crying to his mommy should have been funny. But hearing his name only revived Jaya's anger.

"Well, Kalite is the closest thing he has left to family. I guess he feels entitled to his emotions," Jaya said, rolling her eyes.

"All the more reason for him to get his head out of the sand, or he's going to lose a lot more."

Jaya tried to stand. "Did he send you here to gain sympathy? You should probably come back when my body has healed from his last round of torture."

A burnt orange lounge sofa sprouted from the floor, throwing Jaya face down onto its plush velvet cushions. She jerked back up, getting her feet on the ground in the time it took Rore to meander over, unbutton the front of his suit jacket, and take a seat in the chair he'd summoned for himself. "Actually, I want you to tell me about this magic you say Brome has acquired."

"Why? So you can tell me I'm lying?"

Rore settled back into his chair, crossing his ankle over his knee. A white pillow appeared at the opposite end of the sofa from Jaya, along with a glass of water.

"I promise to keep an open mind."

Strange. Unlike Aquillo, Rore's hands didn't glow when he used his power. She had been banking on that visual warning when things were about to turn violent in the meetings. Yet another sign that she'd been destined to fail all along.

She snatched the glass of water from the sofa, ignoring the pillow. The cool liquid soothed her dry throat and shocked her aching ribs on the way down. He waited while she finished the entire glass and replaced it with another afterwards.

"What's in it for me?" Jaya asked.

Rore's eyes dropped to her tattered dress. They muted a shade of red that resembled rose petals when he got to her thighs. Seriously? Did he really think she'd use this one opportunity for sex? Rore's low laughter echoed in the dome.

"It was worth a shot." He shrugged. "You want to get out of here, right?"

"Yes."

"Unfortunately, that's the one thing I can't do. Freeing you would be considered an act of war. And as tempting as you are, Aquillo is my oldest friend. I'd hate to have to kill him. *But* if what you say about Brome turns out to be true, and he is behind the attack on Kalite, I could convince Aquillo to let you go."

"Why would you do that? Why do you even care what's happening here?"

"Like I said, Aquillo is my oldest friend. An attack against him is an attack against me. Plus, it's not like you have any other options. I'm your only chance of getting out of this dome."

He was right. Brome knew there was little chance of Aquillo believing her. If there was, he would have stabbed her in the back when he had the chance. None of the royals were particularly trustworthy, but Rore at least seemed motivated to find who was really behind all this.

"Okay." Jaya sighed.

She told Rore everything, from Brome secretly stalking her to him sending one of his men off minutes before Lenille came into the meeting room and stabbed Kalite.

"You didn't hear what he said to him?"

"No. I was talking to Kalite, but the guard wasn't comfortable with whatever he'd asked him to do."

Strands of Rore's curly black hair escaped his crown- which sat haphazardly towards the back of his head- and dangled near his brows. Jaya hadn't realized until now how much he resembled Kalite. His roasted hazelnut skin was a shade darker than hers, but the similarity was undeniable. Maybe Kalite's parents were from Eroni.

"This is all Brome's fault. Lenille didn't deserve to die."

"Lenille's not dead."

"Yes, she is. Aquillo killed her in here. I saw him do it."

Rore laughed. Actually started laughing. This was who she was depending on to get her out of this.

"Sneaky bastard's using my tricks now." He shook his head. "Lenille is fine. Trust me. It'd take an army of demons to kill that woman."

Jaya wasn't sure if she trusted him, but she hoped he was right. "How do you think he did it—controlled Lenille?"

Rore sighed and slouched down in his chair. It was the most unkingly thing she had seen him do. "Probably got a hold of some potion magic. A spell. Who knows? With connections and the right amount of money, you can come up on just about anything here, Princess."

He was taunting her again, which meant he didn't want to tell her what he really thought. Rore's seduction and arrogance act was easy to see through when you weren't affected by it. And Jaya had been through too much over the past few hours to be brushed off.

"Why would he want to kill Kalite?"

"Potion magic is unpredictable and temporary. Maybe he wants something more permanent."

A plate of seared meat on top of a purple puree of some sort appeared on Jaya's lap. The fragrant steam wafted up, caressing her nostrils. She set it aside on the sofa, far out of reach, and locked her hands together.

"Like what?"

"That Inestar discipline runs deep, I see." He smirked. "You'd make a formidable queen. Maybe after all this is over, you can spend some time with me in my kingdom. My palace is much bigger than Aquillo's, or so I've been told."

Jaya waited. After a full minute had passed, Rore sighed. "Brome's after The Gift."

"And how does killing Kalite get him that?"

"The Gift isn't always a random act of divine intervention. Sometimes it can be swayed if a connection is strong enough."

He opened his palm, spreading his fingers wide. Fragments of the destroyed table floated in the air, melding and reshaping into intricate forms: a bear cub, a mace, an ocean wave.

"It's been in my family for nine generations. Each person it passed to had a close relationship with the last recipient, a bond. I received it after my older brother died in a boating accident."

The wave crashed down on itself, dissolving back into a pile of wood dust. "I think Brome is trying to ensure he's the only one left standing in Aquillo's inner circle."

THE VEGETABLE PUREE wasn't bad. She'd had better. Spending time with Quielle had turned Jaya into a closet food snob. Now every time she took a bite of good food, it came with a memory of him, shirtless, handing her a spoon to check the balance of sweet and spicy in one of his dishes. Or him, shirtless- he was always shirtless in her memories- teaching her how to hold a knife when slicing carrots. *It's different from holding a knife to someone's kneecaps. We're going for precision here, not permanent disfigurement.*

The likelihood of Rore convincing Aquillo to let her out was slim to impossible. So Jaya could only imagine what she would say if she had the chance to talk to Quielle again. She'd start with how sorry she was, and she hoped she hadn't done too much damage to his heart because she had thoroughly wrecked her own.

The small light Rore left behind flared near the center of the dome, then sputtered out, leaving Jaya in complete darkness.

32

The meal Jaya had been so grateful for earlier stirred like violent winds in her stomach. A low whirring sound was coming from somewhere inside the dome. It started out soft, rising steadily before it fell silent. Each time it grew louder and sharper. She sprang to her feet, quieting her breath while she tried to pinpoint the direction it was coming from.

The dome vibrated as another wave of sound rocked it. This one was keening, nerve-shattering. Jaya covered her ears and stumbled back, flipping headfirst over the back of the sofa. Her knees slammed down on the hard floor, and her face hit the cushion. The sound continued to build until her ears were numb, and she was seeing stars.

It started again, then abruptly cut off. Dead silence followed. After ten seconds passed, Jaya lowered her hands.

Air was whistling from somewhere, and she felt a cool breeze on her right leg. Jaya closed her eyes and got down on her hands and knees. She let the breeze guide her, stretching her hand out and feeling around for sharp objects before shuffling forward. It was slow going, and sawdust scraped against her knees as she crawled across the rubble. But eventually, her fingers grazed the smooth concave surface of the dome. The whistling was easier to pick up now. It was close. She rose toward it, stretching to her full height plus her tiptoes. *Please don't let it be coming from the top.* Hairline fractures littered the thick surface of the dome. None big enough to make it through both sides.

"Did you get it?"

The question came from the other side of the glass, close to where Jaya was standing. It was clipped, but the voice was clearly male. It wasn't Quielle. But who else would be trying to break her out? Aquillo and Rore had teleported in and out. No one else knew she was in here except–.

"Yeah." Brome's gravelly voice sent an icy blast through the dome wall.

"So where is it?"

"Open the portal first."

A moment of silence passed, then someone sighed. "It's open. Now give it to me before I open one in here."

Faces flickered through Jaya's mind, all the people she'd seen around Brome. He spent most of his time barking orders instead of talking. Jaya had never spoken to any of the guards, and they had probably been given strict orders not to speak to her, so the other voice could be anyone.

"I can handle myself."

"Oh really? I heard about your scuffle with the princess. A female was too much for you. You had to sneak up on her like a little bandit."

"Who told you that?" Brome shouted. "*Huh*? Answer me!"

"Keep your voice down. Listen."

"To what?"

"Silence. Are you sure they'll attack? From the sounds of it–"

A shrill cry echoed from somewhere in the palace.

"Of course, they attacked," Brome said. "It's what they do."

"Hmm, or maybe one of your paranoid guards drew first blood. If I'm not mistaken, their orders tonight are to kill at first sight, right? Not capture or incapacitate."

"Their orders are always to defend the palace at all costs. What are you doing? You're letting her *out*? That wasn't part of the plan!"

"It's my plan. You're just along for the ride."

A blast rocked the dome, and the keening sound returned full force.

The dome shattered, and thick shards came crashing down around Jaya. She fell to the ground, folding her arms over her head and face as large pieces of the dome rained down on her.

When everything stopped falling, and she was somehow still alive, Jaya peeked from behind her elbow. Glass littered every inch of the meeting room's sunken floor, except for where Jaya had balled up in the fetal position.

Brome stood outside the field of glass, glaring at her. His teal guard's uniform was immaculate. The rust-colored breastplate he wore over it slanted from his right shoulder to his lower ribs. His captain's emblem winked at her from across the room like a jewel caught in sunlight.

"Grab her. Aquillo felt his shield break. We don't have much time."

Jaya scrambled to her feet, but there was nowhere to run. She was surrounded by glass and shoeless, so she wouldn't get far. There was no point in risking sliced up feet and infection for two seconds of freedom. So she stood her ground as Brome walked across the glass. He circled to her back, and she heard the jangle of handcuffs.

"Afraid to leave my hands free, kitten?"

Brome yanked her back by her hair. "Don't think this means you're safe."

"Hey!"

Brome's death grip on Jaya tightened as the other man, who had retreated to the corner of the room as soon as the dome collapsed, bounded back over to them. The light from Dewar's full moon illuminated his combat boots first. They were worn and covered in white sandy residue. His muted gray pants and hooded shawl were drab even by Inestar standards, but they covered him completely, up to his clean-shaven face.

He was on Brome in four strides. His scarred hand clamped down on his wrist with enough force to break it. "You better get yourself together because if you so much as scratch her, I'll fold you inside out by your ass."

His coal-black eyes were flat and void of any emotion other than rage. Brome let her go, and the stranger snatched the handcuffs from him, shoving them in the hem of his pants. He smelled like heat and salt. It would be easy to imagine he had just come down from a long day on the wall and stopped by the river to cool his face. Everything, except for the glowing symbol peeking out of his shawl, gave the impression to those who didn't know better that he was from Inestar.

He didn't allow Jaya's inspection to go on long. He turned and went back to his position near the door just as Brome's calloused hand covered her mouth. He hoisted her up like a sack of wheat and carried her away from her ruined cell. She hadn't even considered fighting. Shock over coming face to face with Mia's killer had thrown her off balance.

The commotion in the other room rose, painting a gruesome picture for them of what was happening. The Okew royals, particularly the twins, didn't require much provocation. For them, even the slightest insult was repaid with death. Lots of it. Whoever was fighting in there was crazy to attack during the summit when all the royals were present. There would be no bodies when this was all over, only a red cloud that crackled with the dark energy of Kani's gift. Brome was insane. He'd fed them to the wolves without an ounce of remorse.

33

The first and second floors of the ballroom were packed with people. Quielle had chosen an empty table near the courtyard.

He was gratefully alone since most of the crowd was at the opposite end of the ballroom, near the dance floor and garden terraces. Here he had a clear view of the room where the royals had their meetings. Most of them had filtered out already and were mingling with the other summit invites. Jaya hadn't come out yet.

What are you doing here? She said she doesn't want to be with you.

Actually, she said she *couldn't* stay with him because she had to return to Inestar to free her mother. That part Quielle understood. And honestly, he would have done the same if he were in her situation. There wasn't much he wouldn't do for the people he loved. And, even if she didn't realize it or feel the same, that included Jaya.

He was still raw over her using him, but he had no one to blame for that but himself. In the heat of the moment, things got confused. Those I miss you's, and I want you's sounded a lot like I love you to him, or close enough. He was too deep in the fantasy to care about nuance. That's what he got for assuming. If a lifetime of rejection had taught him anything, it was to never assume. Things didn't go your way just because you desperately wanted them to. People were entitled to make their own decisions. They were entitled to walk away.

That was Mia's credo, why she always put extra effort into her cases involving abuse or abduction. She would not be pressured into being with someone, and neither should anyone else.

She'd had every right to reject him. Mia deserved someone who loved her with every breath in his body, and maybe that person was Aquillo. Quielle had no way of knowing. But the shallow love he had offered, the one that stemmed from that lonely and broken place in him- he knew she deserved more than that. It took him falling hopelessly in love with Jaya to realize the difference and that he deserved more, too.

While things didn't turn out how he had hoped, his heart still belonged to Jaya, and he would do everything in his willpower to make sure she was happy, which meant helping her free her mother.

Bas was a pitiful excuse for a man, but Quielle was almost sure he could be reasoned with or paid off. Men like him always had a price. He'd give all the money he had earned traveling and his royal stipend if that's what it took.

A woman's hand tapped his shoulder. His heart sank when he turned towards a short, chubby-cheeked woman who was definitely not Jaya.

"Hi," she said with a half smile.

"Hi?"

"I'm Anui. We met a while ago at your appointment ceremony."

"Oh, yeah. You're one of the king's or—children." He didn't remember her. But aside from his family, who insisted on coming, and a few royals, they were the only others who attended that sham of a ceremony.

"Right. Is he here? I wanted to make sure he saw me before I left."

"Umm." Quielle looked around the crowded ballroom. The royals were all over, followed closely by their personal guards, advisors, family, assistants, servants, and royal food in teeth checkers. An army of guards in varying royal colors lined the walls, covering the exits and archways. How could these people be in such a partying mood when it looked like a war could break out at any minute?

The foreign royals stood out with their unique clothes, odd customs, and strange entourage that included creatures from their home planets. He'd even seen a man with four arms, floating casually above a dark pit that contained a giant monster of some kind. Quielle had only seen the thing's silver claws when they dragged across the surface of the pit before he got the hell out of their way.

Ormiez must have had a golden tongue and balls of steel to have earned these people's respect. The fact that they traveled across the galaxy for his son's banquet said a lot.

The more Quielle looked around, the less familiar faces he saw. Not only was Aquillo missing, but so were Lenille, Kalite, Nyro, and Brome.

"Look who decided to show."

Spoke too soon. Nyro brushed past him, planting himself between Quielle and Anui, nudging her out of the way. He unbuttoned his suit jacket, drawing attention to the silver bracelet on his wrist. A jagged blue line zipped across, ending at a button that, if pressed, activated a video call to the patient rooms in the healing center.

"Came to see your runaway mom finally gets hers? She'll burn tonight for what she did to Kalite. I'll make sure of it. So will–"

Whatever else he was going to say was between him and Kani. He could tell him when he met him. Quielle's hands closed around Nyro's neck, lifting him off his feet. They slammed onto a table hard enough to send it sliding back across the floor.

"*Have you lost your fucking mind, Nyro*?" Quielle roared in his face.

Cold rage clawed through him, raising the hairs on his neck and arms. Around them, the guests had gone quiet. Aquillo's guards moved as quickly as they could around the shocked and grinning royals to get to the king's son before his lungs gave out.

Nyro was busy throwing punches. He wasn't concerned with air. His brown skin had turned bright red, but still, he fought. If his mission had been to inflict maximum damage, mission accomplished. Quielle was in such a murderous fog his vision had gone black around the edges. The only clear point was where his hand gripped Nyro's throat.

The ground rumbled beneath him, and a large crack split the air like lightning. A portal materialized, filling the archway leading to the courtyard. Quielle squinted as dry air and heat poured into the ballroom. Nyro shoved him off, gasping for air. He cocked his fist back to throw another punch and inhaled a large gust of sand that sent him into a coughing fit.

"What is that," someone asked.

A giant rocky arch was just inside the portal. Beyond it, a crowd formed a loose circle and cheered as a big man knocked another to the ground. They were so caught up in the brawl that they had yet to notice the portal or Quielle. One of them, a man sitting beneath the arch, turned and frowned at him. Space shriveled and closed in on him as he took in the rough terrain and faces of the Inestar army.

"Move! Move!"

Quielle was pushed back by one of Aquillo's guards. They bulldozed the rest of the way through the crowd and formed a barricade around the portal.

"What are you *doing* in here? The palace is under attack!" Aquillo appeared out of nowhere.

His skin was black as soot. His eyes were the color of magma and bulging from their sockets. The air smelled of cinder and billowed in cauterizing waves around the edges of his black suit. Jaya had never seen this version of him and would not have guessed that it existed. This thing standing before her was more myth than human.

Aquillo took in the scene: his dome in pieces, Jaya somehow freed. He paused, tilting his head to one side. She could see the moment everything clicked into place for him. The numerous mishaps: Mia's death, Lenille stabbing Kalite, and now, with his palace being overrun, he finds the head of his guard with an escaped prisoner. Rore must not have told Aquillo his theory about Brome trying to steal The Gift, but seeing him here with her was the final nail.

"I'm going to ask you again. What are you doing here, Brome?"

Brome stood motionless, saying nothing. His heart was pounding through his armor and into Jaya's back. She tried to shuffle out of the way, but he tightened his grip and jerked her back in front of him. Boots scuffed against the tile, catching everyone's attention. Aquillo turned. His power flared, forming a shield, but not fast enough. The dark liquid sailed through the air and splashed in his face.

"Ahh!" Aquillo stumbled back, rubbing at his eyes. He struck out blindly, sending a blast of yellow light into the wall just right of his attacker.

The soldier circled him like a hawk, turning the vial he held upside down to pour the last drops of liquid on his fingers. With it, he drew patterns on the inside of his forearms, trailing along his veins, turning and weaving in a way that was clearly familiar to him. By the time he finished drawing the symbol, Aquillo had gone still.

"Do you see them?" The soldier asked. His voice was quiet, and it dripped with venom. He pointed at a blank space on the floor. "*Look* at what he did to them."

Aquillo's face held that same lack of awareness that Lenille's had earlier. He stared down at the floor, squinting and shaking his head.

"No, that's not... what happened." He stepped back, repeating the denial over and over. His voice grew softer, younger, with each word. The potion had not just taken hold of his sight. It was altering his very life. He paced the room, tracking the movements of someone or something only he could see. "Don't do this. They did nothing to you."

"What is he seeing?" Brome asked.

The soldier was drawing symbols again. They grew brighter with each pass of his fingers. Aquillo paused in front of Jaya and Brome, staring past them at the shattered dome.

"Father, wake up!"

He took off running, and Brome followed, dragging Jaya along by her arm.

"Dad, you have to wake up now! DAD!"

Aquillo lunged forward. His chest collided with the floor so hard he'd probably bruised his ribs. He spread his arms out wide, using as much of his body as he could to shield what he thought was his father. His back heaved with shaky gasps and silent tears, but he kept his head low, muttering assurance that *they* were going to be okay. Jaya felt sick. Brome shoved her away and rushed to Aquillo's side.

"*What did you do to him*?" He glared at his partner, who remained by the door, watching Aquillo with dispassionate eyes.

"I gave him the truth. He deserved to know."

Aquillo's head lifted, and his mouth fell open in shock. He blinked hard. Once. Twice. His quivering hands reached out and hovered above the shattered glass. Blood poured from his busted lip as he opened his mouth and let out a loud cry. It came from the base of his soul, beseeching and excruciating, like his heart was being pried from his chest.

"Hold on. I'll get help. Just hold on," he said. His voice was hoarse with tears.

"You were supposed to make this quick!" Brome yelled at the soldier. "Not this! This is.."

Torture.

"Stay with me, Mom. Open your eyes, okay? Help is coming. Just hold on." Aquillo wrapped his arms around himself. "Don't leave me. Please. Don't leave me."

"Aquillo, look at me." Brome kneeled down and grabbed his face." Focus on my voice, okay? It's not real. What you're seeing is not real."

"*Somebody help them*," Aquillo screamed, staring over Brome's shoulder at Jaya.

She stepped forward, unsure of what to do. She had to do something. Aquillo's grief was a conduit, dragging her into the hallucination as sure as if the potion had been thrown in her face. She found herself standing over her father's dismembered body. It was her voice, not Aquillo's, asking why everyone was just standing there.

"Why won't they help him?" she asked.

"They were already gone." The soldier's gruff voice answered next to her. He grabbed her by her shoulders, pulling her away from Brome and Aquillo. "We need to get back."

They had just crossed the threshold of the door when white light blanketed the room, and the delayed sound of the blast hit them.

34

The ringing was deafening, worse than the dust clogging her throat and eyes, but not the pain in her shoulder. It had taken a beating in the blast. Jaya shuffled forward, pausing as the world tilted sideways. She leaned back, trying to correct it, but everything continued to shift past her.

Somehow, she ended up back in the room, which no longer resembled a room at all. The stucco walls and a few tattered drapes remained, but the floor had been hollowed. The nested tile work and foundation had been blown away, leaving behind a circle of exposed soil. Jaya stumbled into the dirt.

The fighting had stopped in the other room. Now the only sound that existed was the ringing in her ears. The closer she got to the center of the depression, the harder it was to see through the dust and smoke. Her eyes watered, and the burning in them intensified. She crouched down and reached through the smoke.

There, at the core of the blast, was Aquillo, or what remained of him.

His charred body was huddled, and his arms were wrapped around him. Still trapped in the delusion. Brome's body had to be somewhere near, mixed in with the dirt. Aquillo's head was tucked into his chest, and his eyes were thankfully shut. Seeing them now, lifeless, stripped of all light and awareness, might be the last straw that sent her over the edge.

Bring me Aquillo's glowing eye.

Jaya snatched her hand back so fast that she fell backward onto the ground. She couldn't do that. She couldn't mutilate his body. Not after everything he'd been through, everything she had just seen.

You're just like your grandfather. Vicious and untrustworthy people.

She clasped her hands over her ears to shut them out. She needed to think. There had to be some other way.

All you want is to slaughter.

No. She shook her head. No, she did this to save her mother.

You are emotionally weak, just like your father was.

I invited you into my home.

Jaya curled in on herself as they pummeled her from all sides.

You're a monster.

We do not survive by carrying the weak.

How many lives have you destroyed besides mine?

You will not fail me again.

She was being buried alive. They heaved in shovel after shovel of dirt, and all she could do was watch. She had nothing left, no fight. Her whole life had been fighting. To please, to be accepted, to survive. Who was she outside of it? Everyone in Inestar had a duty. They were who they needed to be. She was what her grandfather told her to be, which was this.

Maybe Aquillo was right. What did it matter anymore? She would do this- this disgraceful, soulless thing- just as she had done everything before. Did it matter that this time she had a good reason?

Jaya uncovered her ears and reached out to open Aquillo's eye. Her hand stopped at his cheek.

It was still warm.

Through all his loss, Aquillo had held on to that for as long as he could. She sat there, holding his scorched face until the last bit of warmth left him.

Small cracks formed then. First across his legs, then his arms and neck. They multiplied until soon Aquillo's entire body was filled with cracks. He fractured like a broken vase, and his ashes fluttered down, settling on the soil.

JAYA SIFTED through the broken pieces until she found a good one. She stuck the broken tile next to the other three on the left side. *There.* She sat back to look at her work. It wasn't perfect, but the shards of emerald looked like a crown to her. They even shimmered a little after she cleaned them with the inside of her skirt.

The mound of ash had gotten smaller. Now there was maybe a third of the man they used to be left in front of Jaya's rudimentary memorial.

This didn't make things better. She knew that. But they weren't allowed to mourn the fallen in Inestar. Those who died in the hexagon were moved out of the way to make room for the next battle and later sent to the pyre. No apologies or well wishes for their next journey. If there was another life after this one, she hoped Aquillo's was filled with love and a big family.

The air shifted, raising the hairs on Jaya's neck. The hall was quiet, aside from voices coming from the ballroom. She could hear them now that her ears had stopped ringing. They hadn't even come out after the blast, which had to have rocked every floor in the palace. What was going on in there that they wouldn't come out to check?

Maybe they couldn't.

She needed to get in there. Too much time had passed while she sat in here saying her goodbyes. There might be people who needed her help.

She leaned forward to push herself off the ground, and a black hoof stepped down into the dirt. The dust cleared, revealing the rest of the horse's muscular body. It stood eight paces away, much taller than any horse should be. It's blazing eyes stared at the pile of ash in front of Jaya. Golden eyes. Not typical for animals or humans, except maybe one human. Its teeth were as black as the rest of its body and sharp as razors. To drive home its otherworldliness, the ground beneath its hooves melted into a pool of lava. Jaya held her breath, caught between paralyzing fear and amazement.

She didn't have long to waver. The beast took a step forward. Jaya scrambled back, kicking up dirt as she tried to escape from the liquified floor. Its nostrils flared, sniffing at the air she rustled. Flames burst down its back and tail, and it charged, leaping over the space in three strides.

Its blazing hooves nearly rammed into Jaya's face as it galloped toward the door. She ducked and rolled as far as she could from the lava trail, grabbing the drapes to pull herself out of the hole. The thick fabric tore from the rods high above, falling into the flames and setting the room ablaze.

Jaya staggered to her feet and took off for the door. As she raced through the burning archways, her legs warmed. Sparked jumped out, catching the tail of her dress and eating up the fabric. Jaya flailed, turning and frantically patting at the embers. They continued to climb until the right side of her skirt was on fire. She stepped on the tail and pulled, tearing it away from the rest of the dress. By the time she'd put herself out, the dress was mostly rags, and her hands were severely burned.

She shuffled out into the hallway, crouching low to avoid the smoke. The fire climbed to the second floor of the courtyard, and chunks of it rained down into the fountain. Terrified screams echoed back to her from the ballroom in the direction the horse had gone. The large double doors were thrown open, and orange light danced against the bronze engravings.

It was the riskiest route but also the fastest to escape. The doors on the opposite side of the ballroom led to the southern garden, to Quielle's ship.

Jaya prayed he didn't come tonight. If any good could have come from their nasty argument earlier, it would be that he was too upset with her to come anywhere near the palace. She pictured him at his father's house, safe and far away from this madness. It was her strength as she raced through the doors.

35

Sweltering heat and smoke had already taken over most of the massive room. Jaya grabbed a tablecloth off a table to protect her skin from the flames. She pulled the heavy cloth around her nose and mouth and quickly went towards the garden doors. As she was making her way through, her foot caught on something large, and she fell to the floor.

Get up. Keep moving.

She braced her hands against the lumpy object she'd fallen on, feeling... skin.

Don't look. Keep. Moving.

Jaya closed her eyes and climbed over the body. There were probably more, countless, between here and the doors to the garden. She got to her feet again and crouch-walked. The ceiling was nothing but flames, and the smoke was so thick she didn't see the man until she nearly walked into his blade.

He jabbed, aiming for her face. Jaya feinted left and grabbed his wrist, twisting his arm and putting weight on the back of his elbow. He turned with her, dodging her kick to his chest and anticipating the second when she jumped forward.

"Jaya?"

She froze. Her very blood stopped in her veins to wait for his next command.

It couldn't be him.

Bas's armor cuffs winked at her as he lowered the mask from around his nose. He had on new battle armor, which was why she didn't immediately recognize him. Beneath his red cape was gold armor woven into his tunic. Gold shields covered his shoulders and much of his legs. His usual battle gear looked like all the soldier uniforms: black robes with a metal chest plate and shield. He must have had this specially designed. Even the knife he had tried to ram into her face was gold and dripping with fresh blood.

"If you find any of their people, kill them," he said, tossing the dagger to her.

Jaya caught the handle and stared at the war credo on the blade. This couldn't be happening. She was asleep. The blast must have knocked her unconscious.

"Jaya, *now*! We don't have time."

"Jaya!" Quielle's voice called from the smoke, sending horror shooting through her. He coughed, and Bas turned towards the garden exit. *Please stop. Just go. Don't let him find you.*

Quielle's coughing increased to one long, uncontrollable hack. He called out to her in between.

"Call him over here," Bas whispered in her ear.

Her body ran cold in the smoldering heat of the room. Her lungs had stopped working. She squeezed and released the knife handle as her skin drew in, feeling too tight for her body.

She followed Bas on autopilot as he stalked Quielle's voice. Memories of things she hadn't known she had been paying attention to and cherishing played before her eyes, blocking out her horrible reality. Quielle looking at her, and only her, while his family laughed and talked around them. Him tying the skytes cape around her neck. Walking into the kitchen to find him sitting on the counter.

Memories phased into unfamiliar scenes. Weekly dinners at Lirhop and Gisete's. Tonure giving her swimming lessons and laughing at her poor coordination in the water. Quielle dancing with a miniature version of himself beneath a sky of moons. His wrinkled hand pulling her close before they went to sleep.

Dreams.

A life she hadn't dared to wish for, but her mind and heart had filled in anyway. Things that Bas would never let her see. Her mother had always had a better understanding of him. She knew all along what it had taken Jaya until now to realize. They would never be free as long as he was alive. Bas would always find a way to punish her mother for his son's death, and Jaya would always be punished for reminding him of what he had lost.

She was never supposed to make it back to Inestar. Like her father, he expected her to die here, alone in a foreign land. His shock and anger over finding her alive were evident when he'd said her name. In that one word, she had heard it all. Bas may be a master at controlling his body, but his rage had always been his tell.

"Jaya!" Quielle's voice was much closer. Too close to Bas and his deadly sword.

They skulked around a burning chandelier that had fallen from the second floor. Flames reached out at them, and Jaya stumbled back, stepping wide over the body of a royal guard. He was burned beyond recognition. His uniform had melted into his skin, and the badge specifying his kingdom was long gone. A pouch was on the floor near his hand, charred but not too damaged. She grabbed it, then rushed to catch up with Bas before she lost him in the smoke.

"Jaya," Quielle yelled, sending himself into another coughing fit.

Bas neared the garden doors just as the coughing cut off, and a heavy thump followed like rocks tumbling down a hill. Jaya was running before she realized it. Quielle was unconscious on the floor, several feet away from freedom and blanketed by the smoke. The fire had eased here, having very little to cling to.

"What are you waiting for?"

Jaya whirled around, holding out her knife. "Stay back!"

She felt along her arm for the pouch. *Where is it?* She spotted it on the floor near Bas's feet, and her heart sank. She must have dropped it in her panic to get to Quielle. Bas scowled down at the knife he had given her, the one she now pointed at him, then turned his burning stare to her. His face darkened with hatred she'd only seen when he talked about the Carye.

"I guess I should have expected this from you."

He removed his cape, revealing the scar that ran from his ear to his armpit. Jaya was there the day he'd gotten it. He'd beaten the soldier who gave it to him to death with his bare hands. Bas was by no means a small or weak man. Oddly, his strength only seemed to increase with age. She threw the tablecloth off her shoulders.

Don't think. Thoughts bring emotions, and an emotional fighter is as good as dead.

It would help if her inner voice didn't sound like Bas, but his lessons were ingrained in her. They played in her head on a loop whenever she faced an opponent.

"Come on, then." Bas stretched his arms out, showing off his sheathed weapons, while she clutched her dagger. He still had body armor. She'd have to be faster and more accurate than ever with her strikes. With that in mind, Jaya rushed him.

She kept her dagger low until she saw the bob of his throat, then she swiped upward. It was meant to push him off balance so she could drive the knife into his thigh at the last minute, but Bas didn't flinch. The blade grazed his face, and Jaya came down hard on his raised knee. Her body heaved upward from the force, and tears sprang to her eyes, mixing with sweat.

"Always hesitant to make the kill. That's your weakness," he said, cleaning the trickle of blood from his cheek.

She shuffled back, still trembling from the aftershock, as he stalked forward. He sidestepped her knife when she lunged at him, hitting her in the face with the back of his fist. It was a light tap, nowhere near his full strength. He was enjoying this.

A railing from the second level broke off and came barreling towards them. Jaya rolled out of the way, and the knife slipped from her slick and blistered hands. She scrambled for it, catching it before it and the pouch could be taken by the fire. The zipper had been warped by the heat, and the metal singed her fingertips as she tried to get it open.

Bas' heavy footsteps approached. She turned and swung. The knife lodged into something, and, without thinking, Jaya twisted the handle. Bas roared in pain.

The pouch. Where is it? She swiped salty sweat and hair from her face. *Where the hell is it?*

Her hands brushed across sleek metal. Gold. Bas' boot slammed into her face, and Jaya went sailing backward through the muggy air. She hit the floor and flipped feet-over-head onto her stomach. Her mouth felt like it had been packed with sand, and she couldn't move her neck. She was too afraid to breathe. The pain alone might kill her. She tried to push herself up, but her arms were numb. The flames danced around her like evil spirits.

Bas stood over her with a dagger sticking out of his thigh. She hoped she'd hit something major. He kneeled down to turn her over and drew his fist back.

Punch after brutalizing punch followed. Thankfully, she was too numb to feel it. Her body jerked from the blows, legs and arms splaying at her side. Soon she couldn't even see his bulging eyes or make out the words he screamed down at her. The heaviness and coldness making their way into her bones took all the pain away. The world slipped away, and so did Jaya. Feeling returned to her only for a moment. Just long enough for her to feel the smooth surface of the orb as it bumped into her right hand.

Last chance.

Bas reared back for another attack. He clasped his hands high over his head in one large fist, leaning back to put all his strength into it. A killing blow.

Last chance.

The portal opened like a trapdoor. Its light flared as Bas dropped back into the abyss and crashed through the ceiling. His body hit the floor with a loud and final thump, and the fire roared with renewed energy before settling into a steady crackle around him.

Jaya struggled to lift herself. She needed to get to Quielle, but her body was so tired. And the pain. Like some final punishment for the damned, she had been given a minute of peaceful numbness, just enough to make her wish for it more than anything else, before every sensation came back one hundredfold. She had always known that it would take everything in her and the help of the gods to beat Bas. They had done their part, and so had her battered body.

Quielle was still passed out on the floor. Only his silhouette was visible through her swollen eyes, but it was enough to tell that he wasn't moving. He wouldn't make it out of here on his own. She couldn't let him die. This world would not be worth it if he wasn't in it.

She would not let him die.

Deep breath, then move. She gathered every ounce of energy she had left, taking three large inhales and pulling her feet towards her. After what felt like minutes, Jaya pried her eyes open to check her progress. Her feet had barely moved, but they were flat on the ground, at least. *Move faster. You need to get him out.*

"I can't."

Jaya choked on her tears. They pooled in her swollen eyes, trailing down through sweat and into her ears. She prayed to the skies for strength. She prayed to the gods, to Kani, to anyone who would save them. But nothing came. No miracle. She was going to have to do this on her own.

Jaya took a big inhale but stopped. She switched tactics and relaxed her body, letting her earlier thoughts return to her, her dreams, the life she'd been putting together in her mind. She let the happiness fill her, the peace, and the overwhelming love. It filled every inch of her, crowding the spaces where the pain had taken over.

Her knees inched up, and she lifted herself with her legs since her arms were still too weak. Once on her feet, she took a second before limping towards the garden doors. The fire sparked in her periphery, bright as a star. It was so close on her left side, but she kept moving. Red and silver spots danced with the flames. They were so bright- like orbs.

They were orbs.

Five silver balls dotted the ground at Jaya's feet. They had fallen from the pouch during the fight. She picked one up and limped as fast as she could to Quielle's side. Jaya kneeled down and cradled his face in her hand. With her other, she crushed the orb.

36

No surprise, Dewar's healing center looked like a forest. Giant tree-like structures took up the first floor. They shot from the port stations at the base of their trunks to the glass ceiling of the facility. The branches flickered with light as they received and transmitted distress signals from around the kingdom.

Quielle's room was on the sixth floor, among the patient rooms that lined the left side of the building. He had been there for the last two days. Lirhop had refused expedited healing, which turned out to be a nice way of saying bolkin feeding, telling the menders to only give Quielle medicine from the Pati kingdom.

"The serum attaches to the base of the oxygen mask. It'll clean the smoke from his lungs as he breathes it in," the mender explained as he adjusted the breathing mask around his face.

The silver star on the mender's coat was identical to the one on the bottle Quielle had sprayed his neck with the night they escaped The Sleeping Forest. It was probably the best treatment Okew had to offer, considering it came from Mavin's kingdom.

"Are you sure you don't want to have one of our menders look at your bruises?"

"No, thank you," Jaya said.

The swelling on her face was all but gone. Only faint bruising remained around her eyes and jaw. Tacius's bolkin had healed the fractured bones in her face and neck and cleaned her smoke-filled lungs before it was uncomfortably full. Rather than waste time that she wasn't sure Quielle had, she teleported him from the palace to the healing center before going to find the creature.

Being fed on for a second time was not ideal, and Jaya worried the creature was developing a taste for her, but her wounds were more obvious and alarming than Quielle's at first sight. She wouldn't risk the people at the healing center deciding to treat her first.

"You should let them look at that eye and make sure your vision is okay," Lirhop said from across the room where he was sprinkling fish food into the tank.

Unlike most places in the central market, the patient rooms were not stark white. The sage walls, soft lighting, and comfy blankets on Quielle's bed gave the room a tranquil vibe that Jaya appreciated.

"I'm okay, Lirhop. I promise. It just looks bad."

She stretched her arm across Quielle's blanketed legs and rubbed her toes in the fuzzy rug. She just needed a good, long rest. She was seeing triple, but that was because she hadn't closed her eyes for more than a few seconds since Quielle had been admitted.

"I told you about that Lirhop stuff. You saved my son's life. You call me Pop."

Olivia gave her a stern nod behind his back, getting a quiet laugh from Gisete, who sat beside her on the sofa. The wooden table in the center of the room was covered with little ugly and misshapen sea creatures, a result of Olivia teaching Gisete to make piercing charms.

Gentle fingers crept beneath Jaya's hair and pressed into her neck, making small circles. She shot up straight, looking into Quielle's drowsy hooded eyes.

"Hi," he said.

She tried to return his light greeting, but all she got out was a teary cough. She lunged for his lips, bumping face-first into the oxygen mask. Quielle chuckled and lifted it for her. Their lips crashed together with more force than she intended. She smoothed it over with soft kisses to his face, but soon she was back to consuming his lips, feeling him breathe between kisses and his heart beat under her hand.

Quielle turned his head to cough. One quickly turned into many.

"I'm sorry," Jaya said, sneaking one last kiss on his scruffy jaw before she put the mask back over his mouth.

She rested her forehead against his. "I missed you."

Quielle caressed her face very gently, swiping her tears away like they were an illusion.

"It just looks bad," she said, "I prom–"

"I love you."

Her eyes flew open, and Quielle was staring right into her. He was talking to her. Those words were for her.

"I love you too."

"Mmh!" Olivia lifted her hand in a 'don't mind me' gesture, then turned to wipe her eyes with her crop top. Gisete and Lirhop turned the other way to avoid being flashed, and Lirhop covertly wiped away a tear himself.

"I'm hogging you," Jaya realized.

She got up, dodging Quielle's grabby hands, and went over to the two people who had been keeping watch with her around the clock. Lirhop's hands were shaky in hers as he sat down next to Quielle's bed.

"Hey, Pop."

"My boy." Lirhop sniffled. "You had us worried."

"I'm sorry."

"We're lucky Jaya was there to save your butt this time." His voice broke, and he rocked back, drumming his fingers on the sheets. "I heard she carried you out bridal style."

Their twin laughter rumbled for a second before Lirhop fell silent. His eyes darted to the three hovering screens behind Quielle's bed, as they had been doing all day.

"I'm alright, Pop." Quielle squeezed his hand to prove his point.

Two dings rang through the room's speaker, signaling an incoming communication, and Tonure's hologram popped up on the other side of the bed.

"Welcome back, bro." He grinned, leaning down to kiss Quielle on the forehead. Half of his face glitched out of focus. "Damn. Don't worry, I got you when I get there."

"You better keep those crusty lips to yourself when you do," Quielle said, pulling down the mask so he could hear him.

"Look who's talking. I bet you kissed Jaya with those ashy lips."

"He did," Lirhop tattled. "It was like watching a zombie feeding."

"Wow. I see you two were working on jokes this whole time I've been in a coma?"

"Coma?" Tonure sucked his teeth. "Man, you were asleep for two days. Relax."

"Is he awake?" Rea's voice called from Tonure's end.

"Yeah. I'm about to head over there now. You coming?"

"Yeah."

"We'll see you in a bit, bro. Love you."

"Love you too," Quielle replied before the hologram disappeared into the floor. "I need a shower and the biggest toothbrush I can find."

"I'll go get your things from your ship." Jaya volunteered before Lirhop could beat her to it. She needed some time away to deal with these feelings that were hitting way too fast and hard at the moment. She had almost lost him. Even when she was planning to return to Inestar, she told herself that Quielle would find someone else and forget all about her. It hurt like a knife to the heart, but it was nothing compared to what she felt seeing him lying on the floor surrounded by flames.

"I'll come with," Olivia said, joining the group around Quielle's bed. "Welcome back, Prince."

She patted him on the shoulder before breezing out the door. Jaya kissed Quielle's temple and followed her out.

The sixth floor was buzzing with activity, and the hall was packed with large men shouldering their way past the menders and healing staff. Through a gap in their tight formation, Jaya locked eyes with Kalite.

She was still as beautiful as the day Jaya met her. Her long hair was gathered up in a messy bun, and her skin had regained its sun-kissed glow. The loose-fitting guard uniform she wore to hide her identity from onlookers was the only sign that this was not the same Kalite Jaya sipped tea with on her balcony. That and the murderous glare she was directing at her.

Word of Aquillo's death had probably reached all of Dewar by now. Jaya wasn't sure what she planned to say, but she stepped towards the wall of guards. Light flashed before her, and when she blinked, she was in Quielle's room on his ship. Jaya looked around in confusion as Olivia strolled over to the fluorescent ocean on the wall. She reached out to run her fingers along the waves.

"Why'd you do that?" Jaya asked.

"Did you see the way she was looking at you? She was about to sic her dogs on you."

As much as she didn't want to admit it, Olivia was right. Kalite hated her, and she had every right to.

"Did I misread that? Are you two, like, friends now?"

"No," Jaya said. They weren't friends, so she wasn't losing anything. Kalite was always going to end up hating her, one way or another. "Thank you."

Jaya pulled Quielle's black duffle bag from beneath the bed and started towards the bathing room. The door was sealed, but he had registered her in all the ship's scanners. She paused mid-step. "How did we get here?"

"What do you mean?" Olivia replied, eyeing the skeleton on the floor next to Quielle's trophy box.

"I mean, how did you get us here? I didn't see you use an orb, and even if you did, this room is shielded against orb teleportation."

"What?" Olivia looked at her like she was speaking another language. Jaya had a feeling she understood perfectly what she was asking.

"I never told you I knew Kalite or about my time at the palace."

Silence filled the room. *No. Please no.*

Olivia huffed and bent down to grab the carcass. "I believe this is mine. My dad gave it to me. I was sick over losing it."

She pressed the bone to her mouth and played a light sequence of notes. Her fingers fluttered across the smooth holes, the complex medley as easy for her as breathing. She finished and gave Jaya a sad smile.

"Why?" Jaya shook her head. Her face grew hot with oncoming tears.

"For this." Olivia pulled a necklace from beneath her top.

"A *bone*?"

"It's not just a bone. It holds the greatest power Okew, and maybe the universe has ever known."

"The Gift?"

"No." She chuckled bitterly. "I used to think that was the greatest power, too."

Her eyes suddenly blazed. The brown in her irises spiraled before being washed away by blue as deep as the sea. "Until I was cursed with it."

"Yehala."

"Yeah. The grand savior himself."

"But his power went into the grid. It's what freed your people. That's what you told me."

"That's just the lie the tour company makes me say. The truth is Yehala wasn't worth the ground he died on. From the first day Ormiez brought his new wife and her power home to Okew, Yehala was plotting on how to make it his. He came to their home the night of the summit and butchered them in their sleep. Cut Exia open like a science experiment. He wanted to see her power for himself. He was prepared to carve it out of her bones if that's what it took."

Jaya's chest tightened as she thought of Aquillo holding himself and sobbing on the palace floor.

"Their guards came running before he could finish. He convinced them Fadiern had murdered them out of spite, and those idiots believed him, even though he was standing there covered in their blood. He actually did lead the hunt for Fadiern. And when they finally caught up with him and Fadiern cut Yehala down like the animal he was, that coward used his last breath to trap us under a dome. He wanted his power to die with him, but it found its way in. I can still feel him clinging to it like a parasite. Who picks a child to rule a kingdom, anyway? The great Kani, that's who."

She walked over and sat on Quielle's sofa, clutching the animal bone close like a safety blanket.

"It's all bullshit. The gods don't care about us. We aren't chosen. We aren't gifted. They're bored. Mezanya was imploding, and Kani was nowhere to be found. People were killing anyone who they even suspected of having an orb. Instead of the council stepping in to stop them, they were out searching for The Gift. If they had found me, they would have taken me away, locked me in that palace, and my parents would have never seen me again. Or they might have killed me then and there. Hope for a better ruler the next time. One who isn't a child. My dad got us out. He did what no one else would, and it cost him his life."

Olivia looked so small and lost. Jaya's heart broke for her. She wanted to offer her comfort like she had done for her, but one thought kept her rooted in place. *She nearly cost me everything.*

"I hid with my mom in the ruins. Aquillo and his soldiers had already killed everything there, so it was the perfect place to hide."

"For three weeks," Jaya said, recalling the story of Olivia and her parents huddled in a dark house, praying not to be found.

"It was more like three years. That's how long it took us to find the potion to hide the evidence of my *Gift*."

Potion magic. That's how she was able to control Aquillo, and change her appearance. She was able to make everyone believe she was a male soldier from Inestar. It was such a good illusion. Even Jaya had been fooled.

"I breathed fresh air for the first time in years, and my mom and I returned to Mezanya. I saw the people of my kingdom for the first time and realized that they had made *him* their god. That murdering piece of shit was just as important to them as Kani."

The floor rumbled beneath them. Jaya braced against the wall as the ship groaned. Just as quickly as it started, everything stopped.

"Sorry," Olivia said, stretching her neck to one side and resettling on the sofa. "I saw then that people will worship anyone as long as it makes them feel safe. So why not me? I could be a true goddess, not some distant idea they have to wonder about. Not someone they have to fear. All I needed was Exia's power- the power of life. There'd be no more Kani. No more death gods or Sleeping Forest. No more Yehala. Life would begin and end with me."

"Starting with Mia's and Aquillo's."

Olivia stood up, hesitating before approaching Jaya. "That was Brome's idea. It's what he wanted in exchange for digging up Exia's bone."

"It was your plan. He was just along for the ride," Jaya sneered.

"I never would have let him hurt you, not you or Qui—"

"*Don't* say his name." Jaya had moved past hurt and sadness, and was now settling into rage. "We almost *died* because of you."

Olivia took a step back, fidgeting with the animal bone. Exia's bone scraped along the side of the carcass, twirling grotesquely at the end of the gold necklace. She hadn't looked Jaya in the eyes once, which only pissed her off more.

"We are mirrored souls, Jaya," Olivia said. "Always have been. On two different worlds, living the same life. I... I thought you would understand."

A portal opened behind her, and she stepped back, tucking the necklace into her shirt. Jaya wanted to stop her. She wanted to try to understand, but that wouldn't be fair to Quielle or her. So she let her go.

The portal was closing when Olivia's body suddenly jerked forward, and she was forced out of the light. A sword jutted out below her crop top. It disappeared, and Olivia staggered forward, clutching the wound in her stomach.

The portal dropped, revealing Nyro holding the bloody sword. His yellow eyes were wide and tinged with madness. He must have been hiding in the bathing room. The door was open now, and empty plates were scattered on the floor next to a charred suit jacket.

Nyro's dress shirt was riddled with burn holes and hung off one shoulder. Soot covered his singed pants, face, and hair, and he wasn't wearing any shoes. Olivia's body slumped. Jaya caught her around the waist before she could fall at Nyro's feet.

"Olivia, you have to go. You have to teleport out of here now." Jaya dragged her back by her underarms, pressing her hands into the wound in her back to stop the bleeding. Olivia kept slumping.

"Y... you," she breathed into Jaya's neck.

"I'll be fine! Just go!" Jaya cried.

She had faced Aquillo's power before. She could do it again, but not if she was split between fighting and protecting Olivia. Nyro had used a sword, not his power, so maybe he didn't know how to use it yet. If he didn't, Jaya could take him.

Olivia's body went limp.

"No. No, no, no."

Nyro lifted his sword, preparing to ram it through both of them. Jaya tripped on the edge of the bed and fell back on the sheets. Olivia went over the side and hit the floor with enough force to shock her back awake, if possible.

Nyro's blade came down, singing through the air like a war cry. The blow was like lightning, harsh and blinding. Jaya jolted. Her limbs went stiff on impact, then fell loose. Every vein in her body lit with electrical current. It rang from her heels and escaped through her pupils. Pure energy crackled from deep within her, gripping her senses and raising the hairs on her scalp. She fisted her hands, fighting to remain conscious. If she blacked out, Nyro would finish her off. She breathed in hot air for an eternity until the pain retreated. Only then was she able to lumber to her feet.

Nyro glared at her from behind a white and silver hex mesh. His sword lay on the floor with the blade sawed off at a straight angle. Jaya reached out, running her finger along the pattern. It sparked under her touch but held firm. Mezanya's grid. Yehala's grid. Only his power could get them out. Jaya turned to wake Olivia.

The ship's blue carpet was scorched with a black starburst where Olivia had fallen.

She wasn't there anymore.

Jaya jumped as knocking came from behind her. Nyro rapped his knuckle against the shield, testing its sturdiness. He stopped and smirked at her.

"Have fun in here," he said, then left through a portal.

37

The central market was dark outside his window, and Quielle was quietly panicking. "They should have been back by now."

He tried not to think of the last couple of times Jaya had gone missing, but it was hard not to. He still didn't know who put those bruises on her face or how she'd found him in the palace and got him here.

"I can go check on them," Tonure offered, just as a portal formed next to the bed.

Jaya stepped through, and the weight that had been sitting on Quielle's chest for the last few hours finally let up. He rushed over and put his arms around her. She was stiff as a rod in his arms, and her eyes were clenched tight.

"What's wrong?" he asked, bringing his hand up to her bruised cheek.

She opened her eyes slowly. There was a collective gasp behind him. They saw it too? He ran his thumb under one glowing eye, still not quite believing it.

"How?"

Blackness spilled into the deep blue.

"Olivia."

What about her? Where was she? Whose power had Jaya taken, and how long did they have before the kingdom council came looking for her? A million questions and scenarios played in his head. So many he couldn't decide which one to address first. Jaya's arms wrapped around him, and she tucked her nose into his neck. Her body shook with quiet sobs.

"We're going to be outside," Lirhop said as he, Gisete, and Tone passed them.

Quielle waited a few minutes after they left, then pulled back to wipe the tears from Jaya's face. "What happened?"

"I'll explain everything on the way," she mumbled. "I need you to take me somewhere."

THE FLIGHT back to Inestar was the longest and shortest trip of his life. The new model crafts were faster than his old one, but that didn't account for the disorientation and hollowness he felt as they landed a mile from the stone wall.

Jaya had given him the whole story, from when Lenille stabbed Kalite to Nyro's ambush on his ship. Tonure had messaged him yesterday saying that Lenille was not in Pati, and he and Rea were on their way to Ziep to look for her.

What a shit show. How had so much gone so wrong in less than a week? On the one hand, he finally knew who killed Mia, but he didn't feel any better. Olivia was Jaya's first friend in Dewar. She had connected with her when Quielle was still in denial about his feelings. Now Jaya was quietly mourning that friend in the bathroom at night when she thought he was asleep.

Three times now, he had awakened to find her side of the bed empty. Each time he'd gone to the bathroom, picked her up off the floor, and carried her back to bed. They usually couldn't get back to sleep afterward, so he'd spend the night telling her about the most beautiful planets he'd been to. Inestar was getting closer by the minute. Soon he wouldn't have any more time left with her.

Jaya closed her eyes and clenched her fist tight enough to leave little red, nailed-shaped marks on her palm. This was another thing he had seen her do often during their trip. Forming portals looked like it took every bit of strength and concentration Jaya had. It was probably because she was forcing it. If it was anything like the orbs, trying too hard only caused it to shut down and the power to recede.

Jaya took three quick breaths and tried again. When she closed her eyes, Quielle pressed his lips to hers. Her fingers loosened and came up to lightly scratch his beard. Jaya had a real fetish for facial hair. He wrapped his arms around her waist, pulling her close so she could feel the effect she had on him. She moaned and dragged her teeth along his bottom lip. Moments like this were going to tear him apart when she was gone.

Quielle pulled back, unable to resist sneaking a few more kisses on the corner of her mouth and chin. Her eyes were a stormy blue-gray when they opened. It didn't take him long to get used to, and even like the eyes. They were his peephole into whatever she was feeling at the moment. He tilted her chin to the side so she could see the portal, steady and waiting for them to step through.

Jaya pushed thoughts of war-torn houses and scattered bodies from her mind and stepped through the portal. Inestar's raging sun was still hard at work, unaffected by the people it nourished from above. The mist of the Bastian swept past them, blowing Jaya's hair up to three times its height. She knelt down, dipping her fingers into the cool, running water. The strange urge to strip naked and jump in washed over her.

That's not what we're here for.

She straightened up and craned her head back. The glare from the sun made it hard to say for sure, but it didn't look like anyone was up in the east tower. If there was, they would have sounded the alarm as soon as she and Quielle came through the portal. Had it always been this quiet over here? Where were the children and the people manning the water purification tanks? Jaya spun around, squinting to see if anyone was walking to or from the houses.

No sign of life.

Had they all been wiped out the night of the banquet? Maybe Nyro had beaten them here. If he couldn't get to her, destroying Inestar was the next best thing.

Racing footsteps caught her attention. Quielle must have heard them, too, because he nudged Jaya behind him and unhooked his curved knife from its holster. The bushes rustled as a small person burst out. The girl was looking back, moving so fast she didn't notice them. She tripped over her robe and tumbled to the ground. At that moment, a boy raced from the bushes and hurled a bucket of water. It hit Quielle square in the chest, splashing water into his and Jaya's faces.

Everyone froze. The boy's teeth started to chatter, loud enough for all of them to hear. He slowly lowered the bucket. The little girl locked eyes with Jaya, and sheer terror blanketed her angelic face. She was about to try teleporting them away when Quielle's shoulders started to shake. He bent back, resting his head against her, and let out a deep laugh. *What the hell?* Jaya rubbed her face into his back and joined him.

The kids didn't stick around to ask questions. The boy pulled his friend to her feet, and they both hightailed it over the bridge. Smart kids.

"I needed that," Jaya said, squeezing water out of her hair, which was now an afro.

"Me too." Quielle grabbed her hand, entwining their fingers. "Come on."

He led them across the bridge, then paused, letting Jaya take the lead. She cut across the compound, taking one of the dirt paths that led to the vegetable gardens.

There weren't many people in the gardens, but even this handful was a weight off Jaya's chest. She scanned the fields and spotted a shock of white hair on a small and perfectly shaped head. Jaya took off down the middle dirt path. Her feet barely pace with her heart.

Subconsciously, she registered the people as she passed. Sellyan looked up from her wealth of greens. Ishma straightened up with a basket of harvested herbs in his scrawny arms. Justen continued watering the plants with his back to them. And Zora was tending to the root vegetable. Her eyes were glued to the crop, checking for pests, when Jaya slid into her, causing them both to fall.

"Ma!" Jaya cried.

"Jaya?"

She couldn't embrace her mother fast enough. Jaya locked her in an awkward hug, squeezing too tight as emotions wrung from her body. She was probably choking her, but she couldn't let go.

"Shh. It's okay." Her mother smoothed her hair back, comforting her like a frightened child- exactly how she felt. Her assurance had always been Jaya's balm, loosening the ties around her heart whenever they got too constricting. They stayed like that, holding each other on the ground until Jaya's breathing evened out.

Zora pulled back and went stiff in her arms. The bruises. They were faint and mostly healed now, but her mom was close enough to see them.

"You've been through some changes," she said sadly.

"Oh." Jaya shut her eyes.

"No, sweetie. You don't have to hide from me."

Her mom kissed her eyelid, then pulled away.

"No." Jaya pulled her back in.

"It's okay. Let me wash up, and then I'll make you dinner."

"Resting time isn't for another three hours," Jaya recited through teary hiccups.

"Are you hungry or not, child?"

Zora helped Jaya up off the ground, and they walked back to the edge of the garden where Quielle had been standing.

He was gone.

38

Quielle inserted the last orb into the fuel lodge, and his wrist scanner flared with a motion-detected signal. He should have left sooner instead of sticking around to watch Jaya with her mother.

They hugged like two people going off to war, not like a mother and daughter seeing each other again after two months. Two months of struggling to survive and wondering if they would ever get that moment. And he had almost asked her to give it up.

Jaya raced across the sand like a bird about to take flight. She had already adjusted back to this environment. Her legs were used to the sink and pull of the sand. Her skin glowed under the harsh sun. This was where she belonged.

He closed the fuel lodge and pulled an orb from his pocket. She could just teleport back to Dewar and find him. Would she? He couldn't take that chance. He was going to have to face this head-on. It was time he stopped running.

"Where are you going?" Jaya huffed. She took one steadying breath through her nose, then another. Her cheeks were flushed, and her eyes were solid blue.

"I'm going home."

"But I thought. You said... I don't." Her shoulders slumped as she struggled to find her words. Eventually, she stopped trying and closed her eyes.

"You and your mom need each other, Jaya. I can't be the reason you two aren't together. Jaya, baby, look at me." He couldn't do this with her standing there like that, like she was bracing for impact.

"I'm sorry," she whispered.

"What?"

"I'm sorry for not telling you sooner. I'm sorry for leaving. I'm sorry–"

"Jaya."

"I'm s-sorry," fat tears squeezed from her closed lids, "for not trusting you to help. I'm *sorry* for using you. I'm sorry for being the way I am. I'm–"

"Jaya, *stop*." He grabbed her arms."There is nothing wrong with the way you are. I l–"

No. He couldn't do that. This had to be a clean break. She needed to know that it was okay to let him go.

"You can't say it." She stepped away, bringing her hand up to her throat. "You don't love me anymore."

"That's not true. I'm just trying to do the right thing."

"Did you mean it when you said it the first time?"

No. He hadn't meant to tell her he loved her.

The last thing Quielle remembered was the fire. When he woke up in the healing center, his mind was still trapped in the burning palace. He could still feel the heat. But there she was. Smiling at him with tears and *love* in her eyes- love for him. He decided then that he wasn't leaving this life without telling her how he felt about her.

So, no, he hadn't meant to say the words to the real Jaya, but that didn't change the way he felt.

"I love you, Jaya. I meant it then, and I mean it now."

"Then stay. Stay with me."

~

Zora was standing near the wall when Jaya walked up to the gate. One soldier patrolled the entire right side of the entrance now. The one to the left had his back to them as he walked two thousand paces to the next tower. Neither was Durand. Yet another loss. And Jaya hadn't even had the chance to fight for him.

"Keep your eyes down," Zora whispered.

She closed her eyes and let her mother pull her across the threshold and away from the wall.

"They'll want to meet with you on the wall to go over the new rotation. We'll have to think of something to tell them before then."

"Wait." Jaya dug her feet into the sandstone path. "Ma, I want you to meet someone."

Quielle's head poked from behind a house. He scanned the empty walkway like it was an assassin's den, taking a second to glare suspiciously at a crispy bush.

"Having fun?" Jaya asked when he finally came out from behind the house.

"Yes."

"Ma, this is Quielle. Quielle, this is my mother, Zora."

He gave her the same smile that had disarmed Jaya that first day on his ship and surprised them both by pulling her in for a hug. "It's great to meet you."

Zora raised her eyebrows at Jaya over his shoulder. "So nice to meet you. Are you having dinner with us?"

"Oh, I don't turn down a meal. Jaya can tell you that."

"Well, good. Come on then."

Quielle walked ahead of them with the confidence of an explorer. His muscles flexed beneath his black t-shirt as he went.

"He smells good."

"*Ma*."

"What?"

Zora made them salt fish and flatbread while Quielle watched from a nearby stool, occasionally complimenting her food artistry. He actually used those words. Jaya had just taken her first bite when someone knocked on the door.

"I'll be right back," Zora said, pushing away from their small dining table.

Quielle groaned, licking a bit of sauce from his thumb. He bit down on his bottom lip, drawing it out slowly.

"Can you not do that in my mom's house?"

He smirked at her and took another bite.

"Sorry," Zora said, returning to the table and her untouched plate. "That was Mikahla. She wanted to know what to do with today's dyed clothes. It's her first week working textiles."

"Ma, why don't you just lock the door?"

That was the fifth interruption from someone asking questions or giving her their summary for the day. At this rate, her mom wouldn't eat until midnight.

"They'd just find me later. Since Bas and Yido disappeared, they've been looking for someone to confirm that they're doing their part. You know he's going to ask when he comes back. The guys on the wall don't even come down to sleep anymore."

Jaya's food hardened in her stomach. Quielle stopped devouring his food to reach over and rub her lower back.

"They're not coming back, Ma. Not Bas or... any of them."

Zora sat back in her chair as Jaya's words sunk in. Thankfully, she didn't ask how she knew. Maybe she didn't need to. She looked around bewilderedly for a moment, then flexed her fingers and straightened her robe, which still didn't seem to settle her.

"Do you two want dessert?" She jumped up, talking while en route. "I can put something together."

"Ma." Jaya stood, catching up to her before she could retreat into the kitchen. "It's okay. It's gonna be okay."

"They're going to find out, and the soldiers... they'll want to take over."

"No, they won't."

Jaya took in her mother's shivering form. Her brave, thoughtful, and strong mother who had stayed after losing the most important person in her life. Who was beaten and made to cower and slave for a heartless man who deserved nothing but the death Jaya had given him. It was enough to confirm that she was doing the right thing.

"I have a plan."

39

SEVEN MONTHS LATER

When Jaya had the bright idea to make Inestar a modern city by the likes of Dewar, she thought it would be as simple as waving her hand. She hadn't accounted for her lack of knowledge regarding underground water systems, sustainable energy, and infrastructure. Pretty much anything that had to do with building a city. Even if she had a good enough grasp on her powers to create what she had in mind, it would likely be a mess of pipes that led nowhere, unstable roads, and a filthy sewage problem.

So far, the only progressive thing she had done was form a council that included her mother, Sellyan, and Mikahla, a noble who came with his wife to Inestar twenty years ago, and a representative chosen by the remaining soldiers.

That had been no easy feat. The noble, Horace, felt his higher knowledge and years of treating various wounds and heat exhaustion qualified him to make decisions on his own. The soldier representative wanted to keep things the way they were when her grandfather was in charge. They both had a change of heart when Jaya made it clear that whoever wanted the title of Bas would have to go through her.

Today was going to be different. After months of imagining and planning, her dream for Inestar was about to take its first steps into reality.

"Hello, Princess."

Rore stepped from the portal into the haunted silence of the hexagon. His smirk was already too wicked for this early in the morning. He wore his usual tailored suit, one shoulder and arm of the jacket embellished with a red and blue tribal pattern. Instead of a crown, he wore a royal blue head wrap. He eyed Jaya for a minute longer than a casual glance before turning to inspect the canyon area.

"I thought there would be more people here… and camels," he said, turning his nose up at a flattened lizard on a nearby boulder.

"Inestar is three miles north of here. *This* is the epicenter for inter-planetary trade, or at least it will be."

"Ah. Aquillo would approve."

Jaya adjusted the split of her asymmetrical shirt. She should have known better than to wear jeans today. She'd have to peel these things off when she got home.

"Still not comfortable talking about him, huh?"

"What?"

"Aquillo used to fidget like that whenever someone mentioned his kids' parents or the ruins. Took him from a powerful ruler to a broken man begging for forgiveness like that." He snapped his fingers.

It shouldn't bother her. Aquillo had tortured her and let the bolkin feed on her. She should be happy he was gone. But she'd meant what she said to him that day in the dome. Deep down, she empathized with Aquillo and his effort to repair some of the damage he had caused. Under different circumstances, Jaya might have taken the same path. She still might.

"It's a little tacky to speak ill of the dead, isn't it?" She asked, folding her hands to prevent them from pulling at her shirt again.

"Even tackier to lie on them. Life is too short to spend it apologizing for every mistake."

"Not every one, just the big ones. It's hard forgiving yourself after taking innocent lives."

"It's extremely hard, but that doesn't mean we shouldn't try. Plus, are any of us really innocent? I'm not. Neither was Aquillo. Dewar has its fair share of murderers, thieves, and deviants, just like any other kingdom. It doesn't make them more suitable for death than anyone else. Death is unavoidable. We'll all have to face it one day. And the death gods aren't going to take the fact that you are a good person into consideration. Your fate is what it is."

What a dismal way of looking at things, but oddly it brought Jaya peace. Maybe Olivia wasn't judged too harshly for her mistakes. They were mirrored souls like she said, but Jaya had defeated her monster. Olivia was left to struggle through life, knowing that the one person responsible for every hardship and loss she'd endured was long gone, forever out of her reach. It would have been too much for Jaya to handle, too.

"He wanted me to seduce you."

"What?" Jaya asked, taken by surprise for the second time in less than five minutes.

"Aquillo. He wasn't comfortable doing it himself. Or maybe he thought you'd turn him down, so he asked me."

"Why?"

"Well, not to brag, but I can be really charming when I want to be. Ladies are often satisfied with my company." A smug grin crept up one side of his face.

"Ugh." Jaya rolled her eyes. "No. I mean, what did he hope to gain?"

"Your allyship. This." He gestured between them. "He saw the benefit of having Inestar's mighty soldiers in his corner, and- unlike your grandfather- you actually have a vision for this place and a devotion to its people. That's what makes a great ruler."

"So you thought getting in my pants was the only way to accomplish this? Did you two, maybe, consider asking me?"

Rore laughed shamelessly. "What would I get out of that? With Aquillo's plan, at least, he'd get his peace treaty, and I'd get a mighty queen to serve by my side and bear me some good-looking children."

Jaya shook her head. No one could be this full of themself. This had to be an act.

"Is it because I didn't run back into the burning palace for you? I would have, but the traveler beat me to it. And honestly, I thought you'd find those kinds of heroics melodramatic. I know I do."

Okay, so maybe it wasn't an act. "How are things going with Lenille?"

"She's driving my staff crazy. I overheard three of them plotting to take one of my ships out at night to dump her notebooks in the ocean." He rolled his shoulders and stood a bit straighter. "They're all stressed enough with these council investigations."

Since the summit and word of Yehala's secret heir getting out, the kingdom council had stationed one of their people at every palace.

"Are they getting close?"

"No. The seeker can't even get up the nerve to ask me if I was invited to the summit. Your secret's safe with me, Princess. Or should I say Queen now?"

Those ruby eyes of his sparked with something. Maybe humor, but she was never sure with Rore. For now, at least, he was on her side and willing to do favors. Who knew when the time for her to repay those favors would come and what he would demand? She couldn't worry about that now.

"Let's get on with the city plan."

IT WAS LONG past nightfall by the time she finished walking Rore through Inestar and going over her plans with him. He'd agreed to return in the next two weeks to check on his team of builders.

Jaya smiled as she stepped through the portal and looked up the winding stairs of her cozy home. Though Quielle had since left Deep Exploration traveling behind, and he no longer received the prince's stipend, they had more than enough to buy the house in the woods. The previous owner was an old man who had defended it during Aquillo's raid on Aoeja.

On the other side of the forest was the ravaged land known as 'the ruins'. Although greenery and life had returned to certain areas of the once desolate place. Jaya sometimes walked the line between the dry, razed land and the new growth. It felt symbolic of her life now between Inestar and Okew.

She entered her front door and stepped right into a battle.

“All I’m saying is, I don’t appreciate you trying to kill my brother.”

Quielle and Tonure were lounging on the couch, and Rea stood behind them, holding a plate.

“Shut up, Quielle. I made it just how Lirhop told me to."

“So you gone lie on Pops now? He told you to burn that top crust like that?”

“It’s not burnt you–”

“Hey!” Jaya said with extra volume.

Quielle was on her before she could blink. He wrapped her up in a big hug, lifting her off the ground by her waist. Jaya was a tall girl, but Quielle always acted like she needed a boost to kiss him.

“I’m gross right now. I’ve been out in the sun all day."

“Hmm.” He rubbed his nose into her neck, sniffing loudly, “Yeah, you’re gonna need a second set of hands in the shower to get all this sand off.”

He set Jaya back on her feet, following on her heels to the bedroom.

“You two aren’t gonna try some of Rea’s meat.. crust.. things?” Tonure called after them.

“Nah. We’re good,” Quielle responded over his shoulder.

“Peasant,” Rea said.

Quielle’s laughter caressed Jaya’s ear as he closed the door.

“Shower first this time,” she said.

“Deal."

EPILOGUE

Nyro walked the familiar hallways of the palace. He didn't slow down or move to the side for the servant coming towards him with her arms full of folded sheets. Her eyes were on the stack she was balancing, and she nearly tripped over her feet when she noticed him.

"Sorry, *King*," she said, catching the sheets before they fell in his path.

Nyro watched her struggle. When she had the sheets steady, he stepped towards her. Her eyes widened as she tilted her head back. He towered over her by half a foot. "Say that again."

She swallowed loudly. Her mouth opened and closed, but no words came out. Nyro sighed, taking a step back to alleviate some of her fear.

"Okay?" He held his hands out to show her he wasn't a threat. "Now, just repeat what you said."

"What I...I don't understand."

"Say what you just said!" Nyro thundered, making her drop the sheets.

"I-I'm sorry. I'm sorry, Your Highness. I didn't—I didn't mean to."

He stormed away, leaving the idiot girl behind, still blubbering apologies. He made it to his office- Aquillo's office- and slammed the door.

Calm down. It's just The Gift. It's testing you, trying to see if you're strong enough to handle it.

He couldn't let this break him. He had been through too much to be broken by voices in his head. But this was the first time they had come from a real person.

When she'd called him king, Nyro could have sworn it came from a male voice- Quielle's, of all people. And his reaction had been visceral. That disrespect and judgment in his voice. It was how he always addressed him, with barely hidden disgust. Saying king like you would say the word rat.

No, that wasn't right. Those weren't his memories. He hadn't seen Quielle since the summit. Although he could easily imagine him being stupid enough to disrespect one of The Gifted to their face. If the memory came from Aquillo, why would he allow it? Why would he appoint him prince? Nothing he did over the past ten years made any sense, and Nyro still wasn't sure how he died.

He rounded the massive desk and dropped into the chair, rubbing his palms over his burning eyes.

Knock, knock, knock.

Nyro sighed. It was impossible to get two minutes alone in the palace. "Come in!"

Fabian, his newly appointed head of guard, came in, tugging a big beast of a man in with him. He was dressed like an Órb Center maintenance worker in coveralls that were too snug for him and stopped high above his ankles. There was something wild and unpolished about him. Nyro couldn't put his finger on it, but it probably had something to do with that grisly scar on his nose.

"We found him in the outer kingdom. He's one of the Inestar soldiers."

That explained it. A rhino was trying to ram its way out of Nyro's head at that very moment. He was sure of it.

"What do you want me to do with him?"

"Put him in the forest," Nyro said, massaging his temple.

"But.. I thought you said we were sending them back."

“Do you think I need you to tell me what I said?” The desk groaned beneath his fingertips.

“No, Your Highness."

“Drop him and any other Inestar soldiers you find in The Sleeping Forest."

THE END

SOCIAL MEDIA

I'd love to hear what you thought of this book. Please consider leaving a review/rating on Amazon and Goodreads. Hearing from you all puts the battery in my back to get more words written.

Join my newsletter to be updated on my book sales, releases, and freebies. You can also find me on social media.

www.sukaliabrown.com

 facebook.com/SukaliaBrown

 twitter.com/SukaliaBrown

 instagram.com/Sukalia_Brown

ABOUT THE AUTHOR

Sukalia is an avid reader of sci-fi and fantasy. She's always longed to see more people of color on the covers and read about them going on epic journeys. Her novels focus on beautiful, three-dimensional Black people who are finding their joy in a magical world.